ALONG
THE
WATCHTOWER

A Novel by
David Litwack

EVOLVED PUBLISHING™

www.EvolvedPub.com
Evolved Publishing LLC
Butler, Wisconsin, USA

Printed in Book Antiqua font.

WHAT OTHERS ARE SAYING ABOUT
ALONG THE WATCHTOWER

WINNER: Readers' Favorite Book Award – Bronze Medal – Fiction Drama
WINNER: Pinnacle Book Achievement Award – Best Literary Fiction
FINALIST: Beverly Hills Book Awards – Military Fiction
FINALIST: Massachusetts Book Awards – Fiction

"War exacts a terrible physical and psychological toll on those who serve. Throughout history, soldiers have devised coping mechanisms to escape their demons and save their sanity. In his sensitive new novel *Along the Watchtower*, author David Litwack explores these themes with the added twist of game theory, a refuge for many whose minds find solace in fantasy. ... Although the term PTSD has reached the popular consciousness, Litwack puts a sympathetic face on it by sharing an unvarnished account of Freddy's progress and pain. The author avoids mawkishness, choosing instead to paint a simple portrait that is all the more effective for it. Freddy represents any or all of us as we reconcile the sturm und drang of life, making our choice to fight or yield. By using virtual warfare and fantasy, *Along the Watchtower* anchors a modern audience to this story without alienating others. In a touch of irony, one wonders if for some insulated politicians warfare is a sort of game without real and immediate consequences to the pawns that live it. Freddy's story vividly illustrates the fallacy in this thinking."
~ *Arlene Kay*

"The book not only helps us to understand the trials of a severely injured returned serviceman, but also highlights the archetypal nature of computer games and the healing power of using such imagery to defeat our inner assassins. All up, this is a book that deserves to be read. It is both gritty reality and magical fantasy, and filled with both love and beauty, and ugliness and despair, but ultimately it is a story of healing, of burying the past, finding hope and taking control of the future."
~ *Awesome Indies Reviews*

BOOKS BY DAVID LITWACK

Along the Watchtower

The Daughter of the Sea and the Sky

THE SEEKERS (3-Book Series)
The Children of Darkness
The Stuff of Stars
The Light of Reason

DEDICATION

In Memory of Dad, Mom, and Arlene

ALONG THE
THE
WATCHTOWER

DAVID LITWACK

"All along the watchtower, princes kept the view,
While all the women came and went, barefoot servants, too.
Outside in the distance a wildcat did growl,
Two riders were approaching, the wind began to howl."
~ *Bob Dylan*

PROLOGUE

I AWOKE ON A SLAB.

No. Too soft for a slab — more comfortable than a corpse would need. More like a stretcher.

A fog swirled in my brain. I picked through its wisps, searching for one thought to cling to, and my combat training kicked in. First rule: assess the situation. I steadied myself and tested my senses, starting with touch, flexing each finger until it grazed the pad of the thumb.

So far, so good.

Next, I listened. Nothing but a dull throbbing, like the beating heart of a dying beast. My sight might reveal more, but I was terrified to open my eyes. Instead, I sucked in air through my nose, and caught the unmistakable smell of jet fuel. Then a wind blew so strong, it rippled my cheeks into folds.

I lay outside on a runway. Alive.

Minutes later, someone wheeled my stretcher up a ramp and locked it into place. A hand rested on my arm, and the soft skin at the crook of my elbow stung as some medic inserted a needle. Then, still in silence, came a bump from below as wheels separated from the tarmac. I knew what that meant.

Farewell Iraq. Hello Ramstein.

While the critical care air transport climbed, my mind churned, still trying to plan the raid. Not that morning's patrol into Al-Nasiriyah, but the *World of Warcraft* raid scheduled that evening with my guild. Gaming was how I coped, at least until that morning, when it nearly got me killed.

I started gaming after Dad died, and kept playing when Joey would go on a binge or while Mom prayed through the garret window to the ocean. I even played after Richie ran off.

But I shouldn't have been gaming that morning. I should've been focused on my job—First Lieutenant Frederick Williams, leading my squad into bandit country. Instead, I'd been channeling Sunstrider, head of the Lightbringer guild, trying to figure out the way past the trolls at Blunderbore's Gate.

What will be the cost of that distraction?

When the IED exploded, I felt the shock but heard no sound. Maybe my eardrums had ruptured as the impact rattled the roots of my teeth. Seconds later, the pain in my legs hit like shards of glass fraying the nerves. My first thought: not the legs. Better to die.

I'd been training to dunk on that old basket at base camp, and had finally managed to curl one knuckle around the rim. Not bad at five feet ten. Now, like everything else I'd hoped for—blown away.

Then I remembered: the archangel collapsing on me, spilling his blood on my chest.

The fog in my brain morphed into a movie screen, replaying images from that morning—the roof of the Humvee blown off, the exposed sky turning from blue to white to red, the medics cutting open my shirt.

"Help the archangel first," I yelled, though I couldn't hear my own words. "It's not my blood."

I read their lips. Concussion, they said. The blast had addled my brain. It must have been my blood, since I was soaked in it.

As I tried to block out the pain, the oddest of thoughts struck me — I'll never make it to level eighty.

Just what I had coming.

Nine months and seven days in Iraq, my squad patrolling a hot zone, and I'd been daydreaming about a raid in a fantasy game.

The IED should've killed me.

I grabbed the edge of the stretcher and tried to roll onto my side. Big mistake. My mouth opened, but I couldn't hear my scream. The CCAT nurse rushed over and fiddled with some tubes as everything started to spin.

It happened sometime after that — dreams of a fantasy world, like in the game. Of course, I was frightened at first, but then, as blackness closed in on me....

What the hell. Can't be worse than this place.

A Ringing in the Ears

I AWOKE TO THE TOLLING OF a bell, but not the sweet chime of vespers or the carillon of noon. This bell had a more somber sound, one that I'd dreaded since childhood. With each clang, my bed quilt weighed more upon me, until it felt like a paladin's shield on my chest.

I squeezed my eyes shut and forced my mind to envision a different place, a garden I'd played in years before. I was nearly there, could picture dust motes floating across the light that filtered through gaps in the pergola. I could almost smell the flowers.

Clang. The garden vanished in a burst of black smoke, the scent of flowers replaced by the stench of charred wood. I pressed my hands to my ears.

Clang. On the seventh toll, I flung off the quilt and jumped out of bed.

Why wait for Sir Gilly to burst into my chamber and announce what I already knew? I'd knelt by my father's bedside the night before, saw his face so pale, his lips struggling to speak.

"Stay strong, Frederick," he managed to say. "And beware the cunning of the spinning wheels."

"But how?"

"Focus on what you hold most dear."

I'd prepared my whole life for this—the trials about to be thrust upon me. They loomed closer with each clang of the bells, for my father, the king, was dead.

I grabbed my sword and rushed into the hallway, buckling the scabbard as I went. Already well into the night, candles along the wall had burned low. Their flickering cast gloom into the corners of the vaulted archways, and their wax drippings sculpted ghastly shapes over their sconces. I hurried past them toward the office of the lord chamberlain, the door to which stood open.

He was waiting.

I'd known Sir Gilbert since birth. He'd been my mentor in all things that mattered, and my father's before me. By the time I was old enough for training, his features had settled with age, most prominent among them the jowls that hung about his chin and jiggled when he laughed. When I was little, they resembled fish gills to me, and so I called him Sir Gilly. I spent more time with Sir Gilly, an affable man, quick with a jest or a magic trick, than with my father.

When I turned seven, everything changed. My mother died that year, and I became sole heir to the throne, meaning the future of the kingdom would someday depend on me.

That time had come.

The gleam had vanished from Sir Gilly's eyes, and his jowls trembled, but not from laughter. "I'm sorry. He was your father and my friend, a great man, but neither of us has the luxury to mourn."

I understood, having been taught all my life about the Burning Legion, and the treaty that kept the Horde at bay. That treaty relied on magic bestowed on the reigning king, but Stormwind now stood without a king, and the magic that protected it would soon fade. For the next thirty days, they would task me with trials. I would overcome them and succeed my father to the throne, or I would fail and the Horde would overrun the Alliance—the end of life as we knew it.

For all my lifetime of training, I felt unprepared. "What happens now, Sir Gilly?"

"For a start, you must stop calling me Sir Gilly. I am the advisor and you the dauphin, until the days of anointment are finished. If you prevail, I will be Sir Gilbert, lord chamberlain, and I shall call you Sire. If you fail, what we are called will no longer matter."

"I won't fail," I said, wondering if failure were possible. For the past millennium, an unbroken line of Stormwind kings had kept the world of Azeroth free.

His gaze bore into me, no longer my mentor, no longer my friend, but every bit the advisor. "Why do you say that?"

"Because of everything you've taught me." I rose to my full height and lifted my chin. "And because I'm my father's son."

"You're a brave dauphin, but you underestimate what's to come."

"But all your teachings, the stories of trials past—"

"Mean little now." He leaned on the oaken table, his fingers splayed wide against the wood grain, the pose of a teacher urging his student to comprehend. "Each generation is different, each trial unique. Every prince must stare into the spinning wheels alone."

A fluttering arose in my stomach, accompanied by a tightening in my chest.

Sir Gilly must have sensed my distress, because he came from behind the table and rested a hand on my shoulder, as he'd done so often when I struggled in training. "Come, Dauphin. Walk with me."

He led me up to the parapets of the castle. Despite the pre-dawn haze, I could make out the land below. Out past Elwynn Forest rested the village of Goldshire, with its thatched-roof cottages and patchwork quilt of green pastures stitched together with stone walls. Beyond them, looming over the houses and fields, the mountains of Golgoreth loomed, high, jagged peaks where the world of the Alliance ended and the realm of the Horde began. Already, storm clouds gathered over the ridge.

As I paused on the ramparts to watch, a wind gusted from the east, an unnatural gale that roared in my ears and rippled in my skin.

"You feel it?" Sir Gilly said. "Their power builds in the hope that you will fail. Everything is changing now, different from what you've come to expect."

"How so?"

He stretched a trembling finger toward the distant mountains. "Their evil flows like fog on a November day, seeping into everything. When your father died, the protection he gave to the countryside began to weaken. It will grow weaker still until only the walls of Stormwind provide protection. At the end of the thirty days, they too will fail." He turned to me, his face inches from mine, his brows wriggled and knotted. "First lesson: you must not, under any circumstances, go beyond the castle walls during the days of anointment. Even the castle itself will not be safe. The mist will enter the smallest of cracks and transform into strange beings, the source of the trials."

I took two quick breaths and steadied myself, as I'd been trained. "Tell me what I have to do."

"Second lesson: you know about the watchtower?"

I nodded. As a child, I'd sneak up there to play, but knew well how it changed during anointment.

"None but you may go there for the next thirty days, for, as you know, following the death of a king, the advisor is charged with mounting two bejeweled disks. One will face east and one west, transforming the watchtower into a dream chamber where the dauphin must go twice each day, at sunrise and sunset. What these disks show you, and how you respond, will determine the fate of the kingdom."

"What will I see?"

"That, I cannot say. No prince before you left word, written or spoken, about what the spinning wheels showed. Most claimed they remembered nothing at all. Others refused to tell. But in some mysterious way, what you dream influences how you'll respond to the trials. The answer lies in the castle, if you have the courage to explore."

"Explore? I know every inch of this castle. I've wandered throughout it since I was a child."

"Ah, but you were never a child during anointment. The castle as you knew it will change. Stairways will come into existence where none existed before. You'll go down them, but when you turn back, they'll be gone. Archways and tunnels will appear, leading to new chambers. There you'll meet strange creatures. Some will be guides—elves or priests or mage. Others will mean you harm—spectral demons, agents of the Horde, assassins."

"How will I know the difference?"

"Trust what's in your heart. If that's enough, you will save Azeroth for another generation. If not—" A sorrow came over him, weighing down his features. "I've lived too long. I put your father through this and now you. I wish I had died before this day."

I'd never seen this man, my source of knowledge and strength, so downcast. I fingered the hilt of my sword, as I had at the start of so many training sessions. My grip on the braided leather tightened.

He looked at my hand and shook his head. "No, Dauphin, you cannot fight this enemy with a sword."

"But to defend against assassins?"

"It's not your body they seek to harm. These assassins can't threaten your being."

"Then what is their purpose?"

"To extinguish your spirit. To make you abandon the kingdom to darkness. Their purpose is despair." He turned toward the watchtower, standing erect, now every inch the advisor. "Come. It's time to begin."

Ramstein
Air
Base

AN ECHO OF AN ECHO—A dream interrupted by hushed voices talking the way people do near the deceased at a wake. One voice sounded gruff, a man's, possibly a smoker. The other was mousy, almost a squeak, a woman's. Three fingers pressed on the inside of my wrist—thick fingers.

"His pulse is strong. Let's give it a try." The man's voice rose. "Freddie, can you hear me?"

I recognized the name—Freddie, short for Frederick, a name that must be me. Then panic set in. I'd been dreaming of castles and kings. Why would I want to be Freddie?

"Try his rank," the woman said. "They're trained to respond by rank."

"Lieutenant Williams."

An image flitted across my mind—Iraq, an explosion. My mind recoiled, and I groped about in the darkness, trying to find the castle again.

"Did you see that?" the man said. "His eyelids twitched."

"Lieutenant," the woman said, louder now; at least I was no longer deaf. "Can you wiggle your thumbs?"

I needed to be somewhere else, bound by duty to do... something important. My mind whirled in a jumble, and when I couldn't fit the puzzle pieces together, I sent a signal to my thumbs.

"Wonderful." Slender fingers touched my palm, the woman this time. "And can you squeeze?"

I did, and she squeezed back. At least I wasn't alone. I'd always worried hell was being alone for eternity.

"Good. Now your toes."

I felt a draft as she removed the sheet.

"Can you wiggle your toes for me?"

I concentrated and wiggled my toes. She sounded pleased, but then I reached for the next level before I was ready. I tried to bend my knee.

My back arched as though an electric shock had run through me. I wanted to scream, but had forgotten how to make a sound.

"A convulsion, Doctor?"

"Don't think so, Mary. More likely pain."

"Should we keep trying to wake him?"

I waited, not understanding the question but feeling it was important. The pain kept distracting me.

Please, send me back.

"No, he needs more time. We've done all we can here. Put him back under and we'll send him home. Let the boys in the States do the rest. He has a long road ahead."

I wasn't sure what "under" meant, but I had questions before I got there. What road was he talking about, and why was it so long? I shifted my weight onto my elbow and tried to sit.

Oh Christ, my legs!

First came the smooth sense of plastic gliding across the small hairs on my arm, and the pain subsided. My mind began to drift.

A bright flash... soldiers screaming... dogs barking....

Where is my castle? Where is my quest?

Then, slowly, sweet darkness enveloped me.

The
Bequest

SIR GILLY LED ME TO THE death chamber, and already
the mist from the mountains crept into my bones, intruding like a
malaise. The trials weighed heavily upon me—that, and the
watchtower—but Sir Gilly insisted I bid farewell to my father
first.

"We're in unfamiliar territory," he said, "and I know little of
the right path. But of one thing I'm certain: we can do no good by
forgetting our humanity."

We stopped outside the entrance. He grasped me by the
elbow and whispered, as if the ghost of my father might hear,
describing the protocol of succession, though he'd explained it
twice before. "The king's remains will lie in a casket on a gold
pedestal. Once the pallbearers remove the cover, you'll see a gray
shroud covering his face, which I'll peel back to below the lips.
Bits of clay will cover your father's eyes and mouth. Look until
you recognize him, then nod. I'll give you a parchment to sign
and seal, your first act as dauphin. Then kiss his forehead, a last
goodbye. Be prepared for the taste of death, like dust in winter.
Take a moment. He was your father as well as the king. When

you're ready, I'll replace the shroud and close the cover for the last time. As a sign of respect, back away from the casket, never turning until you're out the door. Do you understand?"

I was too numb to do anything but nod.

"You must answer, Dauphin."

"Yes."

"Say 'I do, Advisor.' I'm sorry, Frederick. It's the law. We must follow the proper form."

"I do, Advisor."

Once we entered the death chamber, Sir Gilly did as he had described. I stared at the corpse, the muscles of my shoulders throbbing as if I'd held them stiff throughout the months of my father's slow decline. I loved him and was heartbroken to see him die, but more than anything... I dreaded becoming king.

Minutes before sunrise, we stood by the portal at the base of the watchtower, an opening so narrow that only a single man turned sideways could pass through. I took a deep breath and entered. Inside, twin staircases spiraled upward around a stone core. In normal times, one was designated for ascent and the other for descent, but as with so many things in the days of anointment, the rules had changed.

"Use the leftmost one at sunrise," Sir Gilly said, "and the right for sunset."

"What if I encounter an assassin blocking my way? May I escape on the other side?"

"Obey the rules, Dauphin. Do not deviate. Any encounter with a spirit or demon is meant to be."

I scurried up the hundred-and-one stairs to the top of the watchtower, pausing on the last landing to wait for a red-faced and out-of-breath Sir Gilly. He needed a moment before entering, giving me a chance to survey the chamber.

I hadn't been to the watchtower in many years, its allure nothing but a relic of my childhood. Age had changed the place. On the surface, it looked less imposing—as all memories of childhood do—a musty room, perfectly round and six paces across. The tangle of beams that supported the point of its cupola was less impressive now, hung with spider webs and covered with droppings where birds had made their nests. The elaborate molding that some artisan had added centuries before had been worn smooth, ravaged by rainwater and time.

One thing remained the same, exactly as it had been etched into my memory when I was little. Two circular windows breached the battlement walls—oculi, as Sir Gilly had taught me, great eyes that looked out across the land from this, the highest point of the castle. One faced east and the other west, and now, two platforms had been placed before them. On top of each sat a disk framed by a golden rim, with a kaleidoscope of gems in the center—amethyst and amber, emerald and bloodstone.

I reached out to touch them, but Sir Gilly stayed my hand. "No, Dauphin, your role is to sit and dream."

He motioned to a wooden stool facing east. Once I settled onto it, he turned to go.

A sudden agitation overcame me. "Wait, Advisor. Stay."

"It is forbidden."

"Stay only this first time."

"I cannot. I must be gone before the sun is up."

Before I could say another word, he fled as if the dawn's first rays might scald him. The sound of his bootsteps trailed away as he raced down the stone stairs.

I was alone.

I left my post and went to the western side to peek past the disk toward the darkened valley below. For an instant, I thought I caught a glimpse of something, two riders approaching through the jungle of Stranglethorn, out of the mist at the base of Golgoreth.

Assassins?

I watched until my eyes watered — nothing but shadows.

I shook off the sense of dread and returned to the morning oculus. A red glow had begun to dance over the mountaintops as the sun began to rise, casting light over the farms of Goldshire and the trees of Elwynn Forest, lands dependent on my protection. I sat once more on the wooden stool and glanced through the gems, doubtful anything would happen....

...and waited.

At once, I was staring into the teeth of a hot wind whistling through the oculus from the mountains, chasing the rays of the sun.

Slowly, the wheel began to spin.

VA Hospital
Stateside

I STARED INTO A PAIR OF Coke-bottle glasses wedged between a green crepe cap and a mouth-and-nose mask. The magnified eyes behind the glasses crinkled at the corners, a hint of a smile.

"You're awake," a muffled female voice said. "About time."

"How... long?" Each word burned as it forced its way up my throat.

"You sure you want to know?"

"Uh-hum." It hurt to talk.

"Almost two weeks. Medically induced coma."

"Where—"

"VA Hospital, West Roxbury, Massachusetts."

"Why...?"

"I guess they couldn't find out much about you—no family, last known home on Cape Cod but grew up in Jamaica Plain. We were the closest, so they sent you here."

I tried to shake my head. Not what I was asking, but I was afraid to move.

"Why...?"

"Oh, you mean why are you here. I'll let Dr. B. answer that. You should drink some water. We'll take it slow. You haven't had anything by mouth in a while."

I nodded, mostly by blinking. The least movement made my head throb.

She brought a plastic cup over and stuck a straw into my mouth.

I took a sip, swished the water around with my tongue, and swallowed. It felt tight going down.

She withdrew the straw and waited—I must have looked like hell. Her eyes narrowed, then crinkled again, and a latex-gloved hand reached out and stroked my forehead. "You've had a rough time, Freddie. Okay if I call you that? I'm Dinah, your nurse. You know, like—," She half sang. "—someone's in the kitchen with... No need for formality here, but we'll do everything we can for you. You've served your tour and you're home now."

Home. An image flashed in my mind—a gingerbread house, one of fifteen around a green with a steepled tabernacle overlooking them all. Ours was the runt of the litter, tucked into a half-lot at the end and farthest from the ocean.

The front door, for some reason, was painted purple. It had frosted windows with palm-frond cutouts. Joey used to tell me they were cannabis leaves, and Richie claimed they looked like snowflakes, but I knew they were palms. The steeply pitched roof had white scalloped trim, and a tiny balcony on the second floor overlooked the green. The house had four and a half rooms, a kitchen and sitting room downstairs and two bedrooms up—one for my parents and the other for the three of us boys. The half was a garret with a single circle-shaped window where Mom used to sit and pray to the ocean.

The first time I saw it, I was ten. Mom was so happy that day—the ocean, at last. The five of us raced each other into the house and scrambled up the staircase to the garret to check out the view—Dad and Mom, Richie, Joey, and me.

Now, only I was left... and not much of me, from the look on Dinah's face.

I blocked out the thought. My mind wanted no part of Iraq, but I wasn't ready for memories of home either.

I mumbled one word. "Morphine."

The eyes behind the Coke-bottle glasses sagged, and the green crepe cap nodded.

I felt a tube along my arm shift... followed by blessed darkness.

I stirred to the sound of Nurse Dinah removing the metal cover from a plate of scrambled eggs. Two days had passed, and I'd managed to spend a fair part of them conscious. I'd graduated from water to juice to soup, and now this. I was actually starting to look forward to solid food.

Dinah's cheerful voice serenaded me as she positioned the tray. "Big day today, Freddie. A hearty breakfast, but we'll need to sit you up first."

She pressed a button on my bed control and a voice responded. "Yes?"

"This is Dinah. Can you send Ralph in?"

A moment later, Ralph filled the doorway to my room, a huge man dressed all in white—white smock, white trousers, white shoes—wearing a mask and cap like everyone else. He almost needed to bow his head to get into the room.

I bet he could touch the rim with either hand standing flat-footed.

"This is our newest patient," Dinah said. "Lieutenant Williams, but he answers to Freddie."

Ralph nodded, then bent down and reached out a latex-gloved hand to shake mine. "Pleasure."

Another mask, another smile... this time I could tell because his great brows slanted upward. I thought I might like Ralph, and suspected I'd be seeing a lot of him.

Dinah and Ralph moved to either side of the bed, grabbed the pad beneath me, and curled its folds into their fists.

"Get ready, Freddie," Dinah said. "Take a deep breath."

I did.

She counted to three and they slid me back toward the head of the bed.

I let out a yelp.

"Sorry, Freddie, best way is to do it quickly."

Then they raised the back of the bed. It was my first time sitting since Iraq.

Ralph started to leave but came back, placed a great, gloved paw on my head, and rubbed the stubble. "Hang in there, kid. It'll grow back." His voice rumbled as if he had his own built-in echo chamber, and it seemed to linger after he was gone.

Dinah helped me with the meal, and though I didn't think I'd be able to eat it all, I managed to down every bite. When I was done and the tray shoved out of the way, she cleaned me up, and then hovered over me. "Are you ready for Doctor B.? He thinks you're well enough to get evaluated."

"Haven't you poked me enough?" I was glad to be speaking in full sentences.

Dinah tapped her head. "Concussion test. Only you can tell us how well your brain's working. I'll let Dr. B. know you're ready." She gave me a little wave and strolled out the door.

Now that I was half-upright and alone, I did my first self-assessment, like evaluating intel before a patrol, or health and resources in *Warcraft* before a raid—only more personal.

I tugged at the neck of my hospital gown, enough to peek underneath. My chest had been shaved and was covered with EKG cups. Tubes ran out of my body in various places, including a catheter, and lines for antibiotics and morphine. I reached up to my head where Ralph had patted.

Peach fuzz.

The CCAT guys must have suspected damage to my brain, and shaved my head. Maybe they were right, given the machines beeping around me. I watched the peaks and valleys of the heart monitor.

No flat line. That's always good.

Finally, I took a deep breath and slipped the sheet back. The good news—both legs were still attached. The bad news—a black brace enveloped the right one from hip to ankle, secured with Velcro, and metal hinges locked the knee straight.

I peeled back a strip of Velcro as gently as I could, wincing at each fraction of an inch. When I'd removed enough, I spread the brace. Scabs and scars decorated both legs, but the major damage was an angry incision held together with what looked like staples running from mid-thigh to below what was left of my knee. It still oozed along the edges.

When footsteps echoed from down the hall, I reset the Velcro and replaced the sheet.

A second later, Doctor B. came in, a chunky man with enough wrinkles around his eyes to tell me he'd treated a lot of veterans. He seemed friendly enough, though it was hard to tell through the mask. He'd been to see me before, but mostly just to read my chart and nod.

This time, he pulled over a chair and settled beside me.

"How are you, Lieutenant?"

"You tell me."

"Okay." He checked my chart for the third time. "Let's start with your eyes." He took a penlight from his smock pocket, tested it on his own eyes, and then pointed it at mine, the light bright but tolerable. "Follow the light."

I did, as he moved it from left to right and back again.

"Very good. Now a few questions. Can you tell me your name?"

"You know my name."

"I'm not the one whose cognitive abilities need testing. Please, we need to follow the proper form."

"Why?"

"About sixty-eight percent of the wounded we see also suffer from traumatic brain injury. It's the signature wound of these wars where you guys are subjected to IEDs and other kinds of blasts. No shrapnel hit your head. That's why they shaved you, to be certain there were no hidden wounds. The brain scan was clear, but you were pretty groggy when they pulled you out. Non-penetrating head wounds can damage the brain without leaving a mark."

"You think my brain's fucked up?"

"Just being thorough, Freddie. We use the Glasgow coma scale to measure consciousness, ranking from three to fifteen. Three is alive but unresponsive. You were a five on the CCAT, an eight in Ramstein. Let's see if I can get you to the next level. Now, please tell me your name?"

Another game. Still trying to level up.

"Frederick Williams," I said. "Lieutenant first class. You want my serial number too?"

He chuckled awkwardly. "No, that'll do. Do you know where you are?"

"Only because they told me. VA Hospital, West Roxbury."

"And who won the World Series last year?"

"You think I'd forget that?"

"Please cooperate. I'm trying to establish you have memory from before the blast."

"Red Sox."

"Thank you." He scribbled something in his notebook, then looked up. "Any headaches?"

"No... yes... I can't tell with all the drugs you're giving me."

"I'll take that as a yes. Now, please count down by nines from a hundred."

"You gotta be kidding."

He tapped his index finger to his head. "Different part of the brain."

"My brain's okay. It's my leg that's fucked up."

"We'll get to that. For now, humor me."

With an honors degree in architecture, this should have been easy, but I'd discovered some things didn't work as well as they used to. I thought a second, then rattled the numbers off.

"A hundred, ninety-one, eighty-two, seventy-three—"

"Impressive. A lot of people can't subtract that fast even without a concussion."

"No more questions until I get mine answered."

He laughed. "Fair enough."

"Why are you all wearing masks? Am I contagious?"

"Just a precaution. IEDs are bad, medically speaking. It's not enough to plant explosives. They pack them with rocks and gravel, stuff that can cause infection. The soil of Iraq is contaminated with nasty bacteria called *Acinetobacter*. Both your legs were pockmarked with debris from the blast, and some of the fragments might have carried the bacteria. It's generally drug resistant and spreads easily. You've shown no signs of infection yet, which is good, but protocol requires we quarantine you for a while longer. Now, is it my turn?"

"One more." My throat tightened, and I had trouble getting the words out. "What happened to the archangel?"

Dr. B. gaped at me and set his clipboard down. "Have you been having dreams, Freddie?"

I began to panic, then realized how strange my question must have sounded. "The archangel's a nickname, a handle for Specialist Sanchez, Pedey Sanchez. He was with me in the Humvee when—" My voice trailed off. "You probably don't know."

He slid his chair closer and took my hand. "I've read the report, Freddie. I'm sorry. Sergeant Sanchez was killed instantly, his whole chest blown—"

I turned my head away, one of the few things I could do without pain. I wished I could walk so I could run out of the room.

"I'm sorry," he repeated. "That was insensitive." Then, after a pause, "The archangel's an interesting nickname. Why did you call him that?"

It took a minute before I could answer. This was a lot harder than subtracting by nines. "He was ugly as sin, with a shaved head that looked like the top of a bullet, and brows that almost hid his eyes, but they were the gentlest brown eyes I'd ever seen. And he wore this medallion, a two-handed great sword on a cross—a warrior and a saint, last guy you'd expect to be religious. He approached every patrol like a prophesied event, used to give each of us a little Bible quote before we headed out.

"He was twenty-five, like me, but married with an eight-year-old son. He'd call them twice a day. Before every patrol, he'd touch the cross with two fingers, say the names of his wife and kid, and then kiss the two fingers.

"Pedey was part of my guild in *World of Warcraft*. His character was a Draenei priest, and his favorite spell was the archangel spell because it increased healing. That's why he took it as his character's name—the archangel. Looked like a demon but had the soul of an angel... and now he's dead because of me."

The doctor waited. It was his turn for questions, but he seemed smart enough not to push it.

I tried to stay quiet too, but the words slipped out. "Can I have some morphine now?"

"Are you in pain?"

"Only if I try to move."

"Then why do you want morphine?"

I closed my eyes. "Just give me some, please."

"We're trying to bring you back, Freddie, and morphine's the wrong direction."

"I can't walk. Morphine's my only way out of here."

"Lieutenant," he said loudly enough to make my eyes pop open. "It wasn't your fault."

"Yeah, well, you weren't there."

"No, but I know you didn't plant that IED, or pack it with gravel to do maximum harm. And you didn't start the war. You just fought in it."

He stood and fiddled with the IV tower, poking at the bags, most likely to give his hands something to do. After a minute, he pressed his thighs against the bed and leaned over me. "I know it's hard, Freddie. I see too many boys sent home like you. But escaping reality isn't the way back." When I didn't respond, he sighed. "Okay, I'll give you something to help you sleep, but first, you should know what happened and what the road back looks like."

I nodded. The dreaded road back.

"You were badly injured. In any other war, you would have died. Today, we're able to get a wounded soldier from the battlefield to a Critical Care Air Transport to a hospital within forty-eight to seventy-two hours. Your leg was hit hard, a 155 mm fragment full force. It shattered the patella and broke off the platform at the top of the femur. The quad tendon ruptured, and it damn near severed an artery too. The medics did everything they could to stabilize you, and then you were taken by CCAT to Germany. You had multiple surgeries there to repair the artery and remove dozens of bits of shrapnel and gravel. They managed to save not only your life, but your leg. Then they flew you to Andrews, and from there to here. We fixed what we could— rebuilt the femur, patched the patella, reattached the tendon."

My throat felt suddenly dry as cotton. "Did it work?"

"That remains to be seen. Your leg sustained a lot of damage, and only time will tell if the nerves are okay."

My brain was well enough to suspect the implications, but I tuned it out. "So no more basketball? Before the attack, I was training to dunk."

I waited for him to answer. I couldn't read the expression under his mask, but his silence was deafening. I forced a swallow.

"Will I be able to walk again?"

He hesitated, apparently not one to make false promises. "That may be up to you. Lots of rehab. You'll have to relearn how, but you're young and athletic, so that will help. Your brain needs to reconnect with that area of the body. Pain is the start of that reconnecting. Think of it as a marathon, not a sprint." I could see him wince under the mask. "Sorry, bad analogy."

He wrote out a prescription for something to help me sleep, and turned to go. "I'll give this to the nurse." Before he left, he grabbed my chart. After flipping to the third page, he shook his head.

"What now?" I said.

An upturn in his crow's feet showed he was smiling. "I was checking your height—five-foot-ten. You're too short to dunk."

"That's what they all said."

He replaced the chart on its hook. "This is going to be a long journey, Lieutenant, but I'll be with you the whole way. Think of me as your guide, and there will be others as well."

When he paused in the doorway, I could see him grappling with something he wanted to say.

When he finally spoke, his voice was pained. "You're not responsible for your friend, the archangel, but you should know that when he fell on you, he probably saved your life. The fragments that killed him were headed for your heart. A lot of people helped save you, Freddie. The archangel was one more. Don't let his sacrifice go to waste."

Night
Elf

THE WHEEL TOOK ONE FINAL SPIN and slowed to a stop. Like the princes before me, I had no memory of what I'd dreamed, only a lingering sense of infirmity, a weakening at the knees, much as I felt after a prolonged fever. I stumbled out of the chamber and down the stairs, grasping the wall for support, wanting nothing more than to retreat to my chamber and collapse into bed. The servants could wake me before the next session.

The staircase down was unremarkable, a spiral of stones with few distinct features. The walls were broken at intervals by arrow loops, the vertical slits cut into the stone through which archers could shoot if the castle came under attack. Since the treaty with the Horde, the loops were more to allow daylight in, along with a breath of fresh air. Between every two arrow loops hung a sconce bearing a candle. By now, the candles had burned low and their diminished flames cast more shadow than light. I'd been distracted by their flickering, struggling to recall what I'd seen through the wheel, when a touch of dread encroached on my thoughts.

The descent was taking too long.

"Beware the castle," Sir Gilly had warned. "It will change in the strangest of ways."

I proceeded more cautiously and began to count. At ninety stairs, I suspected some sorcery. At a hundred and twenty, I knew... the stairway was not letting me out.

I reversed direction and started the long climb up, but no sooner had I rounded the bend than the arched entrance to the chamber appeared. Sunlight streamed through the oculus, so much brighter than the light in the stairway. Inside, the spinning wheel lay still, its task for the morning complete. I became lightheaded at the sight of it and turned away, settling on the topmost stair and hoping to clear my head.

Should I break the advisor's rule and take the sunset stairway down? He'd said any change had been fated, that the castle would confound me but not betray me, that I only needed to understand its purpose.

I descended more cautiously this time, searching for markings in the wall, waiting until I'd noted an image in the stone, a brown watermark in the shape of an owl. Then I continued my count.

After twenty more stairs, the watermark reappeared. I kept going—the same after another twenty. I spun around, poking at the wall and searching for a way out. At the midpoint between arrow loop and candle, where the stairway was darkest, I paused to listen.

Is that the thud of boots coming from the sunset stairway?

I drew my sword and faced the center core. Improbably, from the stone, a light breeze came, then the wall before me bulged and took shape. I turned to flee.

"May the Goddess watch over you, Dauphin," a rumbling voice from behind me said.

I looked back to see an elf emerging from the stone. He was tall, over seven feet, with broad shoulders, a slim waist, and a bare torso that in the dim light appeared to be purple. I stared up at him. As a child, I'd been told stories of the

Sin'dorie, blood elves, who'd betrayed their heritage to ally with the Horde. This one had amber eyes—a night elf and friend.

He broke into a grim smile, bushy brows extending beyond his face, pointed ears quivering.

"And may the stars guide you," I responded.

He bowed his great head to be level with mine. At once, I recognized him from the face painted on the ceiling mural above my bed, the one I'd contemplated since childhood. I looked deeper into those amber eyes, preparing to pay homage, but he announced himself before I could acknowledge him.

"I am Malfurion Stormrage," he said.

Not merely a night elf—the Arch Druid of the Moonglade himself.

I bowed, bending at the hip, but kept my eye on him. "Milord."

"Rise up, Dauphin. These are the days of anointment, and titles mean nothing to us now. Only the present matters."

"Have you brought me a weapon to fight the demons?"

"Weapons will not save you."

"Then a spell." I offered my sword. "Enchant this blade. Recast it into a demonslayer. Engulf it in flames."

He shook his great head sadly.

"Then what must I do?" I said.

"You must speak the pain that can't be spoken."

"Don't talk in riddles. I need magic, a way to battle demons."

"You lack faith, Dauphin—faith in yourself."

I lowered my chin to my chest, chastised by the great elf. Yet what did he know of my burden? I was alone, the fate of Azeroth resting on my shoulders.

I tried again.

"You are Malfurion, shan'do, honored teacher. You know Druid magic from the Well of Eternity. Can't you give me something to help with the trials?"

The ancient one watched me plead, his face revealing nothing. "My magic is useless during the days of dread. You must find answers within yourself."

"Then at least tell me what to look for."

He straightened, appearing as tall as the tower, and stared past me, as if his gaze could pierce the stone and see all the way to the mountains of Golgoreth.

"You will be confronted by four trials. Only after overcoming these, will your life resume. Only then will you be crowned king."

Four trials. Each would be more difficult than the session I'd spent in the watchtower, and I must overcome them all within thirty days.

"Tell me, shan'do, how will I know them and what must I do to prevail?"

"With this I cannot help. The trials are conjured up anew for each generation, conceived from within your own heart. What you confront will depend on who you are." He turned to go, his cloak beginning to merge with the wall.

I reached out and grabbed his wrist, my hand like the hand of a child next to his. "I pray you, Milord, tell me more."

When he glared at me, I let go but continued to implore.

"Very well, Dauphin. One last piece of wisdom."

I bowed more deeply. "Anything, Milord."

He stepped back, now almost indistinguishable from the stone. As he faded from view, he called out in a voice that echoed down the stairwell. "Seek the white rose."

Flowers
and
Jell-O

AFTER A WEEK, I'D GAINED BACK some of the weight I'd lost and swapped the catheter for a bedpan. Best of all, the quarantine had ended. I got to see Dinah's rosy cheeks, and discovered Doctor B. had jowls that shook when he noted my progress. When Ralph came daily to turn and bathe me, I found I'd been right—he wore a perpetual smile beneath that mask.

Today, he strode into my room with an even bigger grin, pushing a wheelchair. "Care to go for a ride?"

I sent a signal to my right leg, trying to flex the muscle, and winced. "You think I can?"

"Hey, Freddie, I do this for a living."

He rolled the wheelchair next to my bed, set the brake, and hooked the IV bag onto the metal tower attached to it. Then he raised the right leg support until it was horizontal.

With his help, I slid to the edge of the bed and balanced on my good leg while he supported the bad. With a couple of nimble moves, I settled into the chair.

"All set," Ralph said. "Let's go find some girls."

I was too busy waiting for the pain to subside to think him funny.

"No?" he said. "Well, how about some fresh air instead? You may not know it, cooped up in here, but it's September in New England, the best time of the year. Gotta enjoy the nice weather while it lasts."

September.

The IED attack had been in July. August had vanished without a trace. How many more months of my life would vanish as well?

He wheeled me into the corridor, my first time out of the safety of my room, and I immediately went on alert. Green tile walls were broken every ten feet by dismal doorways, portals to more misfortune like my own. IV towers cluttered the sides of the hall, with oxygen tanks and ominous machines with wires snaking out from behind them. Between all that, strangers bustled about—nurses and attendants in hospital scrubs, and patients shuffling along with walkers and canes, marching to a more somber beat. Most of them had the thousand-yard stare, young people turned old in an instant.

Do I look the same?

When we came to the elevator, I glanced up at the lights above the door, numbered from one to twenty, the exception being the topmost floor, cryptically labeled "RA." My first thought was "Royal Apartments," but it was more likely roof access.

Ralph reached into his pocket and pulled out a key card, which he swiped across a black box. Then he pressed the down arrow and the mechanism began to whir.

"What was that for?" I said.

He watched the light flash through the numbers and cleared his throat. "Restricted floor. Need a key to leave."

"I'm a prisoner?"

"Naw, Freddie, it's just that some of the guys here have had it pretty rough, rougher than you. Traumatic brain injuries, or bad PTSD. The doors are alarmed so we know where everybody is."

A bell sounded and the elevator doors slid apart. Ralph blew out a stream of air and steered me inside.

On the ground floor, the center of the hospital opened into a small courtyard, an insecure space with too many places for insurgents to hide.

I took a quick breath and tensed. "Wait up, Ralph."

"It's okay, Freddie. You're safe here."

"Give me a minute. It's my first time out."

I surveyed the perimeter—a few benches, a flower garden dominated by hydrangeas, but not like the softball-sized blossoms my mom used to grow. These were small and paler than the Cape Cod variety, which were a blue that could compete with the sky.

At once, I could see my mom, hands buried in the hydrangeas, grooming her flowers. It was one of the few memories I could bear to recall—me and my brothers in the driveway shooting hoops, and Mom telling us to keep the ball out of her garden. She was happy then, surrounded by her family, her garden, and the ocean.

I looked past the hydrangeas to purple asters, and some lilies too, but no roses. For some reason, I'd been hoping for roses.

Despite the nice day, the courtyard was deserted, except for a woman about my age who sat on a wooden bench, finishing up a brown-bag lunch. Her eyes were closed and her head tipped back to take in the sun, making her appear to be dreaming. Sitting alone on the bench, her face seemed framed by flowers.

When she heard us coming, she sat up, straightened her scrubs, and smiled. "Hey, Ralph, what do you have there? Another victim for me?"

"Becky," Ralph said. "What's up? This is Freddie, Lt. Williams, our newest patient. We're trying to bring him back from the dead. Freddie, meet Becky Marshall, one of our physical therapists."

I nodded a greeting to her, not much in the mood for small talk.

She tilted her head to one side as if evaluating me. Then she gave me the kind of look that said we'd met before, if not in this world, then in another, and that she intended to make a difference in my life. "Is he ready for me?"

"Soon. If he's assigned to you."

My attention was drawn to a soda can on the bench next to her. I'd seen too many IEDs in soda cans.

She caught me fixating on it, and grinned. "Just my Diet Pepsi, Freddie. See?"

She chugged what was left and tossed the can into a nearby trash basket. Then she crumpled the bag into a ball and, to show off, stepped off exactly five paces, and shot the bag into the basket in a perfect arc.

"Nice shot," I said.

"I make that shot every time."

"Yeah, right."

She came close enough that our knees were almost touching, and hovered over me, sizing me up. "You'll be mine," she said finally. "I can tell. I get all the hard cases."

As she walked away, light as a dancer on her feet, I fumbled for the wheel of the chair, trying to spin it around so I could watch her go, but Ralph had set the brake.

"I hope you get her," he said. "She's one of the best. If anybody can fix you, she can."

The next day, Ralph let me solo so I could get used to maneuvering the wheelchair by myself. I tried to reach the solarium around the corner and at the end of the hall, but my arms were weak from disuse, and I was uneasy being in the cluttered corridor with so many people.

By the time I arrived, my breathing was labored and my fingers cramped. I unclenched my fists and checked my hands.

Angry grooves ran along the crease of both palms—I must have been gripping the metal rims too hard. I flexed my fingers to ease the stiffness.

When the redness had faded, I checked my surroundings, relieved to be alone, and wheeled myself to the window, grasping the rims more lightly now. I was high up, fifteen floors according to my room number, and could see a long way, but the view had little to offer, nothing but houses and highways, a golf course, and a stretch of cemeteries. I tried to let my mind wander, but there was nowhere I dared let it go. I didn't stay long.

Heading back, I must have taken a wrong turn on the way to my room, number 1522. I tried to follow the numbers, but became lost in the maze of corridors, rolling along until my arms got tired, at which point I stopped.

I'll be damned if I'm gonna ask for help!

I tried again, paying more attention this time: 1542, 1541, 1540... numbers descending, which was good. But at 1529, the numbers started going up again. I became disoriented and started to panic.

Maybe Dr. B. was right about the concussion.

I pressed my eyelids shut and wished for a white butterfly. Sometimes, in *World of Warcraft*, during a quest where I'd become lost in a cave, a white butterfly would appear and show me the way out or lead me to help—a priest, who'd offer an herb to increase my healing, or a mage with an enchanted ring.

I waited.

No butterfly, no magic.

I began counting down instead, from a hundred by nines. I got to twenty-eight when I heard a voice.

"Whatcha doing?"

I looked up to see a young man dressed in a warm-up jacket and loose-fitting jeans. He looked healthy enough from the neck down, even athletic, but on his head, he wore a white plastic hockey helmet covered with decals of American flags and well-wishing autographs in purple marker. Deep eye sockets suggested he'd once had more flesh on his face, and his wild, blue eyes wandered as if they could see more than his brain could process.

"Nothing," I answered. "Just resting. First time on my own."

"You're lost, aren't you? Can't remember your room number?"

"Fifteen twenty-two," I said too loudly.

He reached into his pocket and pulled out a slip of paper. "I'm in 1563. I can never remember the number, so I carry this reminder with me. But I can show you the way back to your room."

"You can't remember your own room number, but you can lead me back to mine?"

He tapped the plastic helmet. "TBI patient: traumatic brain injury." He drew the words out, then lowered his voice. "The brain works in mysterious ways. Follow me." He turned and headed off.

I had to scurry to catch up.

He walked hunched over, focusing on each step as though his feet couldn't proceed without deep concentration. Every third step, he'd lurch to the right and grab the handrail that lined the hall.

I called after him. "Who the hell are you?"

"Jimmie," the boy said, smiling a bit. "Or that's what they tell me. I don't really remember." The grin came easily to him, but didn't make him look happy. He looked more like a quest giver in *Warcraft* about to reveal a secret.

"You don't remember your own name?" I said.

"I lost a lot of words. They tell them to me in speech therapy, and sometimes I remember, sometimes not. I remember the word for my name and trust they're telling me the truth, but I don't recall anyone calling me that before...." He stared down at me with a blank expression.

The pause was infuriating. "Before what?" I said, mad at myself for giving in and asking.

The boy's hands flew to the sides of his helmet and his fingers straightened. "Before boom."

"You mean the explosion?"

"I guess. I don't know that word."

"IED?"

The boy shuddered. "I know that one. Improvised... explosive... device." He said each syllable with care, as if it might detonate.

My attitude softened. Jimmie reminded me a little of my brother Richie, slow and simple but with a magnificent innocence. "So why do you wear the helmet?"

"Part of my skull's missing."

"From the IED?"

"No, the doctors cut a hole to let my brain swell. I was asleep for six weeks. Medically... induced... coma. My brain's healing now. Two more months and they'll patch my skull with plastic. Then I won't need the helmet anymore. How about you?"

"My head's fine, but I may never walk again."

The boy smiled. "And I may never think right, but my legs are fine. I can even dance." He spun around and did a little jig in place.

I turned away. "Great. Glad to hear it."

The boy looked distraught, as if he'd said something wrong. "Maybe we can help each other. You've lost your leg and I've lost my words. I can be your legs and you can be my brain."

"What other words have you lost?"

The boy thought a minute and finally said, "Jell-O."

"Jell-O? But you just said the word. How can it be lost?"

"Someone told me the word, but I don't know what it means, unless someone shows me." When I looked puzzled, he explained. "Did you ever use one of those vending machines for drinks, where you punch in a number and the little basket slides around looking for your drink, and then dumps it into the opening?"

"Yeah?"

"Well, did you ever see one that was broken, where the basket wanders around and can't find what it's looking for? My brain's like that. The words are in their slots, but I can't find them. I hear 'Jell-O' and my little basket should find a picture, a taste, a color, but my brain wanders in circles instead."

I watched him intensely now. "Do you remember the IED attack?"

"Yup. I can find that picture easily — the sounds, the smells."

"And the death?" I said softly.

The incongruous grin spread across the boy's face. "I don't know 'death.'"

"You mean no one died in your attack?"

"No, I mean I don't know the word. Like 'Jell-O.' My little basket can't find that picture."

I envied him — like Richie, with that magnificent innocence, but with the ability to forget.

The
Watershed

7

FOR THREE DAYS, AT SUNRISE AND sunset, I trudged to the watchtower to stare into the void, but I remembered little of what I saw. An image here, a shadow there—like the restless dreams I had as a child, on nights when the moon was dark, the rain battered the castle walls, and the wind howled outside my window. I could recall no person, place, or deed, nothing but the sense of an illness slowly sapping my strength.

In between, I huddled behind the oaken door of my bedchamber, fearful of what might lie beyond. I'd gazed at the mural on the dome above me since childhood, but had long since stopped thinking about the significance of the painting. Now I studied it, searching for hidden clues. It bore the image of an ancestor, a heroic dauphin from centuries past, with the Goddess to his right and the great elf to his left, challenging the thunderclouds over Golgoreth.

Like the prince in the painting, I too had had been advised by the Arch Druid of the Moonglade, yet his riddles stayed beyond my grasp. *'Speak the pain that can't be spoken. Seek the white rose.'*

By the fourth morning, I'd had enough. I was the newest dauphin, and my people needed me.

Following my session in the watchtower, I set off to explore as Sir Gilly had advised, hoping to meet a new ally who could shed light on the trials. I headed down a rarely used passageway that led beneath the castle. My ancestors had built Stormwind Keep upon the ruins of an earlier structure destroyed by the Horde in the Great War, and so its foundation was honeycombed with ancient chambers. I'd explored them all in my youth, but in these strange times, memory or magic may have changed them.

For my first venture, I chose the watershed, a favorite place to play as a child. No one ever went there except on the solstices. On each of those two days, in great pomp and ceremony, the lord chamberlain would reverse the huge iron lever. At the start of summer, this released waters formed by the melting snows, which would cool the castle. In winter, this would let loose steam from the subterranean hot springs to provide heat. The kingdom was naturally mild in the spring and fall, but in the more extreme seasons, the watershed tempered the elements.

Since my father's death, each day had grown hotter. I looked forward to the cooling air below, but resisted the urge to rush my descent. Though I'd encountered no mischief since that first day, I proceeded with caution, relieved upon reaching the watershed unchallenged.

The river rushed before me, slapping the walls of the channel and sending up spray, refreshing me with cool, moist air. Where a ray of light streamed through a crack in the roof, rainbows formed in the mist.

An arched bridge spanned the river ahead, providing access to the lever that controlled the flow. Many a day I had stood on its peak, gazing at the water frothing beneath my feet, wishing my mother were alive, or imagining I had older brothers who would save me from the trials.

I mounted the bridge, careful not to slip on the slick planks.

How absurd to fall and drown in the torrent below. Frederick the Fool, they'd call me, after the Alliance was defeated due to my childish whim.

I was so busy watching my footing that I'd failed to notice an ornate arch on the far wall. As a child, I'd dreamed of being a castle builder rather than a warrior or king. Sir Gilly had humored me and given me access to the plans, which I used like a treasure map to explore the vast structure. Although I hadn't been on this bridge in many a year, I was certain no archway had existed before.

The work of a demon, or my own forgetfulness?

I shuffled down from the peak of the bridge and peered inside.

The archway framed the entrance to a narrow stairway down. After a moment's hesitation, I knew what I had to do; the curse of the dauphin: confront the trials, or submit to the Horde.

I started slowly, counting each step down, keenly aware I was heading below the waterline—fifteen... sixteen... one more to a landing with a closed door at its end. I pressed down on the latch and the door gave way with little effort. Beyond it lay a dead end, a circular room no bigger than one of the round tables in the royal banquet hall. It sat empty except for a moth-eaten garment, the cloak of a peasant, lying in a heap as if dropped in flight. I reached down to examine it, but no sooner did I touch it than it disintegrated in my hand.

I heard the click of heels on the stairs behind me and turned. Despite the possibility that the first trial was at hand, I remained undaunted. After all, I had the great sword by my side and years of practice in its use. I started to call out a challenge....

...But no sound emerged.

I strained, swallowed to moisten my throat, and tried again, but only the weakest wail emerged—more "nooo" than "hello."

Some sorcery at work.

I calmed myself as trained, and inhaled the cool air. When my breathing had slowed, I ran back up the stairs, taking them two at a time, remembering to count again — seventeen as before. At the top, I paused to listen — a thump of boots, the hollow thud of someone on the bridge. Not wanting to be trapped on the far side of the river, I rushed through the archway and back into the watershed.

No one there, but the coolness had vanished, replaced by dank air and a hot breeze that brought a flush to my cheeks. I strode to the crest of the bridge and gaped at the river below.

To my surprise, the water had begun to steam — wrong for the season. As I watched, the sparkling blue turned blood red, water no more, but lava, swirling and boiling, threatening to set fire to the wooden bridge.

I dashed off and escaped to the far side, but once safe in the watershed, a deep foreboding overcame me, as if I could hear death's footsteps rustling the dried leaves on the cavern floor. Then something appeared in my path, a shimmer at first, a fluctuation of light too insubstantial to identify. The leaves gathered in a pile, drawn together by some strange power. They began to swirl, driven by the swelter from the lava, forming a whirlwind that rose to the height of my shoulder, and the whirlwind took shape — leaves no more, but a grotesque little man.

Assassin or ally?

An assassin seemed unlikely, given his less than imposing stature. He stood a full head shorter than me and not nearly as broad, with hunched shoulders and withered arms. He wore a rusted helmet tipped low, concealing his eyes, more foot soldier than knight. More comforting, he appeared unarmed.

I stepped forward to confront him, relieved that my voice had returned. "Are you friend or foe?"

"I am what you would have me be." His voice sounded strangely flat, as if it would not have produced an echo even at the bottom of a well.

"I would have you be friend. Can you help in my trials?"

"In that, I am the best you could meet, because only I can grant you peace."

"Then tell me where I may find the white rose."

He took on an unnatural expression of joy—unnatural because no color showed in his cheeks, and his teeth, though visible, gave no hint of a smile—as he reached into his tunic. He pulled out a white rose and offered it to me, but as I came closer to accept it, the rose transformed into a poor man's dagger, with no sharp edges and a dull point extending no more than a hand's length. With such a weapon, only a direct thrust to my heart could do harm.

I yanked on the hilt of the great sword.

One blow, and the first trial will be vanquished.

I'd trained all my life for this encounter, my muscles thickened by a thousand hours of swinging heavy steel. Yet when I pulled at the hilt, the sword held fast, stuck in its scabbard.

I shivered, not as from the cold but as a stretched cord vibrates—a thrilling rather than a trembling. Although I'd been taught never to look into an assassin's eyes, I could not turn away.

The rusted helmet slipped back, and empty brown sockets stared back at me as the demon's laughter pierced the air. "Behold, I shall dispense with your world of swords and castles, and in so doing, I shall tire no more than if I quenched a candle in its sconce. Poof, and it's gone."

He waved his free hand and an image came into my mind—my father as he lay in his coffin, the clay fragments covering his lips and eyes. My shoulders sagged as if weighed down by a great burden.

What is the sense of it? One day, be it now or in a thousand years, some prince will yield to the assassin's stare and fail. Stormwind will fall, and the demons will prevail.

I gave a violent shake of my head, the only part of me that could move, and imagined instead a delicate white rose, held in the hands of a young woman in a garden. She offered it to me with encouraging eyes, so different from the gaze of the assassin. I gave another tug on my sword, and this time it budged, but no more than an inch.

The assassin took a step forward, within easy reach if only I could draw my blade.

The vision flickered and changed, my father's funeral bed transformed. This time, the young woman rested upon it, clutching a withered rose to her breast. As with my father, pieces of clay covered her eyes and mouth.

The assassin came closer, the dagger now within reach of my heart.

I placed myself in the vision, reached out, and removed the clay from the young woman's eyes. They opened as I took the last piece of clay from her mouth.

She beamed at me, and the white rose bloomed at her breast.

The assassin thrust his dagger, but suddenly my hand was free. The sword flew from its scabbard, and I swung the blade in a sweeping arc, tensing my muscles as taught, preparing to slash through bone.

Nothing. The blade passed through as if slicing through air.

The assassin divided into two parts, the edges of each nothing but wisps, and evaporated like smoke in the breeze.

Physical Therapy

MY HIGH SCHOOL GYM APPEARED IN a dream. It *had* to be a dream, and not just because of the gym—I could walk, run, maybe even dunk. I went out the door of the locker room and down the runway to the brightly lit basketball court. It was empty—no cheering fans, no bouncing balls—just my quick breathing as the adrenaline kicked in. I broke into a jog, admiring my reflection as it raced me across the polished floor. The squeak of my sneakers echoed off the rafters where the high scoreboard hung.

A basketball rested at mid-court, in the center of the team's logo. I picked it up, fingered its seams, rubbed the nub along its surface. The basket loomed ahead, the front of the rim forty feet away. I dribbled once, twice, bouncing on my toes, then took off and launched a step past the foul line. I was airborne, holding the ball high over my head as I floated toward the basket, the ball just above the rim—and the hoop pulled away.

I willed myself to stay in the air, to rise higher—it was my dream, after all—but the rim kept receding. Then the stench of something burning hit me and I fell hard, a sharp pain in my leg.

I woke up to see Dinah at my bedside, staring. "Another nightmare, Freddie?"

Breakfast sat on the bed tray in front of me. I shifted it a little so the watery light streaming through the curtain would fall on the meal—orange juice, a hard-boiled egg, and toast, slightly burnt. I smelled the burning and pushed the tray away.

"Not hungry?" Dinah said.

I shook my head.

"Anything I can do?"

I just glared at the tray, trying to make it disappear.

She headed for the door, but stopped and turned. "You're starting PT today, nothing too heavy, but you should try to eat. Want me to order something else?"

"No." I sighed. "Thanks, anyway."

After she left, I thought about my dream. I used to love that gym, until that November day when the coach came in—the new coach, who had replaced my dad. An unsettling premonition struck me while showering after practice, and I was in a hurry to get home.

As I toweled off, the door to the locker room opened and the coach called my name. "There's been an accident," he said. "Your dad. Some kind of fall from a ladder." He placed a hand on my shoulder, and his coach's voice quivered. "It's not good."

He told me he'd fetch his car to drive me home, but I couldn't wait. I took off, running so fast I could hear my heart pumping in my ears. By the time I reached the gingerbread house, my legs had started to cramp.

Joey had taken some of his pills and was sitting on the front steps in a stupor, giggling to himself. Richie wandered in circles in the backyard, crying and calling out my name.

I rushed inside and yelled,

"Mom, Dad!"

No answer. I climbed to the second floor to check the bedrooms, and then, when music drifted down from above, I went up to the garret.

Mom sat there staring out the oculus at the ocean. A Bible lay open on a table near her, its pages fluttering in the breeze. Her favorite Christmas carol played on the music box Dad had given her, and she was singing softly to the tune.

"Angels we have heard on high, sweetly singing o'er the plains — "

My mother had a little girl's voice and the face of a ten-year-old who'd never grown up, but now, shadows flitted across her features and lingered until they'd blotted out the light. Her eyes took on a distant look, as if she were seeing another world.

"Dad?" I said, the only word I could get out.

She nodded toward the stairs without looking at me. "He's sleeping, Freddie, in the living room." Then she picked up the tune again.

"What the gladsome tidings be, which inspire your heavenly — "

In the living room, I found his body on the sofa and covered head to toe with a white sheet. I reached out and peeled it back, so I could just see from above his eyes to below his lips. His head was tilted at an odd angle, and he wore a wry expression, as if enjoying a private joke.

From upstairs, the music still played, Mom singing the chorus now.

"Gloria, in excelsis deo, Glo-o-o-o-or-ia."

The neighbor, the one who'd brought my father home, later told me what happened. He'd been cleaning out a gutter, one of the odd jobs he took to make a few bucks after losing the coaching job.

"I was holding the ladder," the neighbor said. "I had a good hold on it, Freddie, honest. It was solid, no wobble to it. Then the strangest thing happened. He lost his balance, but only a little. The ladder never wavered, but he kind of let go and drifted to the ground like he didn't really care. I called 911 right away, but when the ambulance arrived, there was nothing they could do."

I went out on the front porch surrounded by the white fence with the little tulip cutouts. Joey still sat on the steps, rocking back and forth and giggling.

Richie had calmed a bit and approached me, oblivious to what had happened. "Did you dunk today, Freddie?" He asked the same question every day when I came home from practice.

I shook my head, unable to answer.

"Well, you'll get 'em tomorrow, Freddie."

I went back inside. I was all of fifteen years old, the youngest of the brothers, and it was up to me. I returned to the living room, to my father's corpse. With the index finger of each hand, I reached out and closed the lifelike eyes, to extinguish that look that seemed to say: *I'm done with it, Freddie. It's all yours now.*

It fell on me to call the funeral home, and they showed up within an hour. Two men rang the doorbell. One looked like you'd expect an undertaker to look — black suit, gray hair slicked back, waxen smile. The other wore the same suit, but it was too big for him. He didn't look much older than Joey. They expressed condolences and asked to see the deceased — had they said "the stiff," I wouldn't have been surprised. Five minutes later, they laid my father on a gurney, zipped up in a black plastic bag, ready to be taken out like the trash.

After they took him, I noticed I was shivering. Sweat from my run home had condensed into a clammy film that made my shirt cling to my skin. I built a fire in the fireplace and sat on the floor warming myself, listening to the crackling of the wood, trying to make sense of what had happened.

In the garret, the music box still played, and my mother continued to sing along.

The funeral a few days later was brief. The minister from the tabernacle stood by the sheet of AstroTurf that covered the dirt pile, and chided my father for not being a churchgoer, intermittently praising my mother for her faith. Then he asked the three sons if we wanted to say anything—my mother was too distraught.

Joey stood there and cried, but Richie kept poking me. "You do it, Freddie."

I tried, knowing my father deserved it. "My father was—"

I was unable to continue as the people around me breathed in, a collective sigh like wind stirring over grass.

Then came the silence.

I tried to go on—it was expected... the good son—but the words caught in my throat. I swallowed and shook my head at the minister, feeling like all joy had vanished from the world.

Little did I know, my life was headed downhill... and picking up speed.

That afternoon, Ralph loaded me into the wheelchair, and we trundled off to PT. He didn't say much until we were in the elevator and had begun our descent to the fourth floor.

"Looks like you won the lottery, sport."

"What does that mean?"

"You got Becky. She's the best. Just don't give her no lip, because she won't put up with it. And do everything she says."

"Sounds like basic training."

"No. Much worse."

The elevator dinged and the doors slid open. In less than a minute, we entered physical therapy. Like the rest of the hospital, the room was green-tile sterile, but someone had made an effort to cheer it up. Porcelain clowns lined the windowsill, stuffed circus animals—lions and elephants and a family of monkeys—surrounded the rack that held the free weights, and a variety of fresh-cut flowers had been set in mugs in the cup holder for each exercise bicycle and treadmill.

When I asked Ralph about it later, he said Becky kept them fresh, paying for them out of her own pocket. He also said she'd deny it, but he'd seen her sneak in on more than one Monday morning with an armful.

Fresh-cut flowers. Mom used to get them every Monday as well, to brighten up the gingerbread house. After Dad died, she started leaving them too long, not replacing them until they'd decayed so badly they smelled. After Joey died, she stopped buying them altogether.

The girl I'd met in the courtyard stood over a rolling aluminum table, organizing things I didn't much like the look of. She was sufficiently absorbed that she didn't notice us until Ralph called out.

"Afternoon, Becky. Brought you some fresh meat."

She turned and grinned. "Always love a new victim."

"Great. I'll leave you two alone. Sounds like you need some privacy."

After he left, she went back to finishing her preparations, making me wait. Finally, she came over and extended a hand. "We already met, but let's make it official. You're Lt. Williams, but I can call you Freddie. I'm your worst nightmare, but you can call me Becky."

I reached out and shook her hand. She didn't seem scary. "Ralph says you're the best, that if anybody can bring me back, you can."

"Ralph's wrong. I'm just the guide. You're going to do most of the work."

"But are you the best?"

"Let's say I haven't lost one yet."

"So I'll be back on the basketball court in no time."

Her grin vanished. She grabbed a chair, dragged it over and sat next to me. "We're going to be spending a lot of time together, Freddie, so we need to be straight with each other, right from the outset. My goal is to get you back to as normal a life as possible. If you work hard, I'll have you out of that wheelchair and on crutches in a month. A month after that, maybe a cane. Beyond that, we'll see. I make no promises other than to work as hard as you will."

She stared at me, and I stared back, captivated by my reflection in her gray-green eyes.

She blinked first and went back to the rolling table. "Let's get started. We'll do some exercises you've probably done before to strengthen your arms and your good leg, but we'll start light, because your muscles have atrophied in the past few weeks. First, let's do a little e-stim on that injured leg."

"E-stim?"

"Physical therapist talk, short for electronic muscle stimulation. We won't be able to do much with that leg until the surgeries have healed. The e-stim will keep the muscles alive until we get to work on them."

She sat down again and undid the Velcro from my brace.

I winced. I hadn't looked at my leg much since my peek the week before. The incision was less angry and the oozing had stopped, but the muscles shocked me. Where once I had bulges, now there were hollows — not the leg of an athlete or soldier, not the leg of a guy who might someday dunk. The leg of an invalid.

Becky's words rattled around in my brain. *Crutches... then a cane. After that, we'll see.*

"It may not be pretty," she said, as if she'd read my mind, "but it's yours. Take a good look. Let it motivate you when you start making progress. And trust me, you *will* make progress."

She squeezed some ointment from a tube onto her hands and rubbed them together. "This will feel a little cold." She spread the ointment, swirling her fingertips over what had once been my quad.

When she started the e-stim treatment, the muscle spasmed and contracted involuntarily, a strange but not entirely unpleasant sensation. As she slid the wand around, humming along to its buzz, I noticed her touch more than the current.

She spoke out of nowhere. "I read the report. Says you have no family."

I kept staring at her making figure-eights on my leg.

She glanced up. "Is that right?"

I nodded.

"What happened?"

"I was born an orphan."

She turned off the e-stim and looked up at me again. "Want to talk about it?"

"No."

"Ralph said you don't talk much."

"I talk when I want to. I don't want to talk now."

"Fine with me." She resumed the treatment, hummed a few more bars, and then spoke without looking up. "Ralph was right about another thing."

"What's that?"

"You *are* a hard case."

She remained quiet after that, going about her job while I focused on the clowns at the windowsill. Every now and then, I snuck a look at her—a beautiful, happy optimist.

Yeah, well, she never lived my life. I focused on the clowns again. *Crutches and a cane. After that, we'll see.*

I was different from her—a realist—and knew exactly what "we'll see" meant. I'd need more than physical therapy to bring me back. I'd need a miracle.

Gardeners
and
Goddesses

9

FOUR MORE SUNRISES, FOUR MORE SUNSETS, eight new encounters with the spinning wheels. Though I recalled nothing of what I'd seen, my strength was evaporating like moisture in the Tanaris Desert. My eyes darted everywhere as I wandered the castle, suspicious of everyone. Loneliness smothered me like the shroud that had covered my father's face.

Late one afternoon, I headed down the tunnel to the armory, thinking I might add a second weapon to my sword. The heat had continued to build since my father's death, becoming rooted in the very stones of the castle. Everywhere was hot, but at least the tunnel offered shade.

Then I saw the butterfly.

The tunnel was difficult to reach from the outside, requiring passage up and down three stairwells and through a maze of corridors. Yet here was a white butterfly, flying with a purpose. It came straight at me and began circling my head, no matter how hard I tried to evade it. Finally, I came to a halt, and without hesitation, it lit on my forearm.

I gaped foolishly, wondering if such a beautiful creature could be a demon. It stayed there, its wings slowly fluttering so I could feel their brush on my skin, its tiny eyes staring at me.

I raised my arm and gently blew.

It took off, flew ten paces ahead, and hovered, waiting for me.

I followed, and each time I stopped, it stopped as well. Before I was aware of it, it had led me out of the tunnel, across the courtyard, and through the main gate of the royal garden. At the center of the garden was a sunken terrace, a circle of stones surrounded by flowers and shaded by the branches of a sprawling elm.

There, beneath its canopy, the butterfly came to a stop.

With the weather so hot, the gardens were deserted, or so I thought, until I heard a song like water tumbling over rocks. I moved closer, wary of another assassin, and caught movement behind a hydrangea bush.

There, hidden among the sky-blue blossoms, stood a girl, humming to herself, so absorbed that she failed to notice my approach.

The white butterfly fluttered before her face.

When she saw it, she reached out and it landed on the curve of her wrist. "Now there's a fine omen for you," she said. "Light knows we need one these days." She whispered some more words, and the butterfly flew off across the courtyard and out over the castle wall.

A fine omen?

Perhaps, but I'd learned to be wary. I stepped forward, scuffling my boots to make noise.

She ignored my presence. Not until I was a pace away did she turn.

It was hard to say if she was beautiful or even pretty, as soil from the garden had splattered her cheeks and marked her forehead with a splotch that looked like a raven. A muddied apron hid her shape, but a glint shone in her gray-green eyes, as if the flowers had conspired to lend their color. Her mouth formed a crescent moon upturned on its side.

The corners of the crescent twitched when she saw me, but only for an instant. Then she went back to her work as if I were invisible. Her hands cradled each bloom as she sliced off the heads with a small knife.

"Are you spirit or demon?" I demanded.

She didn't answer.

I drew my sword, relieved it slipped so easily from its scabbard, and stretched it in her direction.

She watched the point from the corner of her eye, but kept her head down and continued to work.

Finally, I nudged her with the tip, and she let out a yelp. Only then did I realize I'd thrust too hard, and the blade had slit her garment. I backed off at once, ready to apologize, but then recalled my encounter with the assassin. I poked again, more gently this time.

"Why do you keep doing that?" she said.

"To see if you're real."

She stood and faced me, feet set wide and planted squarely on the ground. "Why shouldn't I be real?"

Tall for a girl, her head rose above my chin, and she possessed a bearing unlike a servant. I continued to challenge her.

At last, she reached out and eased the point of my sword to one side. "Would you put that silly thing away?"

I began to back off, then remembered the circumstance and held firm. "Why didn't you say anything when I first approached you?"

"Because we servants aren't supposed to talk to you royals." She lowered her gaze and turned back to the flowers. "I'm sorry... Milord."

"What's your name?"

"Rebecca."

"Rebecca. My name is Frederick."

She paled and then bent in a deep curtsy, her brashness collapsing into two whispered words. "The dauphin."

"Tell me," I said as she composed herself, "what were you saying to the butterfly?"

"SMOG."

"What is SMOG?"

"You don't know?"

"No."

She eyed my sword. "Put that away, and I'll tell you."

"Answer first."

She took a step toward me, until her breast was an inch from the tip of my blade. "How do you expect me to answer a question—one that any *child* in my village knows—when you're frightening the life out of me?"

Heat rushed to my face, and I slid the sword back into its scabbard, but stayed at the ready.

She sighed and wiped her hands on her apron. "It's short for Save Me Oh Goddess. I wanted to give the butterfly a message, just in case it had been sent from a spirit. You've never heard of SMOG? My people say it all the time to ward off evil."

"Why don't you say it out full?"

"Because poor folks like me don't have time like you royals. We're always in a rush and it's quicker to use the initials."

"What were you doing with that knife?"

"Cutting off the heads of hydrangeas."

"Why?"

"To hang them upside down from a nail in my cottage."

My jaw tightened, and I edged closed. "Some demonic ritual?"

Despite her bravado, she fell back a step. "No, Milord. To let them dry so they'll stay beautiful in the winter, after the shrubs have stopped blooming. It's something *gardeners* do, not demons." She fingered the rip in the apron where I'd poked her, then took it off, revealing a summery dress underneath. She waggled a finger at me through the hole. "Now look what you've done. You've gone and torn my gardening apron. I have only one, you know."

"I'm sorry." I wandered in a circle, hands folded behind my back, and inspected the flowers, unsure of what else to say. Then a thought occurred to me. "Do you have roses in this garden?"

"No roses, Milord. I have asters and hydrangeas, some fall crocus, and climbing the wall to the watchtower, sweet autumn clematis. There's a bit of monkshood underneath, and tulips in the spring, but no roses."

I must have looked disappointed, as she came closer and reached out, but not enough to touch me. "It must be lonely, Milord, a terrible burden. Every morning, as I walk from my village to the gardens, I see the darkening clouds and wonder where my strength will come from. Then I remember. The dauphin will protect us. Save Him Oh Goddess, I pray. If only I could do something to help."

I mumbled a thank you and turned to go, but stopped when I saw her examining her damaged apron. "Are you here every day?"

"No, Milord, I have other gardens as well."

"Come tomorrow, and I'll bring you a new apron to replace the one I tore."

She curtsied more deeply this time. "I'd be so grateful, Milord, but I have nothing to give in return."

"No need."

"Ah, wait." She took her small knife and clipped off a bulging blossom at the stem, and handed it to me. "Now place it in water the first chance you get."

I accepted the gift and admired her through its petals. "Thank you. Tomorrow, at noon."

As I walked away, I glanced over my shoulder to get one last look at the gardener.

She'd returned to her work, resuming her song and snipping away, so light of hand and foot. As she blew away a curl that had drifted across her face, the summer dress rustled against her skin.

I inhaled the scent of the flower and thought I caught the sun peeking through the clouds over Golgoreth.

For the first time since my father died, goddesses seemed possible.

The Ruins
of
War

RALPH DRAGGED ME DOWN TO SEE Becky every afternoon. After a few days, my arms and good leg felt stronger. I learned to transfer to the wheelchair on my own, and maneuvering became easier, but the e-stim treatments had little effect on my injured limb. Becky assured me that was normal, that the purpose of the e-stim was to keep the muscles alive while the surgery healed. The hard stuff—the real fun, as she called it—would come later.

On the eighth day, as I dozed after lunch and waited for Ralph to take me to PT, Becky appeared in the doorway carrying a drab, military-issue box. She seemed subdued.

"Good afternoon," she said, more formal than usual.

"No Ralph today?"

"He's here, but I wanted an excuse to visit you."

I responded with a weak smile. "What's in the box?"

She became flustered and shuffled her feet, half-turning to leave, but it appeared someone out of sight in the hallway was egging her on. "Okay if I come in?"

My guard went up as if I were on patrol in Al Anbar, about to enter a blind alley. "It's your hospital."

She came forward and set the box down on the bed. "They're your personal possessions, Freddie. You know the army. They need a month of paperwork before they ship your stuff back to you."

I eyed the box and struggled to breathe. *My old life before....* "I don't want any of it. Throw it away."

She placed a hand on my arm and tried to turn me. "Look at me, Freddie."

I gave her a look that made her flinch. "Is that an order? How'd you get stuck with this detail?"

"It's not easy for any of the guys. So much has changed for them. Ralph and Dinah thought I should be the one to bring it to you."

"Why? You draw the short straw?"

"They figured I'd make it easier." An uncharacteristic flush rose in her cheeks. "They claim you're less gloomy after PT."

My anger subsided. I reached out and ran a finger along the top of the box. "Did you look inside?"

"I wouldn't do that without your permission, but I'd be glad to sit with you and go through it. We can skip PT today. This is part of your rehab too."

I knew what was in the box: my odd collection of memories and totems that I'd brought with me to Iraq—remnants of a life that was already shattered before my body joined it. She'd think I was a weirdo when she saw the contents, but I didn't want to face them alone. I lifted the cover.

On top of the pile was my spiral gaming log with the all-weather army pen stuck through its spine. *World of Warcraft* was complex, and as the leader of our guild, I was the one to plot strategy. I always carried the log with me in case an idea popped into my head, and I had it in the Humvee that day on patrol, folded open to the plans for that night's raid.

The plans were unreadable, splattered with the archangel's blood. I tossed it aside.

I fumbled through the rest, a bunch of junk—keys, the dog tag the medics had cut off my boot—and my wallet with a plastic photo sheath tucked inside. I slid it out. On top was a picture of the five of us in front of the gingerbread house—Dad and Mom, Richie, Joey and me. I'd salvaged the dog-eared picture from Dad's hip pocket before they took him away.

I looked up to find Becky staring.

She nodded almost imperceptibly. "So you weren't really born an orphan?"

I shook my head and went back to the box. I pulled out the diamond ring on the gold chain and held it up, letting it sparkle in the fluorescent light.

Becky's brows turned to question marks. "You were married?"

"No."

"Engaged?"

"It was my mom's. I wore it around my neck for luck—a wonder it wasn't stolen."

Next, I found the metal bracelet I used to wear in high school, an old joke I could never decide whether to scrap or keep. I smirked at the date engraved on it and threw it back in the box.

Becky laughed at my reaction. "And that was...?"

"A story from long ago and far away."

When I refused to elaborate, she reached into the box and retrieved two larger objects wrapped in newspaper. Some well-intentioned clerk must have figured they were fragile and tried to protect them.

I knew at once what they were.

"Can I open them?" she said, like a kid on Christmas morning.

"Just a couple of keepsakes from people who are gone."

She held the first one up and ruffled the paper, trying to guess what was inside. "My father used to say any memento of the dead is precious—that is, if you valued them when they were living.

May I?" She picked up the picture of my family and studied it for a long time before looking back at me. "Did you value them, Freddie?"

I took the picture from her and rubbed the pad of my thumb along the plastic sheath. A friend had taken it when we first moved to the Cape. I was ten years old, the youngest of the three. Richie was twelve, although he never behaved more than five and never would. Joey was fourteen. Mom wanted the ocean, and Dad loved Mom, so after seven consecutive winning seasons, he gave up his coaching job in the city so she could raise us near the beach. He took a pay cut to coach at a smaller school, which meant all we could afford was the gingerbread house, a half mile from the water, with only one place with a view — the garret.

"Yeah," I said. "I valued them."

I braced for her to ask more, but she seemed to know better. When the silence grew awkward, she unwrapped the first package. Inside was a turquoise statuette of a mermaid the color of the sea on a summer day. The mermaid's hair flowed into waves and formed a circle around her that she dived through, arms extended and toes pointed. She was bare from the waist up.

Becky picked up the statuette and rotated it in her hands. "You *have* to tell me the story behind this one."

"That's Gloria, my mother's favorite mermaid."

"Why's she called Gloria?"

"Open the second package."

She removed the paper from the next one, revealing a music box with a clear plastic pedestal that left the mechanism exposed. When Mom used to play it, Richie would watch mesmerized as the pins on the revolving drum plucked the gold tines of the comb. Above the pedestal was an old-fashioned snow globe, but this one had glitter instead of snow, with two baby-faced cherubs floating inside. When you wound the key, the two cherubs would dance with each other while the music played.

"Your mother's too?" Becky said.

"She loved music boxes, and Dad liked getting them for her. Since they had little money, that usually meant finding one at Pick of the Litter."

"Pick of the Litter?"

"The second-hand shop at the town dump. He'd browse there Saturdays after dump runs. Most of the music boxes he found were broken, but this one caught his fancy. The drum wouldn't rotate and it had no label, so we didn't know what song it played. After he lost his coaching job, he took a book out of the library on repairing music boxes and tried to make it work. One day, he burst into the kitchen, cradling it like a crown jewel. Then with great pomp, he wound the key and slid the lever forward. Out of this little box came that Christmas carol: 'Angels We Have Heard on High.' Mom would bring the mermaid and the music box up to the garret, set the statue on the windowsill, and sing the verses, while the three of us joined in the chorus. 'Gloria, in excelsis deo.' My brother Richie thought the mermaid's name was Gloria."

Becky held the music box up to the light. Then, before I could stop her, she flicked the lever in the pedestal with her fingertip.

The music started to play, but the spring had wound down. The first notes groaned, more dirge than carol, and stopped.

I grabbed the box away before she could rewind the key, and clicked the lever off. "I don't want to hear it."

"I just thought—"

"Maybe you're a good enough therapist to fix my leg so I can limp along with a cane, but you can't fix this part of my life. Please don't try."

She glared at me, her lips stretched into a thin line.

"I'm sorry," I mumbled, trying to make up for being such an ass. "I know you're trying to help."

When her glare persisted, I raised the music box between us, shook it, and viewed her through the glitter. "Mom knew all the words. After six notes, she'd begin to sing, 'Angels we have heard on high.' Joey made fun of her, but Richie snuggled to her side, too big to fit on her lap, and tried to sing along. All he knew was the chorus. In between, he'd hum. But he loved that song. He'd sing it all year round."

"What happened to them, your brothers?"

"Gone. Joey's dead, like my parents. Richie? Who knows?" I dropped the music box and collapsed back onto my pillow. "Now the archangel's gone too, and I can't even take care of myself."

I figured she'd stomp away. Why would anyone want to stay with me?

Instead, she reached out and placed her hand in mine. She must've held it there for a full ten seconds before speaking. "Your old life's in the past, Freddie, but we'll get you better. And then you'll have the rest of your life ahead of you."

I looked at her hand and squeezed. "Thanks for the optimism, but you don't understand."

"What don't I understand?"

"It wasn't just my old life. It was all I ever had."

I clammed up after that.

Becky waited for more, and when nothing more came, she rewrapped the mermaid and the music box and went to put them back in the box. "Wait. There's one more thing." She fumbled with something stuck in the bottom flap and pulled out a Ziploc bag with a sealed envelope inside.

She looked at me, questioning, but I couldn't remember what it was. When I struggled to recall, my head throbbed as if the air in the room had become thin. My brain whirred in a panic, like Jimmie's vending machine, frantically searching.

"Are you all right?" she said.

"Fine," I lied.

"Should I throw it out?"

My brain cramped with the strain. All I could recall was a card with charred edges and a flower in the center. "No!" I said it so loudly, she must've thought I was mad at her. "Just leave it."

She bit down on her lower lip, suppressing her response. For the next minute, the only sound in the room was the soft thud as she placed each item back into place. Once she finished repacking, she stored the box in my closet. Before she left, she came over and patted my hand, then told me tomorrow would be better than today.

I was skeptical.

After she'd gone, I felt like a glow had left the room, leaving it bare and sterile. I sat alone on the bed and stared at my left hand, the hand Becky had touched. All she wanted was to help, and I'd driven her away.

One more time, I eased into the garret of my mind, into that place I was terrified to go.

A flower in the center....

And then I saw it—a white rose—but no matter how hard I tried, I couldn't remember anything more. Instead, Mom's Christmas carol started playing in my head. I could hear Richie as if he were standing next to me, singing along. I pressed my hands to my ears to stop it, but the music kept on, a song not of glory but of false hope.

In excelsis deo.

Mementoes
of the
Dead

11

I LEFT THE ROYAL GARDENS WITH a lighter step and found my way to the armory without further incident—no assassins, no elves, no butterflies. The armorer greeted me at the door as a long-lost son. He'd been a lot more vigorous when I began my training, but the years had not been kind to him. Now he stood hunched over and walked with a limp.

"Dauphin." He bowed. "May the Goddess be gracious to you in these dread times. How may I serve you?"

"I seek a second weapon, something I can slip into my belt, one that comes free easily and is nimbler than a sword."

"Then you seek a dagger." He rubbed the scar that crossed his face from ear to chin, and hobbled over to a wooden chest. He sorted through a pile of weapons inside, all the while mumbling to himself, "A dagger worthy of the dauphin." After clattering about for a few moments, he straightened. "Ah, I know."

He pulled at a key ring on his belt and picked the largest one, then wagged a finger at me to follow. At the end of an alcove stood a stout wooden armoire. He managed to slip the key into the lock, but his knobby fingers had trouble turning it.

He beckoned for me to come closer. "If you please, Dauphin."

I twisted the key and snapped the lock open with no effort.

He took out a plain-looking dagger, and must have noted my disappointment. "Don't be fooled by appearance, Milord. This is Kingsbane, the dagger that killed King Llane Wrynn, master of Stormwind in the First War." He extended it to me, but as I reached out, he pulled it back. "A caution: Kingsbane has great power, but only one of equal skill may wield it. And it comes with a deep sense of sorrow."

I snatched the blade from him before he could withdraw it again, and whirled it through the four ready positions. The dagger lacked beauty but had a strong heft and good balance. "Thank you, master armorer. This will do."

He bowed his head, once again beseeched the Goddess to protect me, and limped back to his work.

With the sword at my side and Kingsbane in my belt—with no sheath to bind it in place—I set off for my midday meal and a rest before resuming the trials. My mind dwelled on the girl in the garden, the way her hair swished about as she shook her head, and how her eyes glanced down but kept returning to mine. I'd fetch her a proper apron from the royal provisions, and something more. I pictured the flowered shawl my mother used to wear, and imagined it lying softly on the girl's shoulders.

I'd become distracted, and suddenly noticed my passage through the tunnel was taking too long. Worse, it had begun to descend.

I was about to retrace my steps when a sound from below made me pause, the voice of a man singing. Intent on not being caught weaponless, as I was in the first trial, I withdrew Kingsbane and continued on. The singing grew louder, an unthreatening tune, not quite cheery but workmanlike, the sort of song a guildsman might sing while doing something mindless and repetitive. As I stepped closer, the clank of metal on metal joined the rhythm of the song.

The tunnel ended at a stone archway, the entrance to a steep ramp leading downward into what looked like an abyss. I peered behind me, thinking I should turn back, but what if at the bottom I might find some weapon or enchanted ring, the secret to overcoming the next trial? I had to risk it, so I started down, setting my boots lightly on the ground, toe first and then heel, so they hardly made a sound.

At the bottom, a chamber spread before me, appearing as vast as Stormwind Keep. It had dungeon lighting, not darkness, but a twilit gloom—a fitting place to find a demon. As I entered, a pungent odor assaulted me. It seemed to be coming from overhead, where a grid of corroded pipes crisscrossed the low ceiling.

I glanced out across the maze above and searched for the source of the song.

Behind a series of valves stood a man with his hands covered in grime. His thick neck supported a massive shaved head, though his face was out of proportion. His warm, brown eyes were set deep in their sockets and stuck so closely together, they were nearly lost beneath an overarching brow. He sang as he twisted a wrench around a section of pipe, making the muscles in his forearms stand out like ropes. Periodically, he stroked his skull, wiping away sweat and smoothing it down as if he had hair.

When he saw me, he nodded as if he knew me, but kept working. He'd tap a pipe, listen for the echo, and then make an adjustment with the wrench.

"Are you spirit or demon?" I said.

"Neither. I'm a plumber, just doing my job."

"And what job is that?"

He tapped once more, and looked me over before answering. "Checking the pipes."

"I... see."

He went back to tapping.

"Where do these pipes come from?"

He squared his shoulders toward me, revealing a hairy chest bearing a medallion. To my surprise, it was an image of Nordrassil, the World Tree—the mark of a Druid.

"Cemtries," he said.

"Sorry, I don't—"

"Cemtaries." His thick lips contorted as he struggled to say the word more clearly. "You know... places where people's buried." He waved his hands across the maze of pipes. "All the cemtries in the kingdom." He wandered around, tapping each pipe with his wrench as he described it. "Sure. This'n be the guild cemtry. Peasants here. Royals. Pets. Livestock."

"I don't understand. Why would there be pipes under cemeteries?"

He came closer and placed a thick hand on my upper arm. "See here, those big muscles of yours. Be sludge someday. Where do you suppose it goes, all that sludge? Into the pipes. Comes together here and flows out to the sea."

Sweat began to run down the small of my back as recognition grew. The pungent odor was the smell of decaying flesh. I breathed through my mouth in an effort to diminish it.

"How do you know?" I finally managed to say. "Are you a demon?"

His forehead furrowed. "Don't think I'm a demon." Then he chuckled to himself. "More likely an angel, though my wife might say otherwise."

"You don't look like an angel."

"Everybody says that, but how'd they know what angels looks like? Besides, somebody's gotta do the dirty work. Can't have all the angels flying about making sunshine."

A Druid? Unlikely. But some Druids are shapeshifters.

I waited for him to say more, but he lost interest and resumed his work. As I stared past him, I noticed a pipe at the far end of the room. Unlike the others, it was shiny and new, with no hint of corrosion. "Where does that one come from?"

He wiped his forehead with a greasy rag that left streaks on his face, and walked over to where I was pointing. "Why do you ask? Does it need fixing?" He tapped the new pipe with his wrench. "Sounds okay to me."

"But where does it come from?"

"You should know. It's your pipe."

Perhaps a Druid, sent by Malfurion Stormrage. A great secret might lie here.

"I don't remember. Why don't you tell me?"

He shook his head and chuckled. "'Don't remember,' he says. More likely wants to forget."

Sir Gilly had cautioned that weapons would be useless during the trials. I began to see why. My sword and Kingsbane together might be of no avail here.

"I've had enough of riddles," I said. "For the sake of Stormwind and all we hold dear, pray tell me."

In answer, he smiled a simple smile and spoke a simple thought. "Your castle, Milord. Your pipe. It's for you to figure out."

I hoped he'd say more, but he began banging the pipes instead, this time so hard, the clanging filled the room. I covered my ears, but the sound still rang in my skull. The stench of decay grew stronger, as if the pipes had burst, and my head throbbed. Black spots swam across my vision and the room began to blur.

The man with the medallion of the World Tree on his chest merged with the pipes. I covered my eyes as a rush of air roared through the chamber. The last thing I heard was the sound of dogs barking.

Then silence.

Somehow, whether by the grace of the Goddess or the magic of the great elf, I had been transported to the safety of my bedchamber. When I could see once more, I was alone. The pounding in my head had subsided, replaced by a more well-mannered knocking. I went to the door, withdrew Kingsbane, and released the latch.

A young page stood before me with head bowed. He fell back a step when he noticed the dagger in my hand. A look came over him I'd seen before — pity for the poor dauphin.

"The advisor," he stammered, "he sent me to fetch you." When I continued to gape, he made a second, deeper bow. "It's nearly sunset, Milord. Time for the watchtower."

A Need
for
Goals

WEEKS PASSED. MY LEG WAS HEALING, or so they said, but with the brace on, I could hardly feel a difference. I still relied on the wheelchair when not in bed. And the dreams continued, lingering effects of the concussion, perhaps, or the pills Dr. B. gave me to sleep. I dreamt mostly of the other world, but more recently, jumbled memories had begun to mix in.

In this morning's dream, I prepared for a patrol in Al Anbar, going over intel with my squad in a haze-filled room. When I was done, they peppered me with questions, but I couldn't recall the details. I fudged my way through the briefing—something I'd never do outside of a dream. Then, with my confidence shaken, I donned my equipment—the Kevlar helmet with the night goggles, the flak jacket, the M-4 carbine, and the M-9 buckled to my waist—but when I stepped outside, I wasn't in Iraq at all, but on the green in front of the gingerbread house.

I ran, scanning for faces in the garret windows and snipers in the trees. I raced up the stairs to the tabernacle, M-4 locked and loaded, and searched under the pews and behind the altar. I called out names: Joey, Richie, Mom, Dad. I even yelled for the archangel.

No answer, no wind, no sound. Everyone had vanished without a trace.

When I awoke, my heart was pounding and my fists were clenched. I closed my eyes again, trying to stay in the dream. I wasn't finished. I wanted to go back to the tabernacle, to overturn the altar and hurl the holy relics to the floor, to watch the candles set fire to the fine linen altar cloth—to destroy it as God had destroyed everything I held dear.

My heartbeat slowed as the dream lapsed into memories.

After Dad died, I'd tried to tell Mom she couldn't mourn forever, that she needed to get back to life.

"It takes a long time for those we love to die," she said. "Like waves to the shore, the memories keep coming, and they only stop when the tides turn back to stillness."

A long time.

I decided enough time had passed, and tested my memory. I eased my mind toward that instant—the flash, the smell of C-4, and then silence. The gentle spirit that had been the archangel lay draped over me, a final act of healing, his blood flowing like a magic elixir to save my life. It was an atomic moment, unique to itself, with neither a before or an after. My time in Iraq had become a separate reality... like the dream.

Then, all at once, I realized it. Other things had happened in Iraq, things that had stayed buried in my brain. I could probe their ragged edges but not touch them. Like Jimmie, the TBI patient, I had memories I was unable to reach.

I shook it off and thought instead about my dad.

After his funeral, we went back to the basement of the tabernacle, where our neighbors had arranged cookies and pies and plates with slices of ham. Beside them sat white bread and rye, fanned out in a circle, with mustard in paper cups. I waited in the receiving line before the food table, next to my mother and brothers, while people I hardly knew offered condolences and assured me my father was in a better place.

Finally, the crowd began to thin as folks offered weak excuses—the kids are home alone, the dog needs walking. Only a few kind souls remained to clean up, leaving the church basement nearly silent but for the echo of the click of their heels.

When all the cookies and pies and cold cuts had been wrapped in aluminum foil, our neighbor, Mrs. Miller, urged my mother to go home. "We'll take care of the cleanup," she said. "Go get some rest."

After Mom was tucked in bed and sleeping, I went for a run on the beach. It was late in the day. As the sun weakened, the fog rolled in. Waves crested from nowhere, and seawater washed across the sand by my feet. As I ran, I contemplated the constancy of the surf, comforted by its alternating roar and hush. In my grief, the ocean consoled me.

My father had taught me about the sea when we first moved to the Cape. The sea, he said, was always in charge. We were only invited guests. Those who did not respect it did not survive. I recalled his stories, ghostly tales of ships that had foundered and crashed on the rocks a hundred years before. He claimed that, if we listened carefully, we could still hear their mournful crews and groaning rigging in the fog.

I tried to remember him at a happier time. Basketball... we were always happy on the court.

He started me playing as soon as my hands were big enough to hold a ball. We didn't have a lot in common, especially as I got older, and we never said much over dinner, but we could always talk basketball.

He taught me how to shoot—push off with my legs, then let the ball spin off the tips of my fingers. After a shoot-around in the driveway, he'd check my hands.

"Only the top joints of your fingers should get dirty," he'd say. If there was dirt in the wrong place, he'd show me again, spinning the ball off his fingertips, tossing it a foot in the air before catching it.

"If you do it well, the ball has backspin, so when it comes near the rim, it will roll in and not clunk off. If you do it *really* well, there's no rim at all. Just strings."

He demonstrated. *Swish.* "And when you do it perfectly, it's like magic."

He set himself, bent at the knees, and shot the ball in a glorious arc. It spun through the air and floated through the rim soundlessly, not even a swish—only a whisper as a few threads from the frayed strings followed the ball to the ground like snow.

A knock at the door interrupted my memories, and Dr. B. entered, followed by Ralph, Dinah, and Becky.

"Looks like a court martial," I said.

"Today, we get you back on your feet," Dr. B. said.

I remembered Dinah telling me something about the brace the night before, but I was too groggy to listen. I gaped as Dr. B. pulled out an Allen wrench from his bag.

Becky laughed. "It's not for you, Freddie. It's for the brace hinge."

Dr. B. poked around and inserted one end into a hole by my knee. "I'm going to adjust the bend from straight to twenty degrees, enough to let you walk. Becky tells me you're ready."

Becky held up a pair of crutches and nodded. "Your arms and good leg are strong enough. Give it a try. Today's goal will be the solarium at the end of the corridor."

Dr. B. raced off to his next patient, while Becky and Ralph helped me stand. I wobbled on my good leg. My balance was awful, and I clung to Ralph for support.

Becky eased a crutch under each of my arms, and then let go.

Panic. For the first time in a month, my right leg was free, and I was terrified it would buckle.

"Don't worry," Becky said. "The brace will support you."

I focused on the floor and gripped the handles of the crutches.

"One step at a time," she said. "Bad leg first."

I swung the crutches forward to a spot six inches past my big toe, then dragged my damaged leg along the floor. Once stable, I brought my good leg even and stopped.

"Wonderful," Becky said. "Now keep going. I won't let you fall."

I took a few more steps, not quite to the door to my room, and a light sheen of sweat had already begun to form on my forehead. "Is that enough?"

"Remember the goal? The solarium."

"Fuck that. I want to go back to bed."

She rubbed my arm. "I'll cut you a deal, Freddie, special for today. Make it one way. Ralph will follow with the wheelchair."

I looked at Ralph, hoping he'd relent.

He shook his head. "Take the deal, Freddie. She's not always this generous."

It was maybe fifty yards down the hall to the solarium, and every inch was agony. Dr. B. had been right: a normal life was a long way off. When I reached the corridor, I could sense everyone staring, but saw nothing but the polished floor. I would have turned back but for Becky, who did everything but walk for me — encouraging, cajoling, rubbing my back when I stalled, and supporting me when I stumbled.

Then, after what felt like an instant and forever, she touched my shoulder and gave me a peck on the cheek, careful not to knock me over.

"You did it," she said.

I was out of breath and my hands throbbed, but I managed to look up. Ahead, sunlight streamed through the entrance to the solarium.

"Wheelchair," I said, the only word I could manage.

Once I settled into the chair, Ralph begged off.

Becky stayed. "You did great, Freddie, for the first time. You might as well enjoy your reward. I have fifteen minutes before my next appointment. Let's take in the view."

She wheeled me in, and we were alone in the room. She slid a chair in front of me, so close her knees were touching my good leg. "Now admit it. Didn't that feel good?"

"Wonderful. Confirms I'm an invalid."

"Come on, Freddie. It's a first goal, and you made it. You'll have others."

"Fuck goals."

"What do you have against goals? My father used to say everyone needs a goal. Otherwise, how do you know where you're going?"

"Yeah, my dad had a goal too, to coach a championship team. He would have made it, but my mom's goal got in the way. She got the ocean, and he ended up at a small school with a crap team. He was hoping to hang on long enough for me to be his point guard, but after they fired him for being politically incorrect, that goal was out of reach. And when he died, my mom's goal didn't seem to matter anymore."

Becky stood and wandered over to the window, her back to me. I released the brake of the wheelchair and rolled toward her, wanting to see her face once more. When she turned, I saw the color had risen in her cheeks.

"If you don't want to walk again, Freddie, there's nothing I can do for you." She leaned down toward me, close enough that I could feel her breath. "Promise me you'll try."

I wanted to get mad, to tell her she had no idea what I'd been through, but her eyes held me. I finally mumbled, "Okay."

"Good. Then at least you have one goal. Everyone needs something to hope for. You must have had others."

"In college? Sure. To be an architect and build funky homes like the gingerbread house. But then I went to war, where blowing things up was more important than building them. In Iraq, I had three goals: to make level eighty in *World of Warcraft*; to work my butt off so I'd be able to someday dunk; and most of all, to bring my men and me home in one piece. Now, playing a video game seems stupid. I'll never get to dunk. And I didn't do such a hot job bringing us all home."

"Okay, so you need new goals."

"Why? So I can be disappointed again?"

Her features tightened. For a second, I thought she'd walk out and leave me alone in the solarium. I wouldn't blame her. I had an urge to do anything to make her stay.

"How about you?" I said to divert attention from me. "What were your goals?"

She laughed a bit, more a nervous puff of air. "I just wanted to get a good education, earn a decent living, and help people."

"Well, you've done those. What's next?"

She gazed out the window, toward somewhere far off, past the houses and the highway and the cemeteries. "I don't know. A home maybe, a family, someone to love."

I watched her as she stared out the window. *Home, family, love....*

My mind whirred like Jimmie's broken vending machine. Nothing found. Home was gone. Family too. And love? That seemed as out of reach as the rim of a basket.

A Flower
in the
Rain

13

THOUGH DEMONS STILL HAUNTED MY SLEEP,
not all of my dreams were dark. Sometimes, the Goddess would
grant a reprieve and show happier scenes from my childhood. I'd
see my father taking a break from his royal duties to visit my
training. He'd borrow a wooden sword from Sir Gilly and
demonstrate a parry and thrust, and then, if I managed so much
as a touch, he'd pretend to die most dramatically. Or I'd see my
mother in the bloom of her youth, taking me to watch the pastry
cook make cakes, and letting me lick the batter from the bowl.

On this night, the Goddess sent me the gardener.

The next morning, I awoke to the fragrance of flowers.
Following my session in the watchtower, I headed directly to the
gardens, carrying a sack with a new apron and my mother's
shawl. I searched through the flowers, but the gardener was
nowhere to be found. I assessed the angle of the sun, shining
dimly through a brown haze—not yet noon—and decided to head
to the castle entrance to wait.

At the main gate, I paced while the guards did their best to
ignore me, but I could feel their pity. Even they could cross the

drawbridge when off duty, but I was bound by the river. Its waters ran high after the prior night's storm, its current angry and loud. I could hear voices as it rushed over the rocks, a race of lost men, my ancestors, kings and princes of old, the damned, or merely those who had passed on. Everything is made to perish, the voices seemed to say.

A cheerful, "Good morn, Milord," silenced the voices in the water.

I turned to watch Rebecca approaching the gate. I'd been harsh with her the day before, wary of a demon. Now, as she came toward me, I wondered how I could have been so wrong. If she were a demon, let Stormwind be damned.

She bowed slightly—a dip of the knee, a tilt of the head—but never lost the bounce in her step.

Aware of guards staring, I returned the greeting formally and turned to go, with her following several paces behind.

As soon as we were alone in the gardens, I opened the sack. With a threatening sky overhead, I wanted to hand over my gifts as soon as possible. "A new apron, as promised."

It was a simple garment I had obtained from a scullery maid, but it pleased Rebecca. She replaced the torn one and twirled in a circle to show the new one off.

I waited until I had her attention again before taking out the shawl. "And a gift to make amends for my bad behavior."

I unfurled it for her. It had bright-colored flowers on a green background, and was made of silk so fine I could see her eyes through the fabric, even in the dim light. They had become round as moons.

I couldn't help but smile. "Well, what do you say?"

"Milord, I cannot."

"But why?"

"I'm not allowed to take gifts from royals. It's not my place."

"You'd refuse a gift from your future king?"

"Yes, Milord... I mean, no."

"At least try it on. What harm in that?"

She reached for the shawl with arms extended, trying to keep as much distance between us as possible, then draped it over her shoulders and looked up beaming.

I drew in a breath; she outshone the flowers.

As I admired her, a black cloud passed overhead, casting a shadow that darkened the garden. A clap of thunder intruded on the moment, and great drops of rain began to fall. Ignoring protocol, I grabbed Rebecca by the hand and pulled her under the eaves of the watchtower.

While we waited out the squall, I became intrigued by the runoff from a gargoyle overhead. Rainwater, which had been leaking for some time from a hole in its neck, had stained the copper grill beneath it a bile green, and old corrosion ran down the wall below like rusted tears. But what most caught my eye was the resulting flow onto the garden. The water trickled down on a single plant, a tall spire covered with hooded purple flowers. The topmost of these would fill until the weight of the rainwater made it bow over and spill its contents onto the next, causing a cascade down the blossoms. The process would then repeat.

"What are you staring at?" Rebecca said.

"At those purple flowers, each filling with rain until it can bear no more, then emptying onto the next and refilling."

"Oh, you mean the monkshood."

"Is that what it's called?"

"Yes. Every child in my village knows monkshood."

"I don't."

"You mean the royal tutors don't teach a prince something as simple as that?"

"I'm afraid I've missed out on simple pleasures."

I turned away from the monkshood to catch her staring. Her eyes had become like the flowers, filling with wonder and pouring over me.

She blushed and looked away.

Realizing I was still grasping her hand, I let go and reached for the flower instead.

She grabbed my wrist. "No, Milord, it's best not to touch. Monkshood is also known as devil's hood or wolfsbane. You may have heard of those. Archers use its sap to poison the tips of their arrows. Monkshood is lovely to look at, but best handled by gardeners, and not princes on whom our lives depend."

"Then you saved me. Now I'm in your debt, and you can accept my gift without guilt." I touched her cheek and made her face me.

This time, she held my gaze. She had strong, unclouded eyes that seemed to know exactly what they longed for, and they were fixed on me. We stayed like that, huddled beneath the eaves, watching each other, until the squall passed.

At last, she stuck out a hand to test for rain. "I think it's safe now, Milord."

She gathered up the knife that had slipped to the ground as we raced to shelter, and dried its handle on her new apron. Then she spoke without looking up. "I don't mean to question you, Milord, but in these days of dread, don't you have more pressing things to do than visit me in the garden?"

I heaved a sigh and glanced up at the tower, as if to check if someone was watching. At once, I knew why I'd come. "I bear a burden beyond imagining, more than I can explain. My time with you in the garden helps ease that burden."

She made her little curtsy. "Then in that case, I'm pleased to lighten your load. May the Goddess grant you strength till tomorrow."

It was time to go, but I couldn't help but wonder. *Is she merely a gardener, or something more?*

"Are you sure you're not a spirit with magic for me?"

"No magic, Milord, though I wish I could offer you more. I'm just a simple gardener who lives her life among the monkshood and hydrangeas, hoping for the flowers to bloom."

"A pity," I said, mumbling to myself. "I'd hoped you could help with the riddle."

"What riddle is that, Milord?"

"'Seek the white rose,' though no roses are to be found."

To my surprise, she laughed. "Oh, I have roses. Not in this garden, but in a bush in front of my cottage."

The words rushed from my lips. "White ones?"

"Aye, Milord, whites and reds."

"Will you bring me one tomorrow?"

The corners of her eyes drooped. "I'm sorry, Milord. It's not the season. But I'll surely bring you one when the roses bloom again."

I thanked her and trundled off, but her words rattled around in my brain—just a simple gardener with an improbable faith in the dauphin. This dauphin, however, had no such faith he'd overcome the trials, and if he failed to solve the riddle, the roses, red or white, would never bloom again.

Faces

AFTER DAD DIED, MOM STARTED GOING to the garret more frequently. Oh, she still cared for the family, buying groceries, doing the laundry and cooking meals. She also cleaned cottages for the wealthier folk who owned second homes on the water. Whenever she could spare the time, though, she returned to the garret.

One foggy day, with visibility so limited I couldn't see the house next door, I asked why she went there so much.

"He moved for me," she said. "I wanted a view of the ocean, and he gave up what he loved so I could have it. Now he's gone. The least I can do is take advantage of his gift."

As she spoke, she stayed focused on the oculus, as if trying to pierce the fog.

"But that fog's so thick," I said. "There's nothing to see."

"I owe it to him." Her voice became harsh. "I have to keep watching."

"Watching for what? That fog might not clear for hours."

"I'm not watching for the ocean, Freddie. I'm watching for a sign from him."

She watched for months, but no sign came.

Joey grew worse. He'd always been out of control, but after Dad died, the wildness that had possessed him turned into something more malevolent. He rebuffed any attempt at comfort, and his sarcasm took on a sharper edge. More booze and pills followed.

Richie was the same as always, a child in a man's body, seeking love like a puppy. Each morning, he'd wake up in the bedroom the three of us shared, turn to me, and ask, "Is Dad coming home today?"

"Not today, Richie, maybe tomorrow."

Joey wouldn't let it be. He'd roll over in a daze from whatever binge he'd been on and shout loud enough that Mom could hear through the paper-thin wall that separated our bedrooms. "He's dead, Richie. Fucking dead. Not coming back. Now let me sleep."

Between the two of them, it took a toll on Mom.

Finally, I decided to give her the sign she was hoping for. I'd taken to tracking satellites as a hobby. A friend from school had put me onto a website that tells you when satellites are visible. If I typed in the latitude, longitude, and altitude, it would tell me what time the flash would occur, and where to look in the night sky.

I tried it, and got so I could precisely predict a burst of light in the sky and then watch it happen.

One night, I sat with mom in the garret and told her I had a dream about a sign from Dad. I pointed to a few degrees above the horizon and counted down. Ten, nine, eight. At zero, the metallic surface of the International Space Station caught the sun and flared like a star right where I was pointing. It hung in the sky for an instant, seemingly motionless—a brilliant message from my father.

For the first time since his death, she smiled.

I sat in my wheelchair, staring at a magazine without comprehending a word, relieved when a tap on my door provided a diversion. I looked up to see Jimmie.

He'd taken to visiting me once or twice a day. I didn't mind his visits, even looked forward to them. Like me, he no longer resided entirely in this world. He was harmless, and occasionally would speak words of wisdom, whether he realized it or not, but today, his grin was gone.

"Got a minute, Freddie?"

"Uh-huh." I put the magazine down. I had all the time in the world.

"I had a visitor this morning. A girl."

"That's nice."

"Not so nice. They told me before she came that we'd been engaged to be married, but when she walked in, I had no memory of her. I said, 'Do I know you?' and she began to cry."

He waited for me to respond, but I was at a loss for words. I had a tough time coping with my own brand of tragedy, and could find nothing to add that would make his better. He just stared, and it felt like he was looking right through me.

"You couldn't remember at all?" I finally said.

He shook his head.

"But you remember me, my name, my face, my room number, even how to find me."

"I can remember faces I've seen since the boom." His fingers exploded around his head as they did whenever he referred to the attack. "It's the faces *before* that I can't remember, all except one. Sometimes, I think that face is blocking the others, but when I try to make it go away, I get headaches."

"What face is that?" I said, afraid to hear the answer.

"A face lying on the ground."

"But whose face?" Getting information from Jimmie was a struggle, maybe because it was a struggle for him.

"I don't know."

"You forgot?"

"No, I never knew. It was a face by itself, blown away from the rest of the body. I remember some arms and legs too, but I don't know if they went with the face. When the headaches come, I close my eyes, but the face won't go away. It keeps me from sleeping until I take the pills Dr. B. gives me."

I released the brake from my wheelchair, rolled over to him, and squeezed his arm.

He perked up. "I have a medal, Freddie. Want to see?"

I nodded.

He dug into his pocket, pulled out a felt case, and offered it to me. "A congressman came all the way from my home state to give it to me. I hoped it would be magic and make the face disappear."

I opened the case to find a five-pointed, gold star with a laurel wreath and a smaller star superimposed in its center. Jimmy was a Silver Star recipient, hoping for magic.

"It didn't work," he said. "Maybe when they close up my skull and I get rid of this helmet—" He tapped the plastic with his knuckles. "—it'll be better, but I don't think so."

I handed him back the medal. "Is there anything I can do to help?" *Shit, I can't even help myself.*

His blue eyes began to fill, battle-weary eyes that must once have been bright and full of hope. "Only if you know the secret."

"The secret?" I thought of satellites flashing across the sky at my command, but what he wanted was beyond my power.

"How do I make the face go away?" he said. "And how do I stop her from crying?"

The
Crypt

THE FOURTEENTH DAY, AFTER A RESTLESS night trying to will the trials away, I rose for my appointment with the spinning wheel. As I staggered across the ramparts, the world below seemed swaddled in gray. The voices of servants stirring for pre-dawn chores sounded muffled and hollow. Smoke from their newly lit cooking fires formed macabre shapes that danced in the light leaking through arrow loops in the battlement. By the time I reached the watchtower, the smoke had thinned into wisps that whirled about like a legion of ghosts.

I took my seat and the wheel began to spin. When it was finished, I awoke from the dream and staggered down the hundred and one stairs, feeling like a knight on the morning after battle. At the bottom, I hugged the parapet wall, whispering SMOG and searching for signs of hope, but the dark clouds continued to gather, and the sun shone dimly. Shadows deepened across the land.

The temperature had increased each day, despite the absence of sun, sucking the moisture from the earth. The willows lining the approach to the castle had turned yellow, and the grass grew brown over the plains. The heat waves were so intense, they were blue in color, and their wriggling made the hills writhe and shudder as if in pain.

A fearsome wind now blew at all times, stirring up whirlwinds that skittered along the road. Riders fleeing to the castle for protection raised dust that swirled about the hooves of their steeds. When the wind gusted, the riders would lean forward in their saddle and spur the horses onward until they broke into a gallop.

A voice from behind interrupted my gloom. "What are you looking at?"

I turned to find a young man sitting on the bench behind me.

He was simply dressed in a rumpled cloak, but wore the strangest helmet I'd ever seen. It clung closely to his head, and was made not of steel but of a white, glassy substance that looked like it would shatter from a single blow. Colorful inscriptions marked its surface, and no curls escaped its edges, as if he had no hair at all. He cocked his head to one side, and seemed to be staring at a leather bag clutched between his knees.

"The storm brewing over Golgoreth," I said.

"There's a storm?"

"You haven't seen it?"

"I never look over the wall. I have no reason to go there, so why bother?"

Wary of demons during the time of the trials, I approached cautiously. "Do I know you?"

"No."

"I haven't seen you around the castle before."

I waited, but no response.

"Did you hear what I said?" My voice sounded too loud, as if trying to outdo the wind.

"Yes."

"And?"

No response.

Not a demon, but a simpleton. I began to walk away.

He called after me. "Why do you need to save the kingdom?"

I turned. *Not a simpleton. Perhaps something more.*

"Because it's the right thing to do."

"Ah, yes, the right thing. I don't remember much, but I remember that. The right thing is a terrible thing to have to do."

I reached for Kingsbane, then withdrew my hand, having learned the futility of weapons. "Are you a spirit or a demon?"

He finally looked up. His watery blue eyes met mine. "A spirit or a demon.... What does it matter? We all have secrets."

"What's your secret?"

"I don't remember. Do you remember yours?"

"I have no time for prattle. Do you have something to offer me or not?"

He fidgeted in his seat, his eyes shifting from left to right as if searching for an answer. Then he squared his shoulders toward me and flashed an unsettling grin. "I remember now. I have something I'm supposed to give you."

He reached into the leather bag and pulled out a scroll. Its edges were charred, like something salvaged from a fire, and it was bound by a soiled string. He offered it to me.

"What's on it?" I said.

"Writing, I imagine."

I curbed my irritation and accepted the scroll, but when I tried to loosen the knot, I found it too brittle to untie. I pulled out Kingsbane and sliced the string free.

My hands trembled as I unfurled the scroll. *Could this be the clue I've been waiting for?*

What I saw disappointed me—a map of Stormwind, drawn by the hand of a child.

I studied the map, running my finger along each passageway to see if anything had changed. All was as I remembered, but when I touched the antechamber to the crypt where the kings of Stormwind were buried, the parchment grew hot. Smoke rose from the spot, and a new symbol appeared—a doorway to a place I'd never been.

I wanted to query the simpleton further, but when I looked up, he was gone.

I'd intended to meet the gardener after breakfast, but this new clue drove me on. Whether the path to salvation or the second trial, I needed to know.

I dashed down the staircase from the parapet and across the courtyard to the entrance of the crypt, but hesitated, reluctant to go in. Before me gaped a doorless archway overgrown with mossy vines, a forbidding portal waiting to swallow me up. I stuck my head inside, but kept my feet planted firmly on the threshold.

The crypt had always been dank, but now a wave of heat struck me, a swelter so strong it made the passageway thick with moisture. I grabbed a candle from a wall sconce, breathed in the last of the fresh air, and went inside.

Immediately, time seemed to slow. Memorials great and small surrounded me—my ancestors, my kin, those who had lived large and died heroes, and those who had passed leaving hardly a trace. All had overcome the spinning wheels. I could almost hear them laughing.

Behind the vault of King Menethil II, who led the Alliance against the Horde in the Second War, I found a doorway exactly where it had appeared on the map. Menacing wrought iron framed the stonework that bordered its frame. The stone itself bore complex carvings. I raised the candle for a closer look—serpents perhaps, or the writhing of souls in Hades. I gave a shudder and entered.

Beyond the doorway lay a tunnel, barely high enough to pass through without hunching over. Its walls looked newly hewn, rough-grooved with loose chips in the crevices, and the ground beneath was soft and fresh. At its end was a smaller crypt with two caskets set on pedestals. Unlike the rest, these were made of polished wood, freshly lacquered and free of dust. Both sat uncovered.

On the right rested my father, the king, as he'd lain in his death chamber. Yet no fragments of clay covered his eyes, and his cheeks were flush with blood. He lay there as if sleeping, appearing as he did in life.

On the left rested my mother, the queen. Nearly eighteen years had passed since I'd seen her last, and I'd almost forgotten how she looked. What remained in my mind was but the fantasy of a seven-year-old. Yet here she lay, looking so alive, a lovely young woman with the face of a child, gone before her time. I knelt over her, bending low, almost expecting to feel the warmth of her breath.

My cheek felt no breath, and her glassy-eyed gaze passed through me.

What mischief is this?

I'd mourned for my mother as a child, and though I'd bade farewell to my father but a fortnight ago, he'd been ill for almost a year.

Didn't I overcome that trial? What do the demons strive for that I should be shown my parents so alive?

I raised the candle high and cast its light about the room, searching for something more, and was rewarded with a reflection from the wall behind the caskets. I walked closer and saw the reason—a burnished brass plate decorated the center of a thick oak door, cut in the image of a hawk with its wings spread. An odd-shaped keyhole gaped where the beak should be.

I bent my shoulder into the oak, but the door refused to budge. I pounded on its surface with the hilt of my sword to no avail. I wedged my dagger into the keyhole and twisted, but the hole was a peculiar shape, with slots radiating out in all directions like the roots of a tree. I'd gain no entry without a special key.

With no way through and nothing left to explore, I sat on King Menethil's tomb, closed my eyes, and prayed to the Holy Light for inspiration.

I listened for an answer, but heard nothing, only my breathing and the beating of my heart. I sniffed the air, but smelled nothing, only the stench of a place abandoned too long. And so, when I heard the rumbling voice, it nearly lifted me off my seat. I turned to see the great elf filling the entrance of the crypt.

This time, Malfurion Stormrage wore a lavender robe. In his right hand, he held a staff, its top adorned with a green gem dappled with flecks of red—a bloodstone, bringer of knowledge and healing. The arm holding the staff extended toward me and his index finger uncurled, pointing toward the locked door.

"The second trial," he intoned. "The Hall of Heroes."

"But the door is locked."

"Try harder."

"I prayed to the Holy Light."

"The Holy Light will not unlock that door for you. Neither will magic help. It's faith in yourself that will show you the way."

"But how can I find that faith?"

"The question you ask has an answer you already know."

I could feel my face grow warm. "Enough of riddles. What torment have I seen through the spinning wheel that vexes me so? Why can't I remember? And how will I know when I've found the secret to defeat the Horde?"

A look of sadness overcame him, and to my chagrin, he bowed before me. "You will know when you've embraced the shadows."

Frustrated, I rose from King Menethil's tomb and rushed toward the great elf, but before I could reach him, the tip of his staff began to glow, and the red gem burst into flames. Though I felt no heat, I raised my forearm to protect my eyes. When the radiance had settled to an afterglow, I looked up and he was gone.

For the rest of that day, I fumbled about the chamber, trying to find a way to unlock the door. I groped at gravestones, hoping to find a crack where a key might be hidden. I looked in the nooks of statues. I even forced myself to probe in and around the bodies of my parents. I searched overhead around the base of the arches, but found only a black spider hanging from a web, its compound eyes taking in the scene of my madness below.

I ignored all meals and forsook my meeting with the gardener. If my fate was to embrace the shadows, I'd search them all. I only stopped when the orange light filtering through the archway called me once again to the watchtower.

The fourteenth day had ended. The kaleidoscope of gems circled one last time and slowed to a stop. Through the gold disk, I watched the last rays of the sun set behind the mountains of Golgoreth.

Too tired to move, I stayed in the chamber and stared through the oculus as the darkness spread across the plains. An owl made great circles in the air, but never stopped to land, for in these days, there remained few creatures to hunt. When the pounding of hooves resounded from the road to Stormwind, I leaned out to look.

A late-arriving horseman approached the castle, towing the corpse of his comrade draped over a second mount—scouts sent by Sir Gilly to no avail. The dead knight's helmet had been shattered by a mace, and two arrows pierced his back. The exhausted rider pulled up and glanced at the watchtower, searching. When his eye caught mine, he looked away.

In the darkened west, an aurora flickered over the mountains from a cold, stony moon. The mountaintops were edged with phosphorous, and a pale light shone through the land, giving the night a force of memory. Visions flowed: my mother saying farewell to her only child; my father on his deathbed, giving me his blessing; and a parade of unknown shadows crying to be embraced. The voice of each floated on the night air—riddles unsolved.

Speak the pain that can't be spoken. Seek the white rose. Your castle, Milord, your pipe. Embrace the shadows.

Then a roar came riding on the wind, a sharp, steady wind that dragged the refuse of dead trees along the ground and pressed in on me from all sides. With it came a new and final voice:

"You will fail, and despair shall carry the day."

I looked back to the horseman. He spurred his horse onward until it lowered its head and clattered across the drawbridge before they raised it for the night.

The roar came closer now, reaching the pine grove. I could hear the tossing of branches, the moan of limbs rubbing together.

And all at once, the wind stung my cheeks and brought tears.

Darker
Corners

AS MY LEG GREW STRONGER, THE dreams grew more muddled. In the light of day, I could pretend my brain had healed, that I'd recalled the worst of my life. The nights, however, held a deeper dread. Despite Dr. B.'s pills, I forced myself to stay awake past midnight, afraid to let my mind wander where it would. I'd recount memories I knew to be real—the roster of my high school basketball team, or the members of my *World of Warcraft* guild—but eventually, I'd drift off, and the dreams of the fantasy world would resume.

Each morning, when the pills had worn off and the light of dawn poured through the window, I'd bury my face in the pillow, hoping to shun the day. Instead, I ended up straddling the boundary between wakefulness and sleep, roaming in a world of familiar things, some real, some not. Some came from my past, some from the here and now, and others crossed over from the portals of hell.

I sniffed. *Is that the scent of royal gardens, or the daisies Becky brought to decorate my room?* I scratched at the bed. *A hospital sheet, or a prince's silk bedding?*

I slowed my breathing and relaxed my limbs, one at a time, until a stream of images flowed.

> *Nightfall.*
> *I stared out from the castle tower. A brown haze had settled over the mountains, but I could almost make out a new moon floating over them — a wishing moon, a light of hope, a wink. Then a dark cloud in the shape of a dragon sped across and swallowed it whole. I looked up to the sky for a sign. As if in response, a shooting star flared into the air and burned up.*
> *What will I do now?*
>
> *Twilight.*
> *Styrofoam packing peanuts skittered across the pavement like snow. I watched my breath glow in a beam cast by a floodlight, and gave up. Richie was gone.*
>
> *A radio crackled.*
> *"Red platoon, second squadron, third armored cav. Humvee three. Where are you?"*

My eyes popped open.

Who am I? A boy who lost his family? A point guard who'd never play basketball again? A leader who failed his men?

Being a prince made more sense.

They paraded into my room, one at a time—Dinah after breakfast, Dr. B. at the end of his morning rounds—both with the same question.

"What's wrong, Freddie?"

The day before, after wheeling me into PT, Ralph had stayed to help in my therapy, as Becky had thought having the huge health aide by my side would make me more comfortable climbing her fake stairway.

"Now remember, up with the good, down with the bad," she'd chanted as Ralph supported me from behind.

Like a baby learning to walk.

I planted my crutches on the first stair and lifted my good leg, then swung my bad one alongside. With Ralph hovering from behind, I tottered there, trying to get my balance and summon the courage to take on the next stair. When I finally reached the top, I stared back down as if I'd climbed a mountain.

My new life. Get used to it.

Back at the bottom, I wobbled on my crutches and looked longingly at the wheelchair.

"Again," Becky said.

"Wheelchair," I muttered.

"Just two more times."

"No," I said, "I'm done." I lunged for the wheelchair, almost falling, needing Ralph to catch me and get me settled back in.

Becky had frowned.

Today, just before lunch, the parade continued as Ralph came into my room, the next advocate in line. I didn't need to hear his booming voice to know what he'd say.

"What's wrong, Freddie?"

Some textbook told them I wasn't making progress fast enough, but none of them knew what was happening inside. Yes, my knee was getting stronger, but I was more than just a knee.

"Did you sic them on me?" I asked as soon as I was alone with Becky in PT.

She whirled on me, her eyes snapping to attention. "You're in my world now, buddy. I'm the queen here, and you're not progressing as fast as you should be. I told you when we started, I can be your guide, but you have to do the work. Well, you're not getting it done. Your leg's strong enough. You should be on crutches by now, not confined to a wheelchair."

I flushed, hating to have her angry with me. "Is this how you talk to all your patients?"

She came over and pulled a chair up next to me. Her eyes shifted to parade rest, and then to a look so tender, it tempered my rage.

"You're not all my patients, Freddie. I want you to get better more than any patient I've ever had, but I'm at a loss for how to get you there. The problem is your leg's healing faster than your brain."

She went silent, staring at me with a look that said it was my turn, and that hell would freeze over before she spoke next.

I swallowed hard. My throat felt thick, like when I took my first drink after waking from the coma. "What do you want me to tell you? That every time I drift off to sleep, I see pictures of war, of a charred pile of flesh slumped over a steering wheel, or a boy with his legs blown off? Yeah, I saw those things, like every other guy here. But that's not—"

I stopped myself, though the memories played on: a dead child with his head split open; a pair of boots with feet still in them, the bloody stumps sticking out; the acidic smell of burning flesh, ordnance, tires; and always the faces.

The faces stayed with me.

Becky wouldn't let it be. "That's not why you won't try to get better? Then what is?" When I clammed up, she slid over and rested a hand on my forearm. "Please, Freddie, let me in."

"There's not much to say."

"Start with that picture, the one of your family. Tell me what happened to your brothers."

I looked at her hand on my arm. I wanted to wheel myself out of the room, to be anywhere else, but I didn't want to lose her touch. I took a deep breath, sucking in the surrounding air and letting every bit of it out before speaking.

"Crazy Joey and Slow Richie," I said. "That's what Mom called them. Joey was crazy, all right, and would try anything. He finally swallowed the next big thing and killed himself."

I felt a tremor in her hand. As if to hide it, she pulled it away and swept a curl from her face. For the first time since I'd met her, she looked shaken.

All the guys she's seen coming back from the war, and my brother OD'ing gets to her?

She steadied herself, a momentary lapse of confidence, and changed the subject. "And Richie?"

"Richie was different, a good kid, but he was born slow. My mother used to insist he had nothing wrong with him, that he was just slower than the other kids. He used to follow me around, even though he was two years older. He always had a dumb grin — perpetual happiness without cause — and he was always humming that song, the Christmas carol from the music box. Never learned the words, but hummed it all year round."

"Where is he now?"

"After my mother died, Richie wandered off. I haven't seen him in six years. Probably homeless, maybe dead."

"Did you try looking for him?"

"What do you think?"

"I think you can use some help, and that maybe I should sign you up for a PTSD group."

I gripped the arms of the wheelchair tighter and half rose. "You mean a bunch of guys griping about how bad the war was? You think that'll fix everything? What happened was real, not my imagination. Talking about it won't make it go away."

She stood and wandered over to one of the treadmills, and picked a flower from the cup holder. When she turned toward me, I thought she was about to offer it to me.

"Would you like to get out of here sometime, Freddie? Out of the hospital for a while?"

"What do you mean?"

"I mean an excursion. I can order a chair car. You haven't been outside in a couple of months. Might do you some good."

"Are you asking me for a date?"

She flushed. "Sorry, we have strict rules against fraternizing with patients."

"Then why are you asking? Can't you take me wherever you want?"

"I need your consent."

"Where would I go?"

"I'll figure something out."

"But you'd come with me?"

"If that's what it takes for you to agree. We're not accomplishing much here."

I watched her holding the flower. *What is it? I used to know. Not a rose. Maybe a lily, like the kind they put around a coffin at a wake.*

Her look was different than someone at a wake, more like someone desperate for a yes.

I was taking too long to decide, and she turned to replace the flower in the cup holder. I called her back. "I'll go."

Back in my room, I sat on the bed thinking. I couldn't dodge the memories any longer.

A month after Mom's funeral, as I was trudging up the walkway at the end of a long day, Richie ran up to me with that silly grin and asked again if I knew when Dad and Mom would be coming home.

I lost it.

He'd sat through three funerals. At each, when the minister had asked if a family member wanted to speak, he'd nudged me and said, "You do it, Freddie." But he still didn't understand that Dad had died, that Joey had followed him eagerly to the grave, and that both of their deaths had devastated Mom.

I tried to temper my words, but they came out hot. "They're gone, Richie, all of them, and they're never coming back."

He'd looked at me as if surprised, but said nothing—just stumbled around in little circles under the basket. Then he began to sob—raw, heaving sobs, loud enough so neighbors opened their windows to see what was going on.

They'd watched for a few seconds, shook their heads, and closed the windows again.

The next day, he ran off.

I'd promised Mom I'd take care of him, but how much could I do? I'd started college, enlisted in ROTC to cover my tuition, and had a long commute. Most of the insurance money had gone for the granite crypts Mom insisted on having—she had a fear of being buried in the ground. I barely had enough left to keep the gingerbread house, never mind pay for someone to sit with Richie, so I placed a necessary bet—that he'd be there every night when I came home.

I lost.

I tracked him to the bus depot at the rotary by the bridge. The man behind the ticket counter remembered him buying a ticket to Boston, which he must have done with the few bucks I'd left him.

I knew Richie liked to ride the T, ever since the summers when Mom used to take the three of us to the beach at L Street. So I spent the next three days on buses and streetcars and trains, crisscrossing the city from Brighton to Mattapan, from Dorchester to Revere, till 12:30 in the morning when the T stopped running. Then I'd crash on a bench in the subway, eat junk food from vending machines in the stations, and hope for a miracle. I showed his picture to anyone who'd listen, the T police, the guys who made change in the stations, the lady sitting next to me on the train.... I'd get off at each stop and search the streets for four blocks in either direction.

No miracle.

At the end of the third day, as I sat on an old packing crate at the edge of an empty parking lot, a torn trash bag from a dumpster caught the wind and released its contents in a gust. Styrofoam packing peanuts skittered across the pavement. I stared at their dance, watching puffs of my own breath glisten under a floodlight, and gave up. Richie was gone, disappeared into the great underbelly of the city. Time to look out for myself.

He was a good kid, Richie, always cared what happened to me. What if some kind soul had taken him in and given him a job? He'd be a good worker if you gave him repetitive chores, like Mom used to do—folding laundry, or picking rocks from a garden.

I wondered what he'd look like now. With no one to cut his hair, had it grown long? Had his fair skin darkened from living on the streets?

I shimmied to the edge of my bed, reached out, and grabbed the crutches leaning against the wall.

If I used them in PT, dammit, I can use them now.

I shuffled over to the closet, and balanced on them while I rummaged through and found the military-issue carton with my personal stuff. I took out the music box and wound the key, then switched the lever on. The Christmas carol began to play.

Wouldn't it be great if Richie heard I was in the VA hospital and came to visit, came walking through that door this very minute?

I listened, and sure enough, footsteps approached in the corridor. When I looked up, Nurse Dinah was there, come to give me my meds. I flicked the lever off.

As I teetered on the crutches like a toddler, she took off her Coke bottle glasses, swished the lenses with the corner of her lab coat, and held them up to the light to check for smudges. Then she put them back on, and the eyes behind the glasses crinkled as she broke into a smile.

Up
with the
Good

BECKY BROUGHT ME THROUGH THE MAIN
entrance of the hospital and down a ramp to the parking lot,
where several other vets were lined up waiting for a ride. I
twisted around in my wheelchair and glanced up, my first
outside view of the building that had been my home the past
two months. It had a decorative turret at its highest point, a
cupola on top, and arched windows staring out in all
directions.

I bet the turret isn't handicap accessible.

"So that's where you've been keeping me captive."

Becky grinned but didn't dignify my comment with a reply.

When my turn came, she wheeled me onto the mechanized
lift. The attendant hit the lever, and the platform whirred until it
was even with the bed of the van. Then they rolled me in and
locked me down.

Once on the road, I badgered Becky to tell me where we were
going, but she insisted our destination should be a surprise. Stuck
in the back, I had no idea where the van was heading. Every now
and then, I'd twist around in my chair, as much as my damaged

leg allowed, and peek through the windshield. After a while, I noticed the trees getting stumpy and the horizon drifting farther away. A childlike excitement grew within me, the anticipation I had as a kid when approaching the ocean.

By the time we crested the bridge over the canal, I knew: she was taking me to Cape Cod.

I didn't know whether to be angry or pleased. It *did* feel good to be outside for the first time since coming back to the States, but I hadn't been to the Cape since going on active duty, and wasn't sure I was ready for a return.

"Why'd you pick the Cape?" I said.

She glanced up into the rear-view mirror and for a moment, our eyes met. I caught the hint of a smirk on her face.

"I like the Cape, don't you?"

"I was thinking something closer. How can you afford all this time?"

"I'm on my own today. It's Saturday."

Saturday. I used to count the days until my deployment ended, marking each box on the calendar with a black X. Now, I'd stopped looking at calendars. Time was no longer my friend.

"Am I the best you can do for a weekend date?"

She chuckled. "I was hard up. Guess you're it."

I eyed the crutches she'd stowed in the corner. "Dinah told you I made it across the room by myself?"

"Uh-huh."

"Is that why you brought the crutches?"

"You never know when you might need them. Maybe a curb or a stair or two."

"You know I can't do stairs."

"I've watched you do them in PT."

"PT's not the real world. I appreciate your taking me out, Becky, but don't get any notions. Across my room is one thing. Outdoors is another."

The smirk widened. "We'll see."

The driver pulled the van into a dirt parking lot. Together, he and Becky maneuvered the chair onto the lift and lowered me. The driver synchronized his watch, as we used to before a patrol in Iraq or a raid in *Warcraft*. One hour.

A couple minutes later, Becky rolled me along the sidewalk.

It was a clear day, mild for October. The Cape got pretty quiet after Labor Day, but the weekend's weather was nice enough that a lot of people were out and about. Becky told me she'd searched online and found a little burger place on the water, just a few blocks away.

On the way, we passed a basketball court where a bunch of kids played pickup, three on three. At the sound of dribbling and the clank of the ball against the rim, my fingers started to twitch.

"Did you know," I said, "that we'd be going past a basketball court?"

"How would I know? I've never been here before. Want to stop and watch?"

I hemmed and hawed, but before I could come up with an answer, she wheeled me to the edge of the court and set the brake.

They were kids of fourteen, maybe fifteen, not all-stars. They looked a lot like the ragtag bunch my dad had inherited when we first came to the Cape. He'd tried to whip them into shape, but there wasn't enough talent in that small school, especially compared to the juggernaut he'd left in Boston. In his second year, after the seventh straight loss, he let them have it, told them they were a bunch of damned losers and would never be anything else. One of the players told his mother, who sat on the school board. Dad made a public apology, but it wasn't enough. At the end of the season, they let him go.

"Want to take a shot?" Becky said.

I turned around to see if she was serious. She had a playful side, but when it came to my rehab, she was a hardass.

"I'm in a fucking wheelchair," I said.

"People in wheelchairs play basketball, some of them pretty well."

She let go of the handles, waited until an out-of-bounds ball stopped play, and then stepped onto the court. "Excuse me."

"Don't do this, Becky."

"Would you mind if he took a shot? He used to be a great basketball player, but was wounded in Iraq. He's a war hero."

I ground my teeth and readied a response, but the kids came over right away. The shortest one, probably the point guard, handed me the ball.

"I can't."

"You don't want to disappoint them, Freddie."

She positioned me in front of the basket, halfway inside the key, at what used to be my launch point when I tried to dunk.

The kids formed a semicircle behind me.

I stroked the nub of the ball, fingered the edge of the seam, and breathed in the leather. How was I supposed to shoot without pushing off with my legs? I tried spinning the ball off my fingertips — once, twice, three times — glanced over my shoulder at Becky, and took a half-hearted shot.

Just short of the rim.

"Try again," she said as one of the boys retrieved the ball.

I did. This time, I compensated for no legs, and it clanked off the front.

The boys behind me shuffled nervously.

Becky released the brake and rolled me a foot closer, whispering as she did so. "You can do it."

I held the ball in front of my face, cocked my wrist, and pushed a little harder. Too much arm to be graceful. This time, it popped over the lip of the rim, rattled around, and went in.

A cheer went up behind me and the boys formed a line for high-fives, as if I'd hit a shot at the buzzer to win states.

Afterwards, I was furious with Becky. "You had no right."

"It proved what you can do."

"That's not your job."

"Helping you get your confidence back is exactly my job. It shows how much you have left."

I pressed down on the arms of the chair with all my strength, and turned around to face her. "You're wrong. It shows how much I've lost."

After that, we both fell into a funk, rolling along without talking, heading to the café. Before we got there, we noticed the ferry to Martha's Vineyard about to depart, and she took me into a small park by the terminal to watch it go.

I compulsively scanned the perimeter before we entered.

Not many places to hide. A few bushes on three sides and Vineyard Sound at the front.

I listened for movement. A gull squawked overhead, and the waves lapped lazily at the shore, murmuring like the hushed voices of drowned sailors telling their stories. I sniffed the air.

No smoke from a discharged weapon. No stench from a detonated explosive.

And none of the hospital odors I'd become used to—disinfectant and hand sanitizer. I calmed myself down and released the breath I'd been holding in. Then I inhaled the salt spray as if for the first time.

The ferry captain blew his horn, signaling he was about to shove off. Overhead, the sun shone brightly, but the Vineyard lay shrouded in mist. The offshore breeze had yet to push the morning fog out to sea. The island that was the ferry's destination rippled and blurred like a phantom world.

Becky rolled me to the center of the park and settled on a bench, stopping first to read the shiny plaque bolted onto its back. The fresh inscription read:

Eva "April" Bryant. A Celebration of Life 1922-2008.

Underneath was a quote:

"So much to do, so little time."

"Now there's a woman with spunk," Becky said.

I was still humiliated by the scene at the basketball court, and the words spewed out without thought. "And you're saying if I had that kind of spunk, I'd be dunking by now. Is that it?"

"I was just saying she had spunk, that's all."

"Fuck spunk."

She laughed. "What do you have against spunk? My father always said he admired a woman with spunk."

"Then fuck your father and all his wise sayings too."

"You know, Freddie, you can be a real pain in the ass."

"Easy for you to say, Miss Sunshine and Light."

Her face turned red and she leaned closer, inches from my nose. "You don't know anything about me. You have no right to—"

Just as she was getting revved up, the ferry's engine grew to a roar as the captain backed the ship out into the harbor. She stopped talking while it executed its turn, accelerated into the sound, and began fading into the fog. By that time, her mood had changed. Despite the breeze blowing hair across her eyes, the difference was easy to see. The color had drained from her face.

I waited, unsure whether to ask her to go on. When she stayed silent, I thought it best to apologize. She was right, after all. I'd been an ass.

"It was being around the court, Becky. I just...."

A half smile. "Apology accepted."

"What were you starting to say before the ferry throttled up?"

She shook her head slowly. "Doesn't matter, Freddie. All that matters is that you get it into your thick skull."

"Get what?"

"How much I want you to get better. If you can't do it for yourself, do it for me."

Following lunch, we returned to the van and drove another half hour. Cape back roads all looked the same, narrow and winding, lined with old trees and weathered houses turned gray by the salt air. I had no way of telling where we were, at least not until we turned onto that familiar, single-lane road, and I felt the speed bump.

I shouted to the driver, "Stop! Turn back!"

The driver tapped his brakes, but Becky waved him on. Then she swiveled around in her seat and faced me. "It's for me, Freddie. I want to see it."

"Why?"

"It's the way you spoke about the garret. I want to see the ocean through that little window your mother loved."

"Did you bring Gloria and the music box too?"

"Come on, Freddie. You won't do anything I ask you to do in PT, even though it's for your own good. At least do this one little favor for me."

She pulled a photograph from her pocketbook, pointed to the far side, and directed the driver around the green and past the tabernacle. She must have had Ralph sneak into my room while I was at PT and rummage through my personal stuff to borrow the picture.

The van came to a stop, the panel doors opened, and the driver shifted my wheelchair to the lift and lowered me to the ground.

There it was: the gingerbread house.

For an instant, I was no longer the wounded warrior but a young architecture student studying for spring exams, hoping someday to build a house as beautiful as the one I grew up in. I recalled the first day I saw it—ten years old, the family whole and together. I thought we were moving into a fairy tale.

The new owners hadn't changed much. Mom's hydrangeas still framed the walkway, but this late in the season, the blue had been bleached out of them, and the blossoms had become ragged.

Everything else seemed the same: steeply pitched roof with scalloped trim; frosted windows with the clear palm fronds; white fence with the tulip-shaped cutouts. Despite the years away and the damage to my brain, all appeared as I remembered it. I almost expected Richie to come running out the front door.

But even he would take one look at me now and realize how much I'd changed—enough to stop asking if I'd dunked. Those days were gone, like the rest of the family.

My daydreaming ended abruptly when I heard a noise from inside, an odd clicking sound like a bolt being pulled back and released. A dog barked, and the war took over. I surveyed the houses surrounding the green, checking for faces in the windows and snipers on the rooftops. A middle-aged couple sat on a park bench on the green, feeding breadcrumbs to pigeons from a paper bag. I strained, staring at the bag, trying to read the intent on their faces.

My hands began to sweat.

A window opened in the house next door, and Mrs. Miller stuck her head out to see what the racket was all about. She was a gracious, silver-haired lady, a deacon in the tabernacle, and a close friend of my mother's.

"Well, I'll be," she called from the window. "Is that you, Freddie Williams?"

A moment later, her door swung open and she came out.

"I heard you were in Iraq. Are you okay?"

Despite my irritation at Becky, I was pleased to see Mrs. Miller. She'd always been kind to my family, though I hated her seeing me in the wheelchair.

"Getting better," was all I managed to say.

"I hope so," she said. "Lord knows your family has had its share."

Becky came out of the van with the crutches, and I glared at them.

Mrs. Miller held out her hand. "Hello, young lady. I'm Helen Miller. Are you Freddie's wife?"

Becky flushed and shook her head.

"This is Becky Marshall," I said. "My physical therapist. She's trying to get me to walk again."

"Well, I'll pray for you to succeed. How is Richie doing?"

"I haven't seen him," I said. "Not for a long time."

"Richie used to follow Freddie around like a puppy dog," Mrs. Miller explained to Becky. "The two of them, different kids, but they looked a lot alike and were always together. Two peas in a pod."

I didn't have the heart to tell her that one of the peas had fled. I thanked Mrs. Miller, told her good-to-see-you.

After she'd god-blessed me and returned to her home, I whirled on Becky. "Now what do you think you're doing with those crutches?"

"Just a quick look inside."

"You know I can't climb stairs?"

"It's three stairs, Freddie. Should be a piece of cake."

"Easy for you to say. Besides, you can't barge in like this. It's not my house anymore."

"I'm not barging. I called in advance."

She left me with my mouth open, skipped up the front stairs, and knocked on the frosted glass.

A young mother answered with two kids hanging off her legs.

Becky explained that she was the one who had called, that I'd grown up in that house, and that this was my first time out of the hospital since being wounded in the war.

I did my best to shrink into the wheelchair.

Then, despite my protestations, Becky handed me the crutches and helped me to stand.

I wobbled, more furious than unsteady. "I'll look like an old man," I hissed.

One of the kids asked his mother why I was so mad.

"Hush, Johnny," she said. "He's a war hero."

"No, I'm not," I muttered as I took my first step.

"Well, you will be to me," Becky said, loudly enough for the whole neighborhood to hear, "if you climb those stairs."

The odd clicking got sharper as I approached the first step. *Clickety-clack.*

A golden retriever ran to the door wanting to play—friend, not enemy. The mother grabbed his collar to keep him from knocking me over.

I had an urge to see the inside again, and started to climb.

For the first time in a while, I neglected to check my surroundings. The gingerbread house had always felt safe, and I didn't want to embarrass myself. I focused on one step at a time, and at the top, I was rewarded with the old living room.

When I lived there last, reminders of my family had been scattered everywhere. Mom's notepad had hung from a hook on the wall, filled with her scribbled proverbs for the day. Dad's reading glasses, which she'd refused to throw away, had been left half-open on an end table, next to the pipe he occasionally smoked. And the sofa... where I'd found him the day he died.

Thankfully, the furniture had changed. A playpen occupied the space where the sofa had been. In the kitchen doorway, a baby slept in one of those wind-up swings. It rocked slowly back and forth. *Clickety-clack.* On the floor sat a box with wooden cars, crayons with a coloring book left open to a half-finished picture, and a dollhouse with dolls inside. Plastic toys and stuffed animals littered the hall. The young mother must have seen how I eyed them, and cleared a path for me.

The only remnants of my family's home were the two paintings that hung on the wall by the stairway to the upper floors. My mother had found the old paintings at Pick of the Litter—portraits of sea captains with their backs and mouths stiff, their caps peaked and tilted to one side, and their eyes narrowed as if staring into a stiff breeze at sunset. The first couple of years after we moved to the Cape, I would fantasize about being a sea captain. Seeing them now felt like meeting old friends.

At the base of the stairway, I stopped and looked up—ten stairs to the next landing, wide enough for my crutches, shallow risers. And I knew the flight to the garret was the same.

Becky caught me staring at the stairway. "You did great, Freddie. I didn't intend—"

I shifted the crutches to face her. "I thought you wanted to see the ocean."

"I was kidding."

"Well, I'm not."

"We can come back another time."

"You said I could do a lot more."

"You can."

"Well, now's the time." I shuffled to the edge of the stairs, so that my shoes touched the riser, and lifted the crutches onto the first stair. "You really think I can do this?"

"I *know* you can."

I took three quick breaths, like I used to when heading into an abandoned building on patrol. "Back me up, just in case." One more breath. "Up with the good."

I stepped onto the stair with my good leg, pulled my bad leg even, and paused to steady myself.

Becky followed like the mother of a toddler who'd recently learned to walk.

"One," I said.

It wasn't easy, but I was driven. I needed to see the garret, to show Becky the ocean through the oculus window. I needed to search for insurgents in my childhood home, to confront an assassin or an elf on the stairway, to know if Richie was hiding in the eaves.

I was in a zone, last ten seconds of the game. *Score tied. Ball in my hands. Freddie the point guard. Pass or take it to the hoop. Clock winding down.*

I was breathing hard, and my hands began to go numb. I looked up.

The garret.

"So this is it?" Becky said.

I nodded, shocked at how small it was, almost surprised my mother wasn't still sitting by the oculus, watching for a sign from my dad.

Becky rushed forward as though she was about to catch me from falling.

When she threw her arms around me, her energy filled me, a life force renewing me.

The trip down was scarier because the zone was gone. I was back to being a gimpy veteran. Neither of us had much to say until I was back in the van with my wheelchair locked into place.

Becky asked the driver to wait a second before driving off. She left her seat and squatted next to me. "You did it, Freddie. See how much you can do?"

I lifted my chin and straightened, getting as tall as I could in a wheelchair. "You win, Becky. Your little scheme worked. But I'm never doing it again."

"Why not? You're only going to get stronger. In a month or two, I'll have you climbing those stairs with a cane."

"That's not what I meant."

"Then what?"

"I meant I'm finished with that part of my life. Time to move on."

Heroes
and
Flowers

TWELVE DAYS UNTIL MY ANOINTMENT OR the end of all things, yet still no progress. The door to the second trial was locked, the key nowhere to be found. Following that morning's session with the spinning wheel, I dashed down the stairway eyeing the shadows, expecting each one to bring doom.

At the bottom, I paused in the archway, held my breath, and listened. The wind whistled through the arrow loops, but neither scrape nor scuffle came from the stairs. I was alone.

I staggered to a bench in an alcove and sat with my sword across my knees, back to the wall—the defensive posture Sir Gilly had taught me. Just when it seemed I might be safe, a chill ran through me, and I shuddered under the sensation of a cold hand on my shoulder.

Impossible. Nothing behind me but wall.

When the feeling persisted, I jumped up and spun around, my sword at the ready, pointing foolishly at the stones.

As I squinted, the stones blurred and a man appeared. A warrior, it seemed, garbed in a uniform I'd never seen before: not the armor of a knight or the chain mail of a foot soldier, but a jacket of blue cloth; not a helmet, but a peaked cap as blue as the jacket. Brass buttons paraded down his chest, and he bore an insignia of gold over his heart. Most surprising, he had shape but lacked depth, and his movements were not movements at all, but ripples, like a tapestry in a breeze.

"Are you the one searching for the boy?" a voice said, though the warrior's lips never moved.

I straightened my arm until the point of the sword scraped the stone behind the apparition. "Are you spirit or demon?"

"They told me someone like you was searching for the boy."

I lowered my arm and relaxed, as he had no physical presence and was deaf to my words. I turned to go.

"I may know where he is," he said. "If you come with me, I'll show you." His right hand reached out in a gesture of beckoning.

Some memory within me stirred, a vision from the spinning wheels — snow skittering across a hard, black surface.

"What boy?" I pleaded.

The wall was fast returning to stone. I took a step closer, desperate for more, but the soldier had faded, leaving no more than a blotch of blue. Then, as I stared open-mouthed, the blue-tinged light rippled one last time and winked out.

"Why is your back exposed?" a more familiar voice behind me said. "Do you expect an attack from the wall?"

I turned to see what appeared to be Sir Gilly, but wisps of gray flew out from his temples, and his face was the color of chalk. He looked more like his own ghost.

"What happened to you?" I checked for the telltale aura of a shapeshifter.

"We must speak, Frederick. I've been visited by a spirit of my own."

I studied his features, then glanced past him, searching behind the pillars for hidden enemies. "What spirit?"

"This morning, when I went to the lord chamberlain's office, I found the door open. I was sure I'd locked it, as I have each night for over forty-one years. Was I less likely to be vigilant in these days of dread? Of course, I entered with trepidation, and what I found.... Only now, after all these years, do I appreciate what the princes of Stormwind endure." He wavered, nearly stumbling.

As I caught his arm to support him, we came close, his eyes inches from mine. I peered into them and my suspicions vanished. Here was my rock and my mentor, but with a weariness as deep as my own. I sheathed my sword and brought him to the bench, warily watching the wall behind.

"What did you find?" I said when he was seated.

His features sagged, making him look old beyond his years. "I often wondered how we go on, with the dreadlord and his Horde looming over us and the watchtower forming but a thin line in between. Yet in the courtyard, the people come and go, taking for granted that each generation will prevail."

"What did you find?" I asked more urgently.

"A spirit with a message for you."

"But why would he give it to you and not to me directly?"

"He said he was barred by the demons from speaking with you ever again."

"Again?" My mind raced. "What did he look like?"

"A large man with an overarching brow and a shaved head that was mostly skull." He stared into the distance, as if he could see the spirit hovering over the parapet wall, and when he continued, his voiced trembled. "His chest was shorn away. No clothing or skin covered it, only the strangest of medallions floating in the air. And behind it... his beating heart...."

I was afraid to ask, but his silence lingered. "The medallion... was it in the image of the World Tree?"

His face brightened with recognition. "Aye, that's it. The World Tree."

"And what did the message say?"

"His words were odd, Frederick, spoken with a deep sorrow. He said he bore a clue to the key you've been seeking, but I'm a poor advisor with nothing to add, not the least insight into what he meant." He stopped, unable to go on.

I squeezed his arm and repeated my question, enunciating every word. "The message. What was it?"

"Just this." He drew me closer and whispered, as if to mimic the spirit. "The new pipe is for heroes."

I led Sir Gilly to his quarters and ordered two stout knights to attend him, making each swear to stay by his side even should the dreadlord himself appear. Once he settled in, I rushed to the lord chamberlain's office in the hope I might find the spirit and speak to him. After finding no one, I sat at the lord chamberlain's table and scratched on a parchment a list of all I had learned.

Seek the white rose. But no roses bloomed in the kingdom at this time of year.

Embrace the shadows. The simpleton's map had led me to the crypt where the shadows of my parents rested. The great elf himself had confirmed the entrance to the second trial. Yet the door was locked, to be opened only by a special key.

The new pipe is for heroes. The clue to finding the key.

The conclusion seemed clear: I was barred from the second trial for want of a key, and the key was connected to the pipes. Therefore, the answer must lie in the chamber where I'd first met the spirit.

I stuffed the parchment into my tunic pocket and headed for the armory. As I strode down the familiar tunnel, I prepared for signs that might foreshadow a change—a draft of air on my face, or the slightest slope downward. I listened for the clanging of pipes or a hint of the spirit singing. Nothing. Only the crash of steel on steel as swords were stacked in the armory.

When I arrived, I queried the armorer to learn what he knew about a hidden chamber.

The old man rubbed the stubble along his scar and gaped at me. "A chamber with pipes? None that I recall."

"Or a tunnel sloping downward to a steep ramp?"

He shook his head. "For thirty-five years, I've come here each morning in service to your father, and the tunnel's always remained level for me. But who am I to say? These are strange times."

He was being kind, but I could imagine his thoughts: the dauphin had gone daft, succumbing to the pressures of anointment.

I thanked him, wished him well, and backtracked along the tunnel, hoping to find a way to make it transform. As if to mock me, the castle refused to change.

Frustrated in my attempt to find the chamber, I went to the gardens instead, seeking a gentler spirit — Rebecca among the hydrangeas — but to no avail.

I settled beneath the sprawling elm tree and stared up at the sky, hoping to catch a patch of blue through its branches; nothing but thunderclouds racing before the wind.

I sniffed the air. The heat had strengthened the fragrance of the flowers, but if it persisted, all the blossoms would die.

I listened. No folk were about, and all the birds had fled.

I rubbed my eyes as if trying to remove a stain. *Seek the white rose. Embrace the shadows. Pipes and heroes.* What did it all mean?

At a sound on the gravel path, I started, but kept my sword sheathed — more the sprightliness of slippers than the crunch of boots, and a voice like a song.

"So low, Sire. Is there nothing your humble servant can do?"

I looked up at Rebecca. "You mustn't call me Sire. I won't become king until I've overcome the trials, if ever."

"But most surely you will."

"I'd have your confidence if I could fight with my sword, but that's not how the battle with demons is won."

A shiver passed through her. "You do battle with demons? You must be brave."

"Not brave. The demons can't harm me. They can only muddle my mind."

She tilted her head to one side, her look questioning. "I don't understand, Milord."

"It's hard to explain. In the watchtower, I see visions that make me question what is real."

She walked over to the wall of the watchtower, where a climbing vine was covered with clusters of white stars, and took a small knife from her apron pocket. She reached up on tiptoes, cut off a sprig, and brought it to me. As she approached, the air filled with perfume.

"Take this," she said. "Touch it, smell it. Then tell me it's not real."

I had no need. The flowers overwhelmed my senses, driving the trials from my mind.

"There," she said, nestling beside me on the bench. "Now that you know this sweet autumn clematis is real, you'll know I'm real as well, and won't go sticking me with your sword again."

I buried my face in the flowers, drunk from their scent.

She leaned close to smell them as well.

"If only they were roses," I said.

"Not all flowers can be roses, Milord. This clematis has a glory of its own. And no rose has ever smelled as sweet."

"But I need to find a white rose."

"Why?"

"I don't know why. That's only what I've been told." I lowered my voice to sound like the great elf. "Seek the white rose, even though no roses are in bloom."

"But Milord," she said laughing, "you don't know one flower from another. Pretend along with me, and perhaps we'll find the magic you seek."

I looked into her laughing eyes. "How?"

"I'll find you a white rose." She searched through the garden and selected a flower. "Ah, here's one, hiding among the others." She snipped it off with her knife.

"That's no rose."

"Yes, Milord, a rose of sorts, and with magic strong enough to anoint you king. Here, no need to kneel. Sitting will do, and besides, you're low enough already."

She touched my forehead with the flower. I could feel its texture, like velvet, but when her hand brushed my cheek, I began to believe.

"What flower is it, really," I said, "this pretend rose of yours?"

"Well, Milord, if you must spoil the moment, it's a fall crocus. But that doesn't mean it lacks magic. Keep my gift close, and it will help you find your way."

She offered me the flower, and I tucked it into my tunic.

"There," she said. "No demon can harm you now."

I smiled weakly. "The dreadlord must be quaking in his boots."

"You make light of me, Milord, but you're in *my* garden now, and no demons are allowed. If they dare approach, they'll be overwhelmed by the scent of my very real flowers."

Weighed down by my burden, my smile settled into a frown. "I wish the trials were so simple, Rebecca, but to overcome them, I'm bound to wander the castle in search of a spirit who can provide me an answer. Yet the days grow short, and I've found no one to help."

"Perhaps," she said, a glimmer in her eye, "the answer is nearer than you think."

"What do you mean?"

"Are you so certain you need a spirit?"

"Why do you ask?"

"Because *I'm* also here in the castle."

I stared at her, unblinking.

She stood before me and made a curtsy so low, the ruffled hem of her apron whispered across the toes of her slippers.

"Your servant," she said with a blush. "Milord and soon to be Sire."

Stories

AFTER THE TRIP TO THE GINGERBREAD house, I threw myself into rehab. Although the brace limited my right leg, I worked the rest of my body as if training for the playoffs. My arms grew stronger, and I no longer needed the wheelchair.

I tried to rehab my mind as well, giving in to Becky's suggestion to attend the PTSD group. At first, I didn't say much — nothing could change the reality of what I'd experienced — but listening to the guys reawakened memories of Iraq, not just of the war, but of the camaraderie.

The trip to the Cape had reawakened something else in me. Now, once again, I wanted to design beautiful places, to build, and not go to war. I might never play basketball again, but I could still become an architect. It would be another long road, made harder by injuries and time away, but I believed I could do it — a few courses, an internship, and then certification. As Becky would say: a goal, something to hope for.

Not only did I realize how much I could do, but I'd exorcised the demons in the garret. In the days that followed, as I sweated through PT, Becky and I talked about what had happened there, things I'd never discussed with anyone. Some were memories my concussed brain had lost, but Becky kept bringing them back—the pain that can't be spoken.

After Joey died, my mother lost it. I came home from school one day and found her and Richie sitting in the kitchen, waiting for me with the table set for five.

"Are we expecting company?" I said.

She smiled a mother's smile that seemed to say I'd understand when I was grown. "You know there are five of us, Freddie."

I waited, hoping she'd remember, and when she didn't, I felt compelled to speak. "Not anymore," I said as gently as I could.

"But of course, we're five, Freddie. Dad and Joey and—"

I started to say, "They're gone," but bit my lip.

Too late.

She'd read the anguish on my face, and opened her mouth as if to scold, to tell me the error of my ways. She drew in a breath, but it escaped as a sigh instead of a sentence.

She stood, took one step toward me, and diminished. First, she folded over with hands on knees, and then her knees buckled and her hands splayed out to either side. She bent until her forehead nearly touched the newly waxed floor, so shiny her face reflected in it. She raised her hands to her hair and began tearing at it, while Richie cowered in a corner. Still no sound, only small and sudden gulps of air.

After a minute, I took her gently by the elbow and helped her stand, but she refused to come back to the table. Instead, she led me to the garret, where she took up watch at the oculus, staring out to sea.

After that, she mostly stayed there, still insisting I always set the table for five, but never coming to dinner.

I'd prepare a meal, wait ten minutes for her, and then Richie and I would eat. When we were done, I'd bring up a tray.

She'd listen to her song and push the food around on her plate with a fork, but never ate much again. Her spirit had vanished... like the family itself.

Day after day, I tried to convince her to join us, but eventually I gave up. There seemed no point to it, as everything she had left was in the garret — the music, the mermaid, and the ocean.

In her last weeks, she hardly ever abandoned her watch. I'd come home from school and try to talk with her, and when she said nothing, I'd sit with her and Richie and listen to the music box, while she hummed softly and stared out at the ocean.

Near the end, she slept a lot and withdrew. Her eyes became narrow and glassy, focusing only occasionally. When I brought her meals, I'd have to let her know it was me. She'd nod, take my hand, and sometimes squeeze. Occasionally, she'd ask where Joey was, or tell me to remind Dad to be on time for dinner.

One day, she asked me to bring her makeup kit and the sundress she always wore when she went to the beach. It was winter, hardly twenty degrees, and a wind howled from the north through the eaves, but I did as she asked. She was barely strong enough to put on the dress, needing my help to slip on the arms. Next, she wanted a mirror, apparently not troubled by the skeleton she'd become, and for fifteen minutes, she put on makeup. When she was done, she asked for the costume tiara my father had given her for their twentieth anniversary, just before he died. She put it on and told me to move the chair closer to the garret window.

It was late afternoon on an overcast day, but as so often happened by the sea, the sun broke through from behind a cloud and shone directly through the garret window. An orange hue streamed onto her face, making the tiara sparkle.

She took my hand, lifted it to her lips, and kissed it three times. "My Freddie," she whispered.

It was all the love she had left. She took one long breath, as if letting the taste of salt air linger on her tongue.

Then she was gone.

I bounded along on my crutches, my confidence growing each day as my arms grew stronger. I'd built up callouses on my hands, so they hurt less, and my good leg supported me without as much as a wobble.

Tomorrow, the brace would come off.

Then, according to Becky, the *real* work would begin.

Looking for a place to show off my newfound mobility, I headed for Jimmie's room—1563, the number he could never remember. When I arrived, Jimmy sat at a table, fumbling with a deck of cards as if playing solitaire.

I swing-bounded into his room. "What's up, Jimmie?"

"Memory therapy," he said.

When I came closer, I saw they weren't playing cards but photos of soldiers, the kind they put in a basic training yearbook. He shuffled through them—eager young men, whole and brave—trying to remember their names. He'd pick up a card, say a name, turn it over and read the answer on the back. Then he'd shake his head. He kept trying, repeating the same name until, after seven or eight more cards, he found the right one.

He looked up and sighed. "Not doing so good, Freddie. I can only get one."

"But you're saying the same name over and over again."

"I know." He grinned like Richie, an innocent grin. "Only one I can remember."

"Who are they?"

"Guys from my squad. Dr. B. claims I was their leader, but I can't recall most of them."

"What's the doc say?"

He laughed. "'Keep trying, Jimmie.'"

We both turned at a knock on the door and watched Dinah come in. I hopped over to show off.

"Getting pretty good at it, Freddie," she said.

"I have a great physical therapist. You need to see Jimmie? I'll get out of your way."

"I'm here for you, Freddie. You have visitors."

Panic. I had no family. Maybe Richie? I'd been down that wishing well once too often.

"Who?" I said, hiding my panic with a smirk. "Someone from the USO?"

Her answer wiped the smirk off my face. "The wife and son of one of your men."

While I hobbled back to my room, I racked my brain. If I were given the same exercise as Jimmie, how would I do? I started listing the guys in my squad by Humvee, working from the gun turret down. Humvee one: check. I had almost gotten through Humvee two when I reached my room.

Seated on guest chairs were a woman and a young boy, maybe eight years old. Someone had been kind enough to offer them soft drinks while they waited. The woman looked vaguely familiar, maybe a picture I'd seen, but I couldn't mistake the boy — the spitting image of the archangel.

The woman stood and took my hand, then brought it to her lips and kissed it. "You're Freddie? Pedey's commanding officer? I'm Maria. I am... was... his wife."

My throat thickened. Nodding was the best I could do.

"Thank you for all you did," she said. "He always told me he had the best squad leader in Iraq." She motioned for the boy to stand and greet me. "Pedro Junior. We call him Pedey too."

The boy looked up at me with the same gentle brown eyes I'd seen every day in Iraq for almost a year — the son of my brother in arms.

I sat on my bed and leaned the crutches against the wall, then motioned for him to come closer. When he hesitated, I held out both arms. What should I say to him, this child I'd orphaned? It was hard to find words, but I had to say something. I owed it to his father.

"Pedro Junior... you should be proud of the name. Your dad was a good man, not just a great soldier, but a great friend too. I hope you'll never know what war can do to a man, but your father never lost his kind spirit. He was like a priest to us all, even in the worst of times. Whatever happens, you should know this, and never forget him."

The boy finally came to me, snuggled close, and began to cry.

What am I doing? I have no right. I should have saved his father instead.

When we separated, he went back to his mother, who rested a comforting arm around his shoulders and patted down his thick, black hair, the only feature that made him look different from his father.

She never took her eyes off me. "They said you were with him that day, Freddie."

I nodded. "He saved my life."

"Was it quick? Did he suffer? I need to know. Otherwise, I have dreams."

"He died instantly," I said, sparing her the details.

She crossed herself, then reached into her purse and pulled out a small package wrapped in crepe. "He told me if anything happened to him, he wanted you to have this."

She unwrapped the paper and held up the archangel's medallion, a two-handed broadsword embossed on a Celtic cross.

I shook my head. "I can't."

"It's okay. I have one of my own. He had a copy made to take with him to Iraq. He was afraid to take this one into battle." She yanked at a chain around her neck and pulled out from her blouse the original medallion, identical to the other except that hers was made of gold. Then she offered the package to me again. "Please, it was what he wanted. You went through so much together, so many of you lost. Maybe this will bring you better luck in the rest of your life."

I accepted the cross and chain and cradled them in my hand, then looked back at her. "I should have done more," I said. "I should have saved him."

She touched my arm and nodded. "He told me you were like this, carrying the burden of others. He told me in emails and phone calls how much he worried about his Lieutenant Freddie, how you were a good man who cared about his troops, maybe a little too much. And when the first attack happened, how you were devastated, how you contacted the families and did what you could to help, how you blamed yourself."

My expression froze, a mask of sympathy for the widow of my friend. I thanked her for her kind words, denying that I deserved them, but... Jimmie's machine in my head began to whir.

First attack?

Time passed in a blur. They stayed a while, and we told stories about her husband, the boy's father, trying to keep his memory alive. Then we hugged and made our tearful goodbyes.

After they left, I collapsed on my bed, forgetting all the progress I'd made. Now I knew: I had gaps in my memory and could no longer trust what I perceived to be real.

I turned the medallion over in my hand and traced the edges of the broadsword.

The first attack. So many lost.

I had no recollection of it—like listening to a story from another world.

The big day arrived, requiring pomp and circumstance. Dinah, Ralph, and Becky stood in formation, while Dr. B. removed the brace. I sat up on the examining table and gawked at my leg. The skin had turned ashen like a cadaver's, and the muscles had atrophied from disuse, but I'd watched it degrade over time, so that wasn't the worst surprise.

Dr. B. had Ralph support my ankle as I swiveled around, so my leg hung out over space. Then the big health aide gradually eased his grip and let gravity take over. I tensed, worried the muscle would tear from the bone again, but my leg bent hardly at all.

Becky saw my disappointment. "It's normal, Freddie. To be expected. You can't lock a leg straight for three months and not have it be stiff. That's part of my job, to fix it."

They lay me back down on the table, and Becky brought over a metal device that looked like a draftsman's protractor. "Raise your knee as much as you can." It was an order.

I did, but barely.

She adjusted the bar of the protractor and frowned. "Twenty-nine degrees. Now raise your good leg."

My left knee popped up effortlessly, a tower intent on humiliating its damaged twin.

She measured again. "A hundred and thirty degrees. Your new goal. I'll get you as close to your good leg as possible, one degree at a time, but trust me: it'll be painful for the both of us."

Into the Void

20

ON DAY TWENTY, AS WAS TRADITION in the final ten days of anointment, the people began placing small wheels upon the parapet, first one or two, then dozens. Each wheel was powered by a series of hand-painted silk sails, and had a parchment woven through their spokes with the craftsman's scrawled prayer. Their greens, oranges, and yellows lit up the parapet wall, challenging the gloom, and unlike the wheels of the watchtower, these whistled when the wind blew, sending their supplications floating into the air.

Save us, oh Goddess, they seemed to say. As their numbers increased, it sounded more like a wail than a prayer.

For the past two days, I'd struggled to discover the key to the second trial. The spirit's message had been clear — I had to find the chamber of pipes once more — but even though I'd traversed the tunnel to the armory many times, the ramp had never reappeared. No elf had sprung from the wall to help, and no butterfly guided my way.

Now, as I stood in the midst of the tunnel and squinted foolishly into the candlelight, I pressed my thumbs to my temples and tried to think what to do. What clue had I overlooked? What spirit had I ignored?

On a whim, I took out the simpleton's map from my tunic and brushed its surface with my fingertips, hoping the chamber might appear in a puff of smoke. Nothing.

As I replaced the map in my pocket, I felt something soft—the gift from the gardener—and pulled out the rose-that-was-not-a-rose. After two days in the growing heat, it should have wilted, but it appeared as fresh as when she gave it to me.

Could she be the spirit I ignored?

I brought the flower to my nose and sniffed the perfume, as strong as ever. When I looked up, I had to blink twice. Either the perfume had confounded my senses, or I'd finally been granted my wish. For now, at last, the tunnel sloped downward.

I followed as before. All seemed the same but the silence—no tapping of pipes, no singing, no sound but the click of my heels.

At the bottom of the ramp, corroded pipes still crisscrossed the ceiling, and the new one—the one for heroes—gleamed in the corner. I called out, beseeching the spirit to appear, and searched in the shadows, but he did not come.

As I traversed the chamber and inspected the pipes overhead, I nearly tripped on something solid on the ground—the spirit's wrench. When I knelt to retrieve it, I found a gold chain wrapped around its handle, and at the end of the chain, the medallion of Nordrassil. I fingered the detail of the beautiful piece.

Could this symbol of the Druids possess the magic I seek?

At once, I saw it. The roots at the base of the World Tree formed a familiar shape.

I had started to grasp its meaning when an unwelcome voice intruded. "That's right," the voice said. "It is what you think it is."

A chill ran through me, as if a winter storm had blown in, as I looked up at the assassin I'd met in the watershed.

He made his little bow and fixed his hollow sockets on me.

This time, I met his gaze. "Why should I believe your words, demon?"

"Because I speak the truth."

"You wish for the destruction of all that's good. Nothing more."

"Ah, yes, I confess, but in this matter, our interests are aligned. Both of us wish you to learn the truth, for no demon can destroy you. You can only be undone by yourself."

I raised the chain so the medallion swung between us, and eyed the assassin through it. The clues had finally converged.

"Yes," he said. "The medallion is the key to the second trial. Go now. We shall talk again."

I wavered, but only briefly, then hung the medallion around my neck and raced off to the crypt.

The crypt remained as I'd left it, with no new footsteps marking the dust. No soul had passed this way. I strode past the memorial of King Menethil II and through the archway of writhing souls, pausing only briefly to pay homage to the remains of my parents.

I came to the door with the brass plate in the shape of a hawk, removed the chain from around my neck, and studied the roots of the World Tree. The complex key would fit in the lock only one way. I fumbled for several seconds before finding the right orientation, but once I found it, the base of the medallion slipped easily into place.

I took a deep breath, turned the key, and....

Nothing.

I tried the opposite direction, and still nothing. I gripped the medallion with both hands and twisted harder, but no movement, even though the key was a perfect fit.

Is this another dead end?

I recalled the words of the elf: *We survive through will alone, through faith in ourselves.*

The blood rushed to my face. *Spirits and demons be damned. I'm tired of mysteries and riddles.*

The days of anointment were racing by, and soon all we held as good would end.

Where can I find the faith to overcome the dreadlord and his Horde? In my father's blessing? In Sir Gilly's training?

I thought of my mother resting in the casket behind me, the bloom of youth still gracing her face, and recalled the fragrance of the gardener's flower.

Click. The lock released.

I entered the chamber of the second trial. At the front stood a casket, draped under a banner with stripes of red and white, and stars on a background of blue. The casket, like those of my parents, lay open, and in it rested the man who'd recently been singing as he repaired the pipes. I held the candle close and read the inscription on the brass plate attached to the side.

I'd been right—not a demon, but an angel. And more—an archangel.

What now?

I'd passed through the door, as both elf and demon had urged, but....

Could this be the end of the trial?

I glanced past the archangel and saw only darkness. When I tried to raise the candle to shed light across the room, a great weariness weighed down my arm. The strongest desire filled me to go no farther, to flee the crypt, but the elf in the lavender cloak had led me here for a purpose.

I lifted the candle high.

Three paces past the archangel, where the light from my candle dispersed, there appeared to be a gate guarding whatever lay beyond. As I drew closer, I realized it was no gate at all, but four spears stuck into the ground. Each had a pair of boots at its base, a helmet resting on top, and hung from the tip, a pair of silver tags.

I slipped through and into the next chamber.

By the far wall lay dark mounds. As I inched closer, the mounds became caskets—four more, lined up in a row, each embellished with the same banner as that of the archangel. In each casket lay a body covered in a shroud. I bent low and swept the candle along the sides. No name plates on these, but instead a mark of honor—a five-pointed silver star.

The new pipe is for heroes.

I reached into the first casket and tried to peel back the shroud, but the darkest of magic worked against me. My fingers passed through as if the shroud were made of fog. I could feel the body underneath, but could see nothing of the face. The next two caskets were the same.

Then, I moved on to the last. This time the shroud came away, but I fell back at what I saw—a gaping void where a face should be.

"Do you know who they are?"

The chill filled the room again, and I turned to confront the assassin. "They're heroes."

"Heroes, but not strangers. Yet you have no memory of them."

I knew he spoke the truth, but pressed my lips together and stayed silent.

"I can show you," he said, "if you but ask."

I looked at the body with no face, then at the assassin with no eyes, and recalled the great elf's words: *Embrace the shadows.* I nodded.

The demon waved his withered hand, and at once, my candle went out. The room became dark, but for no more than an instant, as the air beside the assassin began to shimmer. A cloud appeared, like a hole in the blackness, and the shape of a hulking creature emerged, all coiled muscle and smoldering flesh, absorbing the darkness around it and producing an indigo light. From its edges came a crackling sound so faint, it might have been no more than a tingling on my skin.

I shuddered.

Sir Gilly had taught me of such a creature, one I'd prayed never to meet. I tried to remember what I'd learned so many years before, and could hear my mentor's voice:

"A voidwalker, Frederick, a servant of the demons created from the chaos of the Twisting Nether."

Young and brazen then, ready to take on any fight, I'd asked what weapon they used, but his answer frightened me.

"Its touch is misery," he'd said, unable to look at me as he spoke. *"It brings your most painful memories rushing to the surface, so vividly that you think of nothing but how to block the source of this anguish."*

"Do you want to know?" the assassin said, his cruel mouth grim.

I fell back a step.

He signaled for his servant to wait. "By the rules of the treaty, you must say yes, or it may not touch you. If you want to find out who they are, all you need do is agree."

The voidwalker loomed, waiting for its master's command. In the center, where a face should be, two eyes glowed in the darkness like burning coals. The tentacle-like mist that served as its arm stretched out toward me.

I shook my head and screamed, "No!"

The glow that defined the creature began to swirl and spiral outward, filling the room. I backed toward the entrance, unable to look away, and my leg hit something solid—one of the spears with a helmet upon it. The metal tags rattled angrily as I stumbled to the floor.

On the ceiling above me, the creature's glow threw spidery shadows, making the chamber swim and reel. The polished brown wood of the caskets merged with the red, white, and blue banners, and all took on an indigo hue. For an instant, a rose appeared in the middle, but then the edges of its petals exploded in a flash. I closed my eyes to protect them, and all faded to a pulsating, velvety black.

When I opened my eyes once more, I was in the watchtower, awakening from the spell cast by the spinning wheel. It made one final turn as the rays of the setting sun vanished.

At once, a profound darkness settled over the chamber. I stared out the oculus for a hint of light, but the sky hung clouded and starless, as if some taunting god had placed a great bowl over the land. Earth and sky had converged into a single seamless mass, offering neither light nor insight.

If the assassin's servant had revealed the names of the heroes, I had no memory of it. My mind, like the light in the watchtower, had gone dim.

Eagles
and
Stars

MY PHYSICAL THERAPY SESSIONS NOW STARTED
with a ritual. I'd lie on my stomach on a padded training table while
Becky knelt behind me, pressing her shoulder against my ankle to
stretch my knee. She'd grunt, and I'd scream. Then I'd roll over and
watch while she aligned the protractor and measured the bend.

On bad days, when it showed no change, the corners of her
mouth would droop and she'd pat my leg. "Scar tissue," she'd
say. "It's stubborn stuff. We'll keep working at it."

On good days, when I'd improved a degree, she'd fetch a cold
drink for the two of us, tap our plastic cups together, and toast to
my recovery.

Today was a good day. After my workout, she put an ice pack
on my leg and we talked.

"I warned you progress would be slow," she said. "But we're
getting there. You may not be able to play point guard again, but I
can say with confidence that you'll be able to walk, to lead a
normal life."

"I know," I grumbled as I adjusted the ice pack to the point of
pain.

"Then why are you still so gloomy?"

She was right; I should be pleased with my progress, painful though it had been, but I had secrets still hidden in my brain and was terrified to find out what they were.

"Talk to me, Freddie." When I clammed up, she brought up an object from the military-issue box. "So what's that story from long ago and far away?"

"I'm supposed to be the one with the head injury. What the hell are you talking about?"

"That bracelet with the date on it, the one you laughed about and almost threw away."

"Oh, that. You sure you want to hear about it? It's just another one of my sad tales."

"I want to know everything about you, Lieutenant Frederick Williams. You know what they say: once you've broken scar tissue together, there can be no secrets between you."

I had scar tissue, all right, and not only in my leg, but this story wasn't so bad. Besides, she cheered me up so much, I couldn't deny her.

"We moved to the Cape when I was ten, a big change from the city. I was an outsider, out of place. The village where we lived had been built in the 1800s as a spiritual retreat, and some of that culture still survived. My dad wasn't religious, but my mom used to drag the three of us to the tabernacle for a rousing service every Sunday. After a while, I noticed all the locals wore these metal bracelets. When I asked my mom what they meant, she said people wore them to commemorate the day they'd been born again. The minister had a machine that would engrave the date on the bracelets.

"Lots of boys in school had them, and wore them with pride, but as I got older, I was let in on an inside joke. The guys would buy a bracelet and have the minister stamp the date when they had their first—"

I blushed.

She laughed. "You're not serious."

"It may have been a small town, but the boys still had hormones."

"That's why you kept the bracelet?"

"I wish. The story's not finished. I had a crush on this girl at school, but she lived in one of the big houses on the water, and those folks didn't have time for those of us from the gingerbread houses. I got a bracelet anyway, and lied about it to impress the other kids. Word somehow got back to her mother, and I was suspended from school for three days."

"That's not a sad story. It's funny."

"Hang on. You haven't heard the rest."

She waited.

I watched my joke fade in the reflection of her eyes. I wanted to tell her something happy, but—

"The girl... her mother was on the school committee. She was the one who got my dad fired."

Becky started to laugh, but quickly covered her mouth with her hand. When she removed it, an uncharacteristic frown had appeared. Tough to stay positive when her young lieutenant was at the center of things gone wrong.

I had an urge to restore her upbeat mood, and decided the best way was to deflect attention from myself. "Your turn," I said. "You never tell me anything about yourself. What was it like for you growing up?"

"Not much to tell. I had a pretty normal childhood."

"And your father and mother?"

"They're fine."

"Then why are you always talking about what your father *used* to say?"

"You're fishing, Freddie. The sayings I quote from my father are things you say to a little girl, not a grown woman."

It felt like she was holding something back, maybe uncomfortable talking about her great childhood when mine had been so fucked up.

I pressed. "Any siblings?"

"Siblings?"

"You know, brothers and sisters?"

She said no, but had mumbled the word and it died in the air. I'd learned a lot about scar tissue, and her expression showed a scar.

When I asked again, she checked her watch and stood. "Story time's over. I have things to do."

Then, in a rush to clean up for her next appointment, she wheeled me to the elevator to wait for Ralph.

Always so efficient.

So I thought, but when I looked up at the clock in the hall, I was surprised to find ten minutes left to our session.

Sometime after we'd achieved a bend of fifty degrees, Becky brought me a gift from the Eagle Cane Project, a volunteer group that hand-carved canes for veterans. She opened the box to display a cane encased in bubble wrap, and pulled the plastic off the top to reveal the impressive head of a bald eagle.

I was skeptical at first, not only because I was unsteady on my feet, but also because I didn't want to think of myself as needing handouts from a charity group.

Becky sat me down and read me the card that came with it. "Apparently, it's a tradition that goes back to the Civil War, a sign of respect and honor for wounded troops."

"What's the bird doing on the handle?" I said mostly to give her a hard time.

"Stay with me and listen. It says, 'The eagle is symbolic. Native Americans believed that warriors wounded on the battlefield returned as eagles. This cane is not to be seen as a sign of weakness but as thanks for personal sacrifice. It's intended to encourage those undergoing a long and difficult rehabilitation.' That would be you, Freddie."

"Send it back."

"You can be a real pain in the ass," she said, then insisted on reading the rest of the card, whether I was listening or not. "'Life will hold a lot of promise still, and you'll be back on your feet doing great things. The path ahead is going to be good.'"

"Sounds like a fortune cookie."

"It's intended well, Freddie, and you're ready to transition off crutches. If you don't want this cane, I can get you one of those ugly, old-man ones from our stockroom. Or you can keep this beauty."

She unwrapped the rest of the cane, and it *was* a beauty, with hand-carved, polished dark wood. When I stared into the eagle's eyes, they seemed to be challenging me to get up and walk.

She waited, and I nodded weakly—she was having that effect on me again—and accepted the cane. She told me the group would be glad to add any engraving I wanted as a keepsake, such as my unit number, medals, or the names of those lost.

Great. If only I could remember them.

Not long after that, Becky started coming to my room for lunch each day. It was a New England November, with all the usual cold and drizzle, apparently too unpleasant for the bench in the courtyard, and she'd never liked mingling with the crowd in the cafeteria.

On Mondays and Thursdays, she'd bring fresh daisies with her, fill a glass with water from the bathroom sink, place them in it, and set the bouquet on my bedside table.

Late one Wednesday, before she headed home to her parents' for Thanksgiving, she brought a new batch. She was in a rush, hoping to beat traffic, but I grabbed her hand before she could leave.

"Why do you bring me flowers?"

She tilted her head to one side and grinned. "Because you're so gloomy. I figure you need something to cheer you up."

"Do you do that for all your patients?"

She picked up a daisy, smelled it, and then winked at me. "No, just you." The flower almost hid her smile.

This visit was serious. Since arriving here, I hadn't dressed up in anything but a hospital gown or a warm-up suit. Today, they had me decked out in dress greens for some bigwig coming to give me a Purple Heart. Because I was a local boy, they also planned to take pictures.

Becky arrived first. "Don't you look handsome."

"Yeah, hides how fucked up I am."

She inspected the buttons on my jacket and brushed the fabric smooth over my shoulders. "Well, I'm proud of you anyway."

Ralph and Dinah came in next, and lined the wall along the window.

I stood up and balanced on my cane, hoping the ceremony didn't last too long.

Finally, Dr. B. arrived with a bird colonel and a photographer from the *Cape Cod Times*.

I saluted as best I could, the first time in over four months. The bird took a felt box out of his briefcase and opened it. Inside rested a Purple Heart within a gold border, surrounding a profile of General Washington. Above the heart appeared a coat of arms between sprays of green leaves. He cradled it in his hand to show me, and then turned it over so I could read the inscription on the back: "For Military Merit."

The bird cleared his throat and read from a cue card he tried to hide in his palm. "Lieutenant Frederick Williams...."

At least he got my name right.

"...I'm pleased to award you this Purple Heart for being wounded in action against an enemy of the United States, in an IED assault on your convoy in An-Nasiriyah, Iraq on July the 22nd, 2008."

For being wounded.

Everything I'd done in Iraq, the guys I'd served with and the things we accomplished, even just those I could remember, were worth more than being wounded. Nonetheless, I accepted the medal and thank-you-sir'd the bird.

"Is it okay if I sit now, sir?" I gestured to my bad leg.

"Can you hold on a bit longer, Lieutenant? I have one more." He took on the look of a parent playing Santa at Christmas. "A special award, a Silver Star for valor during a roadside ambush in Al Anbar province, where..."

The machine in my head whirred and clicked, finally finding its slot. I smelled smoke and burning flesh, and heard the sounds of dogs barking. An image emerged from the fog of my mind—a dime-store greeting card, with the corners charred and a single white rose in its center.

I tried to focus on what he was saying....

"Your quick actions... courageous leadership... the remnants of your squad... four men had died."

...But his voice became garbled, as if my head were underwater, and the room began making slow circles, like a carnival carousel slowing down.

I glanced past the bird to the audience around me and wondered why they weren't spinning as well.

Becky's smile faded. Everyone else nodded approval— Freddie the hero—but she knew something was wrong.

After the bird colonel finished his speech, he propped me up by the elbow, while I held the Silver Star between us and did my best to look proud. The photographer from the *Cape Cod Times* crouched in front and clicked his camera, then asked us to hold the pose while he checked the picture.

As everyone else in the room applauded, the bird let go, and I collapsed onto the bed with a single phrase rattling around in my brain:

"Four men had died."

After the ceremony, they stood in line to congratulate me. The bird shook my hand, followed by Dr. B. and Ralph, and then Dinah bent over with her plump cheeks and Coke-bottle glasses and gave me a kiss.

Becky held back, simply patting my arm.

Then the bird and his entourage exited, leaving me alone.

I waited until their voices merged with the clamor of the corridor and faded away, then tossed the medals on the bed, pressed down on the head of the eagle, and struggled to my feet. At the closet, I slid out the olive drab box, flipped off the cover, and fumbled inside— notebooks and pictures, Gloria the mermaid, and the music box.

Where the hell is it?

Finally, at the bottom, a Ziploc bag with an envelope inside.

I tried to unzip it with one hand, but to no avail. It felt like peeling away layers of my brain. Then I leaned against the wall and let the cane drop to the floor. Now, using two hands, I fumbled with the plastic, but the bag slipped from my fingers and floated down alongside the cane.

It taunted me there, only three feet away, but I was too unsteady to reach for it. Then a hand appeared, a hand I knew so well from weeks of rehab.

Becky grasped the Ziploc bag and held it up to the light. "What is it, Freddie?"

"The white rose."

"What does that mean?"

I stared at the bag, straining my brain. All I could think of was the ambush, the four men who had died, the Silver Star I didn't deserve.

"I don't know," I said.

"Do you want me to open it?"

When I kept glaring at the bag as if it were an IED, she picked up my cane and handed it to me. Then, always the physical therapist, she led me back to my bed, encouraging me but letting me get there by myself.

I sat down, rested both hands on my knees, and studied them as if I'd never seen them before.

"I'll open it, if you want," she said. "All you need is to say yes."

I didn't respond.

"Do you want me to leave?"

I looked up at her. Leaving was the last thing I wanted her to do. "Stay, please. I don't want to see it alone."

She settled on the bed beside me and undid the Ziploc bag. Inside the envelope was a card with burn marks at its edges and a painting of a white rose in its center. She opened it and studied its contents, then turned it toward me.

Before me blared a photograph of four soldiers wearing full battle gear, standing in front of their vehicle. Underneath, the words: Humvee three.

Becky watched, waiting for me to react. When I said nothing, she turned the picture around and looked again. "Who are they, Freddie? The four who died in the ambush?"

I tried to answer, but my throat had gone dry. She offered me a glass of water, and I drank half of it before setting the glass down gingerly, as if afraid it would shatter.

Then the words spilled out. "I always took pride in my attention to detail, first in basketball, then in *World of Warcraft*. I'd frequent blogs, research every raid, but it was as a soldier and leader that I left no rock unturned. My men trusted me, a trust I didn't take for granted. I had one priority—to get them out alive."

I looked away at the Silver Star half-hidden in the folds of the bed sheets.

Becky reached out to touch my cheek but her hand stopped short, poised in the no man's land between us. She waited, her lips pressed together, her question unspoken.

I turned back and my eyes locked with hers. "I failed, Becky, and now I can't even remember their names."

A World
with
No Soul

22

THE NEXT MORNING, I SOUGHT OUT the gardener, though she wasn't due to work there that day. I'd come to imagine her as an enchantress who could sense my need from afar and appear. Her make-believe rose had led me to the archangel's key, and despite the encroaching gloom, she always maintained a good cheer.

Might she possess magic enough to help me solve the second trial?

To my relief, I found her in the garden desperately drizzling water on the parched flowers.

She looked as if the mists of Golgoreth had seeped into her soul. When she saw me approach, she set down her watering can, ran her fingers around the inside of her skirt to check that her blouse was tucked in, and patted down her hair. Then she focused on the ground and bent at the knee, a curtsy too deep.

"Milord," she said, without looking up.

"Is something wrong, Rebecca?"

"Oh, Milord, I tried to do something good, and it turned out all wrong."

I took her by the hand and helped her up, then led her to the bench. "Tell me about it."

"I only wanted to help. You bear such a burden, yet all you ever asked of me was a white rose, and I had none to give. So I bought a piece of parchment with the few coppers I'd saved, and drew a picture of a white rose on it. I thought to give it to you today."

A foolish notion. How could an image of a flower possess such magic?

Still, her action moved me. "How kind of you," I said, trying to be gentle, "but a drawing of a rose is unlikely to save the world."

She looked up at me with fire in her eyes. "Then why did the demon try to destroy it?"

Heat rushed to my cheeks.

This is my *battle. Let the dreadlord and his minions attack* me, *and stay away from this innocent girl.*

I glanced about the garden, past the hydrangeas and high up to the arched windows in the castle wall. We were alone.

"You were visited by a demon?" I said, hardly able to control my words.

"Aye, Milord. I'm sure of it. He had a voice one might imagine coming from a snake, and his eye sockets were hollow."

The assassin. "And what did he say?"

"He said—" She lowered her chin to her chest and deepened her voice to add a gruff sound to it. "—'Where is the white rose?' When I refused to answer, he brushed past me as if I were a feather. As he grazed my arm, I felt as though I'd been touched by death."

An encounter with a demon, and exposed, beyond the protection of Stormwind's walls.

I grasped her by the shoulders and made her face me. "Did he harm you?"

"No, Milord, but he found my drawing on the kitchen table and cast it into the fire."

I forgot the trials, so relieved she'd been left unscathed that I found myself clutching her to my chest. She slipped into my arms, allowing me hold her for some time, before remembering her circumstance and pulling away.

"Forgive me, Milord. I had no right."

"No right? You faced down a demon for me. Thank the Goddess you were unharmed. And as for the picture, it was well intended, though now it's lost."

"Oh no, Milord. Not lost. I was able to save it from the demon."

She reached into her apron pocket and pulled out the parchment with the picture of the rose. Its corners were blackened and its surface charred, all except for the image of the flower in the center.

I stammered, "But how?"

"Fool that I was, I reached in with my bare hand to pull it from the flames."

"Your hand?" I checked both her hands, but aside from the dirt of the garden, they were unmarked.

"I wanted so much to save it," she said, "my gift to you. Seeing that, the Goddess protected me. I felt neither heat nor pain as I plucked the parchment from the fire."

"And what did the demon do?"

"He laughed, for as I dropped the parchment on the ground, it continued to burn."

"Then how did you stop it?"

"That's where I went wrong."

"But you must have done well, because the picture of the white rose is here within my grasp."

"Aye, but I had to do something terrible to save it. I was so upset at that demon, standing in my kitchen and laughing as my gift to you burned, that I went blind with rage. Without thinking, I grabbed the first thing at hand and smothered the flame. I'm so embarrassed to tell what I chose, but by the grace of the Goddess, it worked, soaking up all of the demon's evil and leaving my drawing intact."

I pictured the grotesque little man laughing in her kitchen, and Rebecca furious at him, tiny fists on hips, conjuring up enough magic to save the rose.

"But why embarrassed?" I said.

"Because the first thing at hand was your gift to me, your mother's flowered shawl. And now it's gone." She stood and walked away, afraid to face me.

I grabbed her, spun her around, and kissed her.

The white rose. What magic it must possess to defy the demon twice....

"So happy, Milord, but why?"

"Because at sunset this evening, your drawing shall accompany me to the watchtower."

The charring of the flower had scarred its surface, leaving blotches where the parchment had thinned. When I draped it over the rim of the bejeweled disk, the rays of the sun shone through, giving the petals of the flower a mystical glow. As the wheel began to spin, the light weaved a pattern that spiraled across my face.

I watched, captivated, and drifted into the dream.

The dream quickly turned to a nightmare, as I found myself in a chamber like the second trial in the crypt. At its center, where the four coffins had lain, a hole gaped in the floor. I inched toward it, my boots scraping the stone so they sent pebbles skittering ahead. As the pebbles tumbled over the edge, I listened for the sound of them hitting the bottom.

Only silence.

Then a crackle behind me, and a tingling on my skin caused me to turn.

The voidwalker reached a tentacle toward me, and I backed away, lost my footing, and fell into the hole.

At once, I plummeted downward into a dark chasm. I lunged for the sides of the walls, clawing at each crack and crevice, anything to slow my fall. The speed of the wind increased with my descent, and I sensed a smell like sawdust after a rainstorm.

Then a firebird flapped by and circled my head, lighting up the abyss.

I steeled my courage and looked below. Something was approaching fast, most likely the bottom and my doom, but then I realized it was not the bottom at all. A dark mass rose toward me, memories flying up like a volley of arrows to pierce my mind.

After the wheel came to rest, I stayed on my stool in the watchtower, unable to stand, hardly able to breathe. For these past days, I'd longed to remember the dream, and at last my wish had been granted.

Now, I wanted only to forget.

What had the wheel shown me? Evil more foul than anything the dreadlord could conceive. My nostrils stung with the stench of burning flesh. My ears rang with the crash of thunder, voices crackling in panic, iron dragons raining down flame, the sound of dogs barking... and then silence.

I'd been to a place without honor, a world without soul.

My teeth clenched and the muscles around my jaw cramped. The back of my head pounded so hard, I thought I might go blind. Yet the dream had opened my eyes. I no longer needed a voidwalker to remember the heroes. I could embrace them now on my own.

I rose unsteadily, anxious to leave the watchtower behind, but when I took my first step, my right leg buckled beneath me and I collapsed to the floor. The candle in the sconce at the top of the stairs burned low as I writhed there in pain, fool that I was to stumble so.

At last, I withdrew my sword and planted its point in a crack in the stones, then pressed with all my might until I could stand. I scowled at the cursed wheels, blaming them for my woes. Finally, with a hand to the wall and my sword as a crutch, I staggered down the hundred and one stairs.

By the Banks
of the
River

SINCE RECEIVING THE MEDALS, I'D TURNED inward, leaving Becky unable to reach me. Whenever she stretched my knee and measured the bend, I kept quiet—aside from the screaming—not even bothering to ask how I did.

On the third day, when I limped into PT, leaning on the eagle cane and wearing my army jacket, she seemed unsurprised. "What is it, Freddie?"

"No PT today. We need to get out of here, someplace outside where we can be alone and no one will disturb us."

"The courtyard?"

"No. Away from the hospital."

No argument. She made a quick call and had someone cover her appointments for the rest of the afternoon.

A few minutes later, after a short drive, we nestled on a park bench among the trees along the banks of the Charles. It was late November, a watery afternoon when the paths in the park rustled with leaves. Streamers marred the cold blue of the sky, clouds mounting from the west and promising rain. We sat in silence, as she knew me well enough to wait for me to start.

"By the banks of the river," I finally said.

She eyed me as if I were a TBI patient. "What's that supposed to mean?"

"It's what my mother used to say near the end. Early on, before she began to fail, I'd try to get her to come down from the garret for dinner. 'Come down, Mom,' I'd say, but she never came. Later, when her mind was going, she'd parrot it back to me.

"'Take me down, Freddie,' she'd say out of nowhere. I'd answer, 'Down where?' Then she'd start singing in that little girl voice of hers. 'Down by the banks of the river, the river Jordan.' Her brain was addled, like mine is now."

Becky looked at me with that optimism that made me feel bad for feeling bad. "Your brain's not addled, Freddie. You've just been through a lot. If your mind's hiding some of it from you, it's to give you time to heal."

I reached out and took her hand, pulling until she slid closer to me, not speaking until I could feel the warmth of her breath. "Dixon, Anderson, Martinez, and Jones."

Her eyes widened. "The four men in the picture?"

I reached into my pocket and pulled out the charred card with the white rose and the photograph of my squad members. Humvee three—four boys from Georgia in full battle gear. They looked menacing with grenades and ammo hanging from their flak jackets and night-vision goggles strapped to their helmets. Anderson was up in the gunner's hatch as they posed for the picture.

Like the photo of my family at the gingerbread house. All gone.

I must have spaced out, momentarily forgetting about Becky, because I suddenly felt her hand on my cheek.

She turned my head until our eyes met. "Tell me about them, Freddie. I want to hear everything, to know them as well as you did."

I looked away from her and stared at the river, almost expecting their stories to flow across its surface like film on a screen, and took a deep breath.

"I may have been the officer, but the whole squad was close, more like a family. When we weren't sleeping, we were doing something together, whether in the real world or *World of Warcraft*. In the real world, we trained, planned, and risked our lives on patrol. In the game, we were the Lightbringer guild—our way of escaping, I guess. I was a warrior, fully armored, leading them into battle, with each of my buddies supporting me. I'd take the first hit. The mages and hunters would pick off enemies that tried to gang up on me, and the priest would heal me if my health got low, even resurrect me if I got killed.

"Dixie was a Druid, Anderson a mage, Martinez a paladin, and Jones a hunter who rode a timber wolf.

"It was like they chose roles that matched who they were in real life. Martinez fancied the call of the paladin: to protect the weak, to bring justice to the unjust, and to vanquish evil from the darkest corners of the world. His favorite weapon was a demonslayer, a sword that shot out flames.

"Dixie's character was called the keeper. Some of us called him the keeper of minds. He was a hulking guy, six foot four, at least, but he was always calm and grounded. If one of us started to lose it in the real world, if our minds stopped being operational, guys would yell, 'Get the keeper over here.' He'd be the one to pull us back to reality. 'You gotta move on,' he'd say in that slow southern drawl. 'You gotta keep going.'"

I paused, breathed in and out, and let my fingertips brush the faces in the photo. "Anderson... he was the gentle one. He preferred to defend himself with magic. Said he had enough violence in the real world. He was a highly efficient soldier who could do what had to be done, but he had an aura about him, like he knew what it all meant.

"Jonesy was a wiry backwoods kid from a small town. He liked the image of the hunter, the call of the wild. He prided himself on being able to slip like a ghost through the trees and set traps in the paths of his enemies.

"And of course, the archangel, a priest who preferred to heal. All gone now. And it never should have happened."

I slumped on the bench and looked away from the river, into the eyes of the eagle on my cane.

Becky began to console me, something about how the war wasn't my fault.

I waved her off. "Don't stop me now." I could feel the rage rising up from my gut, a fury suppressed too long. "Back then, all units were switching from Humvees to the better armored MRAPs. We were due to get them, next on the list, but some fucker higher up got in the way. Army politics. Somebody owed somebody a favor. I knew we were in bandit country, and that it was just a matter of time before something bad happened. I *knew*. I went into the CO's office and screamed at him until he threatened me with insubordination and threw me out. I knew, Becky, but there was nothing I could do."

My breath came in bursts now, and I didn't know if I could go on.

She took my hand and squeezed with her physical therapist strength until I turned back to her. "Tell me, Freddie. I'm here for as long as it takes."

"Our shipment went to another unit, and we were left with our Humvees. Would the MRAPs have saved their lives? Maybe. I'll never know. Christ, it was a five-hundred-pound bomb. I knew we were headed for a hot zone that day, and had requested a route clearance team, but none were available. What more could I have done? We had orders.

"One minute, our three-Humvee convoy was on patrol on a road in Al Anbar. The next, a thundering boom. A voice crackled over the radio from the second Humvee—Sergeant Billy Wilson, twenty years old.

"'It's not there, Freddie. I can't see Anderson's truck anymore. It's gone.'

"What was left of my squad went out to check. The bomb had torn away the guts of the third Humvee. As the smoke settled, the only thing I could see was the engine block and the front and rear axles.

"And then they were all over us, not just a bomb planted in the road, but a coordinated attack. I pulled my guys back. I wanted so badly to help the others, but I had to save the rest of them. They were running around crying out names, like saying them loud enough might bring them back. But real war isn't a game—no magic, no healing, no Druid resurrection. We had to defend ourselves, to fight or die. I managed to get them inside the Humvees. We engaged the gun turrets and fought back with all we had. I fired my M-9 with one hand while I called in close air support with the other. A Silver Star for that? Big fucking deal. I was trying to save what was left of my men.

"After the choppers had driven them off, we all wanted to go help our buddies, but the brigade commander ordered us to stand down while the EOD team checked the area for other explosives. Only after that did they let us recover the bodies of our friends. But what we found—"

Something caught in my throat and I couldn't go on. The silence around us became deafening. The soughing of the wind in the trees merged with the traffic on the VFW Parkway, forming a dull hum, at the same time too soft and too loud.

Becky reached for a little backpack she'd brought and pulled out a bottle of Gatorade.

I thanked her, took a drink, and felt the cool liquid loosen my throat. I hadn't realized how dry I'd become. She waited, never saying a word, until finally, I was able to continue.

"When I returned to the base and was alone in my tent, the archangel knocked on my door. The air was thick with heat, the fumes of Baghdad burning. He rolled in like one of the dust storms that kept us inside most of the summer, when we weren't on patrol. He hadn't bothered to clean up from the attack. He smelled like an infantryman—of blood and grime, of gun solvent and spent ammo. Sweat channeled down the dust on his face and curled across his skin.

"He sat next to me, needing to talk. A big guy, he barely fit into the folding camp chair. He heaved from side to side, his rifle still slung over his shoulder. Four of our friends were dead, and he just sat there, head in hands, struggling to find words.

"'We seen some bad things, Freddie,' he finally managed to say. 'Bad. I mean, I can't describe it.'

"He cradled his shaven head the way a mother holds a newborn, fighting back tears. A period of silence passed—no idea how long—but I didn't think I should break it.

"Finally, he did.

"'I hated to shoot the dogs,' he said."

"The dogs?" Becky's said, her words more breath than sound.

I looked up at her, almost surprised she was still there. "He meant the stray dogs that were gnawing at the dismembered body parts strewn about the road with bits of Humvee and fuel. They had us put on gloves so we could collect as many pieces as possible and wrap them in ponchos.

"Iraq's full of wild dogs. I don't know whether they're really wild or orphans of war. They were trying to stay alive like the rest of us. We tried to shoo them away, but they weren't afraid of us. When I watched them going after what was left of our buddies, I kind of went nuts. I started yelling, 'Shoot the damned dogs.' When none of them responded, I pulled out my M-9 and started firing. The others joined in, more than we needed to. The archangel was the gentlest of the bunch, a good soldier, but I'd never seen him like that before. We fired until we emptied our clips, then slammed in a backup and fired some more. I couldn't stop it. I couldn't—"

Becky raised a hand, fingers extended to touch me, but the hand paused mid-flight and withdrew. Her lips parted, but no words emerged.

I looked at her and knew she heard and understood. It pained me to be the one to show her the fragility of goodness, but I had to keep going, to finish the story, to confess my sins.

"The next evening, they had the entire battalion at the memorial. They set up rickety wooden bleachers and plastic chairs. Each soldier walked past the four sets of dog tags dangling from the upended rifles, and the four pairs of desert boots representing the men who'd died.

"I wore my game face, and fired my carbine when I was told to, in salute to the dead. But a part of me died that day too. Before the attack, I thought I could smell trouble. I'd convinced myself I had a sixth sense that would keep my guys safe. After they were gone, I lost my edge. Sure, I did my job, more than just going through the motions, but I played *World of Warcraft* every chance I could get. It was like... like I was hoping to meet my buddies again in Azeroth, and maybe heal them if I could find the right spell. But you know what? There's no magic in the real world."

I stopped and looked up.

Becky had never taken her eyes off me. "What are you trying to say, Freddie?"

"I'm trying to say... if I'd kept my head screwed on, maybe I could've saved the archangel. Maybe. I'll never know. But one thing's for sure: I let them down, just like my family. Now they're all gone. Forever."

A Gesture
of
Beckoning

24

I'D VANQUISHED THE FIRST TWO TRIALS, but success had brought me no peace. My family was gone. Now, I knew the heroes had perished as well. Though two more trials awaited me, I needed time to mourn.

For the next few days, the hours passed like prisoners on their way to an execution. With the help of a page, I limped to the watchtower at the appointed times and performed my princely duties, but by the grace of the Goddess, I remembered nothing of what I'd dreamed.

Between the rising and setting of the sun, I stayed in bed, nursing my injured leg and searching for answers in the faces painted on the dome above me. Servants brought food and drink, but I ate little. I made no new forays through the castle, unable to parry and thrust with my usual skill, to run away or walk without pain. I even shunned my visits to the royal gardens.

Mostly, I wondered: if the encounters with the assassin had thus diminished me, and the remembrance of the heroes had brought me so low, what challenges would the next trials bring?

To distract myself, I envisioned a nobler dream than what I'd seen through the spinning wheels. I imagined the five heroes as I would have as a child, when the promise of glory filled a young prince's head and goodness pervaded the world.

I pictured them as knights mounted on mighty steeds, riding shoulder to shoulder, each armored in bronze and bearing a shield that gleamed in the sunlight. One shield bore an image of a timber wolf, the second a demonslayer in flames. The third had five bands of black enamel, forming a chevron that pointed to the sky. The fourth, a serpent with two heads, put forth from a single trunk and intertwined. The fifth showed a cross of gold with a great sword inlaid upon it. All wore helmets, double-ridged with white horsehair crests that bounced proudly above them as they rode.

As their leader, I stood before them, holding a staff topped with a bloodstone, spouting encouragement and urging them on into battle.

Then some dark magic overtook my dream. Angry flames leapt from the gem and consumed the five as I watched.

A pounding on the bedchamber door interrupted my nightmare. By the light streaming through the window, I could tell it was too early for the watchtower.

"It's not yet time," I shouted.

I heard a fumbling at the lock. Whoever was outside had a key. With a grimace, I swung my legs to the floor and struggled to stand. Then I withdrew Kingsbane and prepared to confront the intruder.

After a click, the door flew wide with such force that it slammed into the wall. Sir Gilly strode through carrying a bundle under one arm, wrapped in burlap and shaped like a sword.

"Seven more days," he said, with an uncharacteristic edge to his voice. "Seven days until the end of all things. The storm over Golgoreth grows. The dark mist creeps across the Barrens and blankets the Twilight Highlands. And yet you lie abed."

Only after his rage had vented did he take in my appearance. How bad I must have looked, to cause him to cock his head to one side and draw back a step.

"Do you know who I am?" he said, eyeing the dagger.

"The advisor." I set Kingsbane down and took a sip of wine from a goblet a servant had left on the nightstand.

"Your friend," he said, "and not an assassin. And do you know what day it is?"

"Day twenty-three. Or perhaps twenty-four."

The corners of his eyes sagged, not a gesture of sympathy but of pity. "Have the trials been so hard, Frederick?"

I attempted to step toward him, but my leg nearly buckled and cast me to the floor. I backed off and grabbed the bedpost for support.

"Harder than I could have ever imagined," I said through clenched teeth. "Perhaps, despite all your training, I'm inadequate for the task. Something lacking in my character."

"No!"

His voice thundered in a way I'd not heard in years, the scolding of a teacher to a young whelp who'd been daydreaming in class.

"These doubts have been put in your head by the demons," he said. "Think of all those living and gone who have believed in you, and I foremost among them. Believe in yourself, Frederick, and you will prevail."

"Words from one who has never stared into the abyss."

He raised the package and waved it in my face. "I've seen more of the abyss than you know, but if you need something other than words, take this. It was given to me by your mother, the queen, before she died. 'Sir Gilbert,' she said, 'he's only a child, and I'm pained that I won't be there to comfort him in the depths of his trials. So grant me this deathbed wish. At the lowest point, when the mists of the dreadlord have sapped his will, give him this gift so he may take strength from me and rise up to defeat the Horde.'"

I gaped at the package, a glimmer of hope returning. "A weapon?"

Sir Gilly shook his head and handed me the package.

I ripped away the coarse outer cloth to find a second protective layer inside—a flowered shawl, a twin of the one that had been consumed by the demon's flames. I ran the pad of my fingers along its surface, stroking the silk, like feeling my mother's love. Then I peeled the shawl away, praying to the Goddess for a demonslayer.

Not a demonslayer, but a polished piece of wood—a walking stick for the limp or lame.

The rage within me grew, and I raised the staff high to hurl it out the window and into the moat below. Yet as I lifted up the bequest, I noticed an eagle head carved into its crown, with eyes that seemed to be staring at me, and I could swear I heard it speak in my mother's voice.

"Your old life is gone, Frederick. Embrace the new as you've embraced the shadows."

I grasped the staff and, with its help, stood on steadier legs. Then I hovered by the open door and thanked the advisor, eager for him to leave.

Now, at last, I knew where my destiny lay.

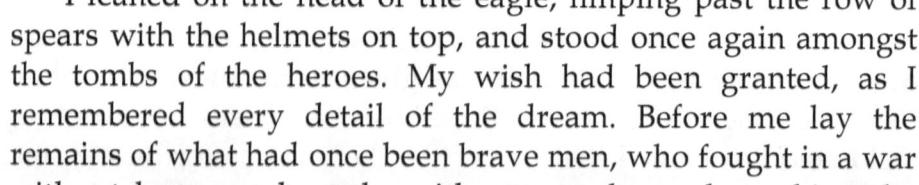

I leaned on the head of the eagle, limping past the row of spears with the helmets on top, and stood once again amongst the tombs of the heroes. My wish had been granted, as I remembered every detail of the dream. Before me lay the remains of what had once been brave men, who fought in a war without honor or bounds, with powers beyond anything the demons could devise. The crypt seemed to roar with their silence.

In tribute, I chanted their names.

"Dixon, the druid, Anderson, the mage, Martinez, the paladin, and Jones, the hunter. And at their head, Sanchez, the priest and archangel. May the Goddess grant peace to them all."

They were my brothers in arms. Instead of leading them into ruin, I should have been there to shield them, to parry their death stroke, and failing that, to die with them. I stood helpless, my weight a useless burden upon the earth, and my eyes began to fill.

No! A white-hot anger stoked my mind, and I shook off the mood. I couldn't afford the luxury of tears.

"Why?" I shouted, my voice echoing through the vaulted arches and dispersing in their shadows. When neither spirit nor demon appeared, I cried out again, this time loudly enough to overwhelm the pounding in my ears. "What more must I do? What new trials must I face before Azeroth can be saved?"

As if in answer, the wall behind the caskets shimmered and took on an indigo hue. I braced, expecting the return of the voidwalker, but instead, the foot soldier in blue reappeared, his arm raised as before in a gesture of beckoning.

At first, I was puzzled, but then I understood—he was the guide to the third trial, beckoning me to follow.

I came closer and reached out to touch the rough stone. As my fingers slid along the surface, they took on the color of the soldier's uniform. I drew back my hand, pulled out my sword, and tapped on the wall, making the chamber echo with the clatter of metal on stone. Then it hit me.

My mother's gift... the staff with the eagle.

I reached out and touched the noble bird's beak to the wall. The blue soldier rippled and emerged, still an apparition but with his features now distinct. Silver hair spilled from the edges of his cap, framing a face etched with a lifetime of kindness.

He stepped aside and waved for me to pass, but when I turned back, the wall remained as solid as ever. I gaped at it, then at the soldier. When he continued to gesture, I raised the eagle head high and inched forward.

The wall remained as sturdy as Stormwind keep, but my body became translucent, like that of the soldier, and I passed through like a wraith, undeterred by the physical world.

On the far side, a blast of cold air prickled my lungs when I breathed in, and emerged as a cloud when I exhaled. Ahead, a single casket floated on vapors, its head tilted upward toward me. White particles skittered about like snow on the floor around it, and inside lay a boy, his face covered in fog.

I edged closer, hardly able to see, my eyes tearing from the stench and the cold.

The blue soldier urged me on. When we reached the casket, he waved and the fog coalesced into a shroud.

I peered in, and a vision came into my mind—a boy with an innocent smile.

"May I see his face?" I said to the soldier in blue.

He reached down and peeled back the shroud.

I peered in, but the face stayed hidden in cloud.

I glanced up to the arches made aery by mist, and down to where the vapors still swirled. Nothing in the chamber seemed real. I'd found the third trial, but what did it mean? More riddles to befuddle the dauphin.

The dauphin. A rank rendered hollow in a mere seven days.

If I solved the trials by then, I'd cast off the honorific and be anointed king. If not, this baseless world would grind to a halt, and all I held dear would burn to ash and be scattered by the blast of a scalding wind.

Styrofoam Snow

"DO YOU HAVE A FAMILY, FREDDIE?"

Jimmie stared at me and I stared back, struggling not to grimace as I shook my head.

The surgery to replace the fragment of his skull had gone well. The hockey helmet had vanished, and enough hair had grown back to cover his scalp. He'd gained a few pounds too, and looked better every day, downright handsome for a young soldier who'd been through so much.

"My mom and dad live in Iowa," he said. "They don't have much money, but they visit when they can, and they email me every day."

"And the girl?" Like Jimmie, I'd forgotten her name.

"Evie," he said. "I wrote it down and read it out loud fifty times a day, like Dr. B. told me to do. Reprogramming the pathways, he called it. Now I can remember. She sent me this T-shirt."

He pinched the fabric at his shoulders and pulled it taut. It bore a picture of a young man who resembled Jimmie—more flesh on the face and more hair on the head, but the same deep blue eyes. Beneath the picture were the words: "Living well is the best revenge."

"Have you seen her again?"

"Uh-huh. She still cries a little but not as much. We're getting reacquainted. She says I'm less nervous now than I was on our first date. I have to take her word for it. She tells me stories, like listening about somebody else. Mostly I just like being with her." He waited for my reaction.

Nice kid. His hope was coming back. I was happy for him but had nothing to add. Maybe selfishly, my own situation weighed on me.

"What happened to your family, Freddie?" he said, as if he'd read my mind.

"All gone."

"All of them?"

"I... think so."

"But you don't know? Did you forget some of them, like me?"

What could I say? He had problems of his own, so no need to burden him with mine, but the question nagged at me. If I could forget what happened to Humvee three, what else was hidden in my brain? I vividly remembered three funerals, standing at the graveside at each and saying my last goodbyes. Mom and Dad and Joey were gone, but when I thought of Richie, a different memory played in my mind—Styrofoam snow skittering across a deserted parking lot in winter, a dumpster, three days riding on the T with little sleep. Was that a memory I could trust?

"I may still have a brother," I said.

"You don't know?"

"Afraid not."

"If I were you, Freddie, and one brother might be all I had left, I'd need to find out. Maybe Dr. B. has an exercise that will help you remember, like with my beautiful Evie—reprogramming the pathways."

A picture of Dr. B. popped into my head, his jowls shaking as he advised me. Another image quickly replaced it—the physical therapist with eyes that could drag me back from the pit of hell.

Becky had smuggled a bottle of wine into PT in anticipation of a breakthrough. My knee was approaching ninety degrees. For three weeks, she'd had me on the exercise bike, trying to pedal. I'd rock the pedals forward and back until my knee screamed, but was unable to spin them all the way around. She'd promised that at ninety degrees, I'd succeed.

"Today's the day," she said. "I can feel it."

"That's because it's not your knee."

"Come on, Lieutenant. Tough it out. On the bike."

I wanted to make her happy, but every time I reached the top of the pedal, my knee would lock and refuse to go further.

Becky encouraged. "You can do it."

Becky cajoled. "A little bit more."

Becky explained. "Your mind's telling you the pain will get worse if you keep going, but it's lying. Once you're over the top, the pain will stop."

I gave a push, winced, and backed off.

"Oh, for Christ's sake, Freddie! I'm going to give it a shove."

She rushed toward me and reached out to push, but never touched my leg. The pedal spun around as if on its own.

She clapped. "You did it. All by yourself. Now again."

Once I got over the fear, spinning the pedal around was easier. I did ten loops for her and then stopped.

"Enough," I said.

"Ten more."

"No."

"Okay," she said as I staggered over to the treatment table. "We'll do more tomorrow. How about an ice pack?"

"No."

She glared at me, then opened the bottle of wine and poured some into two plastic cups.

I accepted a cup from her and watched the wine swirl and settle to stillness.

"Toast?" she said.

When I didn't respond, she tapped her cup to mine and took a sip. I set mine down without drinking.

"What's wrong now, Freddie?"

"Nothing."

"You're over the hump. Ninety degrees. With more hard work and some luck, you'll hardly have a limp. Why are you still brooding?"

I stayed silent, slumped on the table.

She came over and sat next to me, so near our shoulders touched. "Talk to me."

I'd been thinking about it for days, but it came out now, like the pedal spinning over the top. "If I could block out the ambush, what else am I hiding in my brain?"

She folded her hands and studied her fingertips. "I shouldn't tell you this. I hope you won't be mad at me."

"Tell me what?"

"I pulled your 201 file to see if anything else had happened, just in case there was more. You had a rough tour, but there was nothing as bad as the ambush or the IED attack. I checked on the rest of your squad. They're all alive and, as of last week, have been redeployed stateside."

I digested her words, grabbed the cup, and took a gulp of wine — a reason to celebrate — but I still couldn't face her.

"You're not mad at me, are you?"

I shook my head, flattered she'd made the effort. "Mad? No. Good to know. Thank you." Another sip, another swallow. "But it's not just the war."

"Then what?"

"I was trained to leave no man behind, but how can I be sure? What if I abandoned Richie?"

She slipped off the treatment table, grabbed me by the arms, and leaned in so close our foreheads nearly touched. "You carry a lot on these shoulders, don't you, Lieutenant?"

Being so close to her, my mood lightened — she had that effect on me — but then I had a new thought.

She performed miracles with my leg. What if...?

"You dug up my war record. Any chance you could find out what happened to Richie?"

"I'd be glad to try, but you'd need to give me someplace to start."

Styrofoam snow swirled in my head, skittering across a parking lot on a cold winter night; a dumpster; a voice behind me.... I waited, letting the images mingle and merge before telling her.

"After Richie ran off, I looked for three days. I rode the subway and searched for him in the stations. I checked beneath park benches, in the lobbies of tenements, and under loading docks in alleyways. I showed his picture to anyone who wasn't too scared of me to stop — I was getting pretty scruffy after three nights without sleep."

"And then?"

"I was poking around a dumpster behind one of those high-end restaurants on Tremont Street. Since I'd left him with barely enough cash to pay for the bus ticket to Boston, he'd be cold and hungry after three days. I thought he might be scavenging for food, but I didn't find anything, and after three nights without sleep, I gave up. I'd had it with my family. Time to look out for myself."

"And?"

"There was a voice behind me — a policeman. I thought I was in trouble for rummaging through the dumpster, but he'd been looking for me."

"What did he want?"

"He asked if I was the one who'd been looking for the missing boy."

She held her breath. When I had nothing more to say, she had to ask. "Oh, Freddie, did you find—"

I dropped my chin to my chest. "I don't know, Becky. That's the thing.... I can't remember."

She emptied her cup of wine and tossed it into the trash. When she turned back, I expected sympathy, but instead her features had hardened into resolve. "If you're right about the policeman, I might have something to work with."

I waited open-mouthed, and she gaped at me as if I was too dense to understand. Finally, I gave in and asked. "How?"

"There'd be an incident report, Freddie. The police might have one on file."

A
Pretty
Flower

26

DAY TWENTY-FIVE, AND AS THE end of anointment approached, the people prepared for a celebration. They piled food high in the courtyard, and stacked casks of wine in pyramids. Servants planted poles with torches on top, and stretched brightly-colored ribbons between them to line the pavilion. Young girls weaved wreaths of flowers, while children played among the ribbons, enjoying their first anointment. They had no doubt: Stormwind would be saved for another generation, and the dauphin would be crowned king.

None of them knew what I'd witnessed in the watchtower.

Their parents had flocked to the castle not for celebration, but for protection. The courtyard teemed with people clutching hopeful totems, along with their earthly possessions packed in canvas sacks. Bewildered livestock wandered amongst them. Confused chickens searched for their coops, and roosters crowed at noon.

Beneath the archways and in the shadows, out of sight of the revelers, people loaded dried meat and water skins onto carts, preparing for flight.

From the walls of the battlement, I watched the scene before me and shook my head. All was self-deceit. If I failed, none of their preparations would matter.

The day before, I'd exhausted myself seeking magic to reveal the face of the boy. I rummaged through books in the royal library, hoping to find a spell. I searched for the archangel's chamber, and limped down the stairs to the watershed, but no ramps or doorways emerged, and no demons or spirits appeared.

In desperation, I went looking for the gardener. Her fake rose had led me to the archangel's chamber, and the drawing she'd rescued from the assassin's flame had revealed the names of the heroes. Perhaps she would have other charms.

When I arrived in the gardens, she was nowhere to be found. Had my foul mood finally driven her away, or had she succumbed at last to some evil?

Then I heard a rustling behind me and turned, expecting Rebecca.

The simpleton sat on the wrought iron bench that Rebecca and I had once shared, his head cocked to one side, his gaze flitting about as if searching for a specific flower. Between his knees, he clutched the soiled, leather pouch that had once held the map.

I stepped toward him, making no effort to be stealthy, but my approach brought no response.

"Why have you come to this garden?" I said.

"The flowers. They're lovely, aren't they?"

"Where is the gardener who's usually here? Have you seen her?"

"Nope. Just me." His deep blue eyes took on a hint of laughter. "Is she pretty?"

Despite my misgivings, I smiled. "Like a flower newly blossomed on a spring day."

"Oh, I should like to meet her sometime. How did you like my map?"

"It was of great value to me, but now I need your help again." I eyed the leather bag. "Do you have any more magic in that satchel?"

"How would I know what's magic?"

"You gave me the map."

"A stroke of luck. A bit of trash I found in a barrel." He lifted the bag, removed the tie from its neck, and peered inside.

I waited, shifting from foot to foot and fingering the hilt of my sword.

Finally, he looked up. "One thing left."

I was growing impatient. "But is it magic?"

"Perhaps... if you believe it is. It's a child's toy, so it might be magic only for a child. Can you see with the eyes of a child?"

I nodded, resisting the urge to grab it away.

He reached into the bag and pulled out a globe, unlike any I'd seen before, with a clear pedestal that exposed a jumble of prongs and gears. Oddly, within the globe floated two dancing angels.

He held it up to the light. "Watch."

He shook it so hard that I feared the angels would crash into each other, but instead, golden glimmers began to fall all around them, glistening in the light.

I extended a hand. "May I see it?"

"Of course you may. After all, it belongs to you."

I cradled the globe in my palm. It felt too delicate to be a weapon, but the dreaded days offered many surprises. I rotated it, studying the faces of the angels, and finally turned it upside down. Sticking out from the bottom were a lever and a key. My finger twitched and I went to touch it.

"Oh no," he shouted, in a commanding voice that belied his appearance. "You mustn't touch the key of remembrance until the time is right."

"The key of remembrance?" When he did not respond, I said, "But when will that time be?"

"How would I know? I'm only a simpleton." He picked up the empty satchel and began to walk away.

I called after him. "Is there a way I can repay you?"

A smirk curled across his lips, an expression somewhere between madness and malice. "May I pick a flower from your royal garden?"

I watched the glitter rain down upon the angels, and waved my hand across the gardens. "As you wish. Take whatever you choose."

Without hesitation, he headed straight for the monkshood, took out a small knife from his pocket, and snipped off a blossom. "A pretty flower, like your gardener on a spring day."

A flash of panic struck me as I recalled the gardener's words: *"Monkshood is lovely, but not for princes on whom our lives depend."*

"Not that flower," I cried.

His smirk transformed into a wry grin. "But you said I could take whichever flower I liked."

"But that one's dangerous."

"I know," he said, and without waiting for my response, he dropped the purple blossom into his bag and sauntered off.

I held the toy up to the light and watched him through the glitter still swirling in the globe. Then I glanced at the monkshood. From the gash where he'd sliced off the blossom, the stem oozed sap.

Dead
Ends

A FEW DAYS LATER, THE VETERAN'S Administration had finished with me. I was well enough to go outpatient, and free up a bed for the next poor son of a bitch being flown in from Ramstein. So I packed up my few possessions into the military-issue box, and headed off to an advanced rehabilitation facility — army-speak for a barracks outfitted with handrails in the showers and bathroom stalls, a place where they could warehouse guys like me until we were ready to resume active duty, or be discharged to civilian life.

I didn't mind. I'd still be on the grounds of the hospital and a short walk to the services I needed. The idea of being more independent appealed to me — a transition to the real world, which I'd have to make sooner or later — and though we were at the start of a New England winter, I was unfazed.

I had my eagle cane, and Becky would still be near.

She came to me one day as I was leading a trash detail, one of the mindless tasks they assigned the recovering vets as they assumed their own care. When Becky appeared in the doorway, I needed a second to assimilate her presence in the barracks.

"I've brought someone to see you," she said.

My heart pounded. "Richie?"

I knew before I said the name that it was a frivolous thought. Miracles were for children and fools.

Becky's face gave nothing away. "Not Richie, but maybe someone who can help find him. He wouldn't tell me much, said he wanted to speak to you directly."

I handed off the detail to a staff sergeant who was getting used to hobbling around on a prosthetic leg.

When Becky and I were halfway down the dingy corridor that served as the main thoroughfare through the barracks, she stopped me and placed a hand on my arm. "I did my best, Freddie." Her voice took on an edge. "Don't expect too much."

An easy request. I stopped expecting much long ago.

She led me to the common room, a place with a pool table, a TV, and a bank of computers for email and gaming, where the guys could gather to relax. It being midmorning, everyone was either at treatment or on details.

The only person in the room was a distinguished-looking man with silver hair who was aimlessly spinning a cue ball on the pool table. He turned as soon as we came in, and stepped smartly toward me with his chin pulled in and his back straight—the classic posture of a military man, but his uniform wasn't military.

I stared at his face, and then at the blue jacket with the brass buttons parading down his chest, and the gold badge over his heart. The machine in my mind whirred and settled—a police officer, a man I'd seen before.

He took a moment, looked me over, and then turned to Becky. "Yes, Ms. Marshall, this is him, the young man I saw that day."

Becky touched the small of my back and eased me forward, knowing how afraid I'd be to hear the news. "He didn't want to tell me what happened," she whispered, "until he was sure it was you."

The officer nodded a greeting to me and extended a hand. "It's good to see you again, Lieutenant. This is a very different occasion than the last time we met."

I shook his hand, trying my best to be polite despite the blood thudding in my temples. "Thank you for coming. Yes, I recognize you, and I hope you can tell me what happened that day."

"It'd be hard to forget. You looked so desperate behind that restaurant, rummaging through the dumpster. I'd have mistaken you for a homeless person, except that you left a wake in your tracks. I'd heard about you from several concerned citizens, so when I took you to the morgue, I was afraid—"

"The morgue?" My heart nearly jumped out of my chest.

"Yes. We had an unidentified body—same time frame, same age. I brought you to see if it was your brother."

My mind darted in and out of shadows, trying to find daylight.

He must have noticed my panic. "You don't remember, do you? Not a surprise. I recall my own war so many years ago. It can play games with your mind."

An image flashed through my mind of a boy in a casket with his face hidden in fog, and of me turning sideways, inching closer, terrified of what I might find. In a few short years, I'd viewed the lifeless bodies of my father, mother, and brother. I wasn't sure I could handle one more, but the face in the morgue stayed hidden beyond the rim of my memory, in a place where hope taunts and teases.

"Was it him?" I said.

He probably answered at once, but I was sluggish to comprehend. Time slowed and his words reached my ears as if filtered through mud.

"No," I heard at last. "You didn't recognize the body in the morgue. It wasn't your brother."

Following the policeman's visit, my mindset began to change. What if my luck had turned? What if the string of misfortunes that had plagued my young life were the result of happenstance, and not because of some dark and forbidding plan? What if I could dare to believe in the future again?

For some reason, my nature had always tended toward optimism... until it had been beaten down by events. Now that optimism was returning. I could have lost my life or my leg in the IED attack, but I didn't. I might never be able to dunk, but I could see a day when, at worst, I'd walk with a barely noticeable limp, using the most stylish cane around. I started thinking about what I wanted inscribed on the cane.

Mom and Dad and Joey for sure. The archangel too, and the others who were lost. But no memorial for Richie. Not yet.

The advanced rehab facility had a modest exercise room, with a treadmill, elliptical, a few Nautilus machines, and a rack of free weights. I became a gym rat. In the evenings, instead of brooding on my bunk and staring at the somber squares on the army-issue ceiling, I hit the weights. What I was unable to do with my injured leg, I made up for with my upper body—bench presses, abs, lats, curls. I'd been in great shape before the attack. No reason I couldn't get close to where I'd been.

I was also drawn to the computers in the common room. When I first transferred to the facility, I avoided them, afraid to reengage with the game. My reality was weird enough without role-playing in a fantasy world. Now, I realized I could use the computers for a new and more worthwhile quest—searching for Richie.

I sat in front of the screen and began to explore. It was a new feeling for me, having a goal. I'd become so attuned to expect the worst that I hardly dared to hope. And yet... what if... for once, I was wrong?

Becky got me access to a slew of websites—local and state governments, hospitals, churches, and other charitable institutions. I spent all my free time browsing, as addicted as I used to be to the game. Hours passed like seconds as I searched databases throughout New England and beyond. But this wasn't *World of Warcraft*.

In the game, I'd encounter a non-player character with a message sending me off on a quest. The bubble over his head would say, "Kill the dwarf who hides in the first tower in the field of strife and you'll be rewarded with..." I'd research the venue, assess the enemy's strength, and then organize my guild for a raid. If I failed the first time, I'd learn from defeat and try again. When I was finally successful, I'd be rewarded with experience points and gold, sometimes even a new weapon or spell. My level would grow.

Well, this was no fantasy game.

I pored through every document I could find—records of homelessness, drugs, and crime, the great underbelly of society. Most were dead ends, but one in ten yielded an intriguing link. I'd get drawn down a rat hole, fascinated by one person's story. I'd get to know them so well, I'd grieve for their tragedies and exult in their triumphs, as if they were members of my own family. Yet in no obituary, hospital or morgue, homeless shelter or halfway house, did I find a mention of Richie Williams.

When I searched for him, the response was always the same:
NO MATCHES FOUND

Trials
Unsolved

I SAT IN MY BEDCHAMBER AND caressed the globe, watching the angels beam at each other as the glitter rained down upon them.

Could this be the magic to vanquish the third trial? Why am I so hesitant to find out?

I staggered to the mirror, an oval of polished bronze that embellished the far wall, searching for an answer in my reflection. What I saw surprised me: pale skin, and hollowed eyes, as if intent on mimicking the sockets of the assassin. This was not the face of a soon-to-be-king, but of a man at the edge of a precipice, leaning into the teeth of a great wind. And the hollowness ran deeper, to where my heart should be — an absence of hope.

I hesitated because I had no hope.

On the morning of the twenty-sixth day, after another futile session in the watchtower, I could no longer wait. After gathering up my sword and dagger, the staff and globe, and all the other enchantments I'd collected, I headed back to the crypt.

I paused before the archway and filled my lungs with the last of the fresh air, then raised my good leg and stepped over the threshold. By the tombs of my parents, I bowed my head and prayed for the Goddess to ease their journey into the next world. At the plate in the shape of a hawk, I inserted the roots of the World Tree and snapped open the lock. In the Hall of Heroes, I paid homage to each by name.

Once again, I confronted the stone wall, and just as before, the surface rippled and the blue soldier appeared. I gaped at his image, gripping the staff more tightly and tapping its tip on the floor.

I longed to brace for battle, to fight the assassin and defeat him in a contest of skill and strength. Failing that, I preferred to flee and fight another day. Yet the way forward wasn't like the dark portal in the blasted lands. No flaming swords blocked the entrance, and no hoofed beasts barred my way. Only a stone wall stood before me, one that would yield to the touch of my eagle's beak.

I blew out three quick breaths, raised the staff high, and stepped though.

The wave of cold stuck me at once, but I trudged on until I stood once more at the head of the casket. I looked in to see the boy's face still clouded by fog. As before, the apparition of the blue soldier removed the shroud, but to no avail.

I held up the globe and peered through it.

Time for the key of remembrance.

I tipped the globe upside down and twisted the key until it became hard to turn. Then I placed the tip of my finger on the lever, but hesitated, knowing all too well how painful remembrance could be.

I pressed the lever.

Music began to play, a haunting melody from another world. The angels spun and danced to the tune, as the glitter fell all around them.

I watched and listened, transfixed. The key of remembrance was magic indeed.

A vision came into my mind — the face of a young boy with an innocent smile. My eyes began to fill with the tears I was unable to shed at the tomb of the heroes.

I turned to the soldier in blue and spoke with more passion this time. "May I see his face?"

He waved his hand, and this time the scrim disappeared.

I stood bewildered, as before me lay the face of a stranger.

The music grew louder, a force of nature that echoed off the vaulted arches, and the fog cleared, as if a gust of wind had blown through the crypt. Beyond where I stood, the final trial came into view — one lone casket, empty this time — but when I tried to step closer, some invisible force barred my way.

I reached into my tunic for all my enchantments: the crocus that never faded; the drawing of the rose; the archangel's medallion. I thrust the eagle forward and poked at the portal with my sword. None would allow me to pass. In frustration, I withdrew Kingsbane and hurled it at the barrier.

The dagger of sorrow was flung back and fell on the ground at my feet.

Tomorrow would be the twenty-seventh day. With the third trial still a mystery, and the fourth beyond my reach, I shuddered for the future. My hope, like the days, continued to slip away.

I slumped in a chair across the table from the advisor. I'd come to question him, to seek all the help I could find. I remembered my father only as king, but Sir Gilly had known him as dauphin. Perhaps he had gained some wisdom from watching my father struggle through the trials.

"Three days," I said, "and we're undone. I'm at a loss and, though I've come so far, fear that I'll fail. Pray tell me, Advisor, what did you observe from my father that might ease my way?"

Sir Gilly leaned upon his elbows, chin in his hands so that his jowls spread through his fingers like dough. "Nothing comes easily during the days of anointment. Our salvation must be earned."

"But you must have learned something."

He regarded me as if the answer were imprinted on my forehead. After a moment, he stood and shuffled to the bookcases that lined the back wall of his office. From a topmost shelf, he pulled down a sturdy volume whose leather cover bore the seal of the lord chamberlain. He dropped it on the tabletop with a thump, blew away the dust, and flipped through the pages.

I gripped the arms of my chair and waited.

"There was one time," he said at last, "when the despair weighed most heavily upon your father, and he bore a look as haggard as yours. Like you, he came to me troubled, stumped by the final trial. He'd found no spell to overcome it. No spirit or elf had appeared, and his unworthy advisor was at a loss for advice."

"Yet he must have found a way through, for here we are. The Alliance prevailed."

"Aye. The Alliance prevailed in the end, but on that day, when he sat in that very chair, he believed he would fail." Sir Gilly licked his thumb and turned a page, and then another. At last, he brightened. "Ah, here it is."

"What is it? Some bequest from my father? A spell handed down from the king?"

He shook his head and released a breath, like a sigh rising up from the bottom of a well. "No, Frederick. You put too much faith in magic. I have nothing but a record of his words as spoken to me days later, after he'd been anointed and the celebrations had ended, when I asked what he had learned."

I slid forward to the edge of my chair. "What did he say?"

"His words struck me then, and so I wrote them down, though I never understood what they meant."

"Tell me," I said, too loud and impatient, all vestige of courtesy gone.

He ran his finger down the page and lingered over a single phrase. His lips moved soundlessly, like a sorcerer reciting an incantation. Finally, he lifted his chin and became every bit the advisor. "These are the words of your father as spoken to me after he was crowned king of Stormwind, and Azeroth had been saved."

He paused to take in a deep breath, making certain he had enough to spare. Then he continued. "'In the end,' he said, 'there was only me.'"

Treadmills

MY LEG IMPROVED STEADILY, AND SO did my outlook. When dawn flickered around the edges of the window shade, I no longer imagined a 155mm white-phosphorus round incoming. No longer did I spend half the morning in the borderland between waking and sleep, dwelling on the past. Instead, I focused on the future.

I had a year of first lieutenant's salary coming, plus imminent-danger pay, all with no income taxes thanks to my earning them in a combat zone. That, combined with the G.I. Bill and a little left over from the sale of the gingerbread house, should be enough to pay for school — enough to get certified as an architect and design fantasy worlds of my own.

But something was missing.

The next day, I arrived at PT a few minutes ahead of schedule and stood quietly in the doorway.

Becky hadn't noticed me and kept going about her chores, bustling from her ointments to her weights and machines, cleaning up after her prior patient. She mumbled under her breath, running through her checklist. "Weights put away: check.

Wipe down the treadmill: check. Reset the flowers: check." She stopped her bustling long enough to glance in the mirror. "Be sure I'm not a mess: check."

After a while, afraid I'd embarrass her, I rapped on the door jam with the eagle head.

She stopped what she was doing and turned. "Freddie, you're early. Come in. I was just cleaning up."

She stole one last look in the mirror, then wiped her hands and came toward me. As she got closer, she caught sight of the medallion I was wearing. "That's new. I don't remember it in the box. Someone give it to you?"

"Maria Sanchez." When she gave me an odd look, I added, "The archangel's wife. It was his. I decided it was time to wear it, to be proud of it and remember him. Better than wearing medals I don't deserve."

"You can be so gloomy, but I'm glad you're early. I have a big workout planned. Today, we get you on the treadmill."

She'd threatened as much before, but I insisted I wasn't ready. My leg was strong enough, but my balance remained suspect. A list to starboard wasn't conducive to staying upright on a moving belt.

I had something else in mind, and she saw it at once. "Something wrong? You look like you're afraid to cross the threshold."

"I have a question before we start."

"What's that?"

"I want you to go out with me."

"You mean like to the Cape?"

"No. Like on a date."

She became uncharacteristically flustered. "Oh, Freddie, that's sweet, but you know I'm not allowed to—"

"A little joke," I said, and felt my face grow warm. I tightened my grip on the eagle head. "If you're still intent on the treadmill, let's get on with it."

First, we did the stretching exercise, which involved much less screaming than it once did, then she measured the bend of the knee—more than a hundred degrees. After that, she put hot packs on both legs. Once my muscles warmed up, it was time for the treadmill.

I walked with my cane to the machine and stepped up, a small step, less than half the height of a riser on the therapy room practice stairs, but it seemed huge.

"You won't be needing this." She took away my cane. "Just hold onto the side rails. We'll go slowly at first, the pace of a snail."

I gave her a skeptical look that turned to panic when she pressed the start button. The belt turned under my feet, and I clung to the side rails.

She placed one hand on the small of my back and the other on my sternum. "I've got you. I won't let you fall. Now stand up tall, look straight ahead, and don't forget to breathe."

As she ratcheted up the speed to one mile per hour, I dwelled on how I used to run home after basketball practice. I could jog the 2.2 miles in under fifteen minutes, even after a long scrimmage. Now, it would take over two hours… if I could make it at all. I began to sweat.

Then she let go.

"You said you wouldn't let go."

"I lied. Physical therapist trick to give you confidence. You're doing fine on your own. You don't need me."

Suddenly, I knew what I was missing. The thought drove me on, wanting to please her. By the time we were done, I'd walked half a mile. Near the end, I even let go of the handrails.

Afterwards, she rewarded me with a towel and a cup of cold water.

I'd done more in that session than I'd ever imagined being able to do again.

Time to raise my sights, to aim for the future.

I took a deep swallow to moisten my throat, then reached out and grasped her hand. "I lied too. It wasn't a joke."

She blinked, a momentary lapse in professional composure. "What wasn't a joke?"

"What I said about a date."

She came closer, but wavered, her usual self-assurance gone. "Oh, Freddie, I can't."

An awkwardness settled over the physical therapy room, but now that I'd mastered the treadmill, I had no intention of slowing down. "You can't turn me down if we're going to search for Richie."

She nodded, her eyes round and wide.

"How about this Saturday?" I said.

"What?"

"I need to check out the cemetery. It's not far from here—my family's plot. To pay my respects and see if a second brother's buried there." I tapped my head. "No telling what's hiding up here. And after that, I'll need lunch and some comfort from my therapist."

"I guess... that might fit my job description."

When we finished and I was ready to make the trek back to the advanced rehabilitation facility, she accompanied me out of the therapy room and down the green-tile corridor to the outside door. My knee still throbbed from the workout.

She rested a hand on my cheek and waited for my grimace to subside. "I won't always be your therapist."

I smiled back. "I know."

The Nature of Flowers

30

THE EVENING OF THE TWENTY-EIGHTH DAY, after finishing my session with the spinning wheel, I hobbled down the stairs, clutching the eagle staff with one hand and clinging to the wall with the other. My descent took so long that I feared the stairway had trapped me again. I began counting steps and scanning the stone for the owl-shaped mark, but no magic was at work this day, only my labored pace.

At the bottom, I leaned out over the rim of the parapet to survey the twilight scene — no signs of progress. Thunderheads darkened the mountains above, and heat blighted the land below. As I looked south across the Barrens toward the lands of the Horde, a bitter wind blew in my face. When it gusted, I could hear the ringing of hammer on anvil — the sound of steel being forged.

I retreated to a corner and slumped against a wall, but was startled to attention by stirrings from the shadows behind me. Angry at being caught unawares, I struggled to my feet and drew my sword, bracing for an attack from a demon. As I stepped into the murky recesses by the entrance to the watchtower, I poked half-heartedly into the gloom.

A voice that was anything but demonic cried out. "Oh no, Milord. It's me."

"Rebecca?"

My arm lost its strength, ashamed of what it had nearly done. The sword slipped from my grasp and fell to the ground. I staggered and would have fallen, if not for the gardener's firm grip. She grabbed my arm and led me back to the base of the watchtower, where I collapsed on a bench, hiding my face in my hands.

I listened to the sweep of her footsteps as she retrieved my sword. When I refused to take it, she leaned it by my side and reached out to brush my cheek with the back of her hand.

"What's that for?" I said.

"To see if you're real."

I looked up; her eyes were laughing.

"Why have you come here?" I asked.

"Because the flowers in my garden were calling your name, but you were nowhere to be found. Then I remembered your appointment with the watchtower, and knew where you'd be in the twilight hour." She waited for me to respond, but when I remained downcast, she exclaimed, "Oh, Milord, why are you here so alone? Look how the color has gone from your cheeks and the light has fled from your eyes. And what offense have I given, that you've forsaken our meetings in the garden?"

I sheathed my sword for fear of alarming her further. "Come, Rebecca, and sit by me."

"I can't, Milord. It's not my place."

I breathed a sigh. "You think I'm more worthy than you? How far would I have come without you?"

"Do you make light of me?"

"You have more power than you know."

Her face darkened with something—a terror with no name. "Yet I'm as frightened as anyone. What wickedness comes this way from the south? The heat's so strong and unnatural. By this late in the season, I should be swaddling the bushes in burlap for the winter, but the weather's so hot, they'd wilt and die before noon."

I bid her again to sit, and when she did, I reached out and guided her head to my chest, to a place where she could feel safe. It was a lie. None of us were safe anymore. How much better might it have been to stay ignorant, never to see what I'd seen from the watchtower?

As we sat there, her head rose and fell with each breath I took, as if I were breathing for the both of us. After a few moments, I buried my face in her hair and inhaled its scent. At that moment, I noticed a change. As I immersed myself in her perfume, the pain in my leg eased, as if healed by a magical spell.

She lifted her head off my chest and looked up at me. "What is it? I felt you start, like a burden had been lifted."

"It's you. Whether you're spirit or mortal, you've helped me at every turn, whenever I was blocked or ready to despair."

"Such words, Milord. You mock a poor gardener."

"Poor gardener, indeed. Your pretend rose let me find the key to the Hall of Heroes, and your drawing on parchment revealed their names. Now, with time running out, you appear again in my hour of need."

She pulled away and slowly shook her head. "But I have no such power. The crocus pretending to be a rose, and the picture on the parchment, were nothing but jests, a way to cheer you on."

"Not jests, Rebecca. Magic."

Intent on demonstrating her power, I reached into my tunic and withdrew the crocus, but the instant I exposed it, the flower withered and died. I stared in horror as its petals decayed into dust and were carried away by the wind, leaving only a few surviving grains nestled in the palm of my hand.

"Now even *your* magic has failed. I fear it's over and the demons have won."

"Oh no, Milord," Rebecca said. "That's not demons, but the gardener's way. It's in the nature of flowers to bloom and die.

Then, when the new season comes, they bloom again. In this way, life goes on."

A blanket of gloom settled over us. I would have called it a chill but for the heat.

When my silence persisted, she stood and wandered over to the parapet, facing to the east, and spoke with her back to me. "Perhaps if I knew more about the trials."

"Why? Has your butterfly returned with an incantation more powerful than SMOG?"

She spun around, and the color rose in her cheeks. "You mock me again, Milord, but don't belittle a gardener's spirit. Pray tell me what I need to know." She hovered over me, not to be denied.

I took in her delicate features, her fierce but fearful eyes.

Is it possible she could yet conjure up magic?

My words spewed forth like the stream in the watershed, fire and ice, all the good and the bad that had transpired. "In these last two days, the world will be won or lost in the crypt. I've overcome the early trials, but two remain — the missing boy with the innocent smile, and the final mystery, an empty casket beyond my reach."

Rebecca looked past me, out over the gray hills and to the mountains beyond. Her eyes narrowed as she lifted her chin and leaned toward me, tilting up on her toes as if about to take flight. "Though my crocus has died, and my heart pounds in my chest, I swear by the Goddess to stand by you. Tomorrow at noon, I shall accompany you to the crypt."

I looked up, wanting to believe. "Have you had a revelation, or encountered some mage who's granted you spells?"

"You misunderstand," she said. "I have no magic. There's only you and I, but perhaps together, we'll be stronger than apart. Perhaps together, we'll find a way."

Grim
Gray
Stones

ON SATURDAY MORNING, I LIMPED OUT the front door of the advanced rehabilitation facility and found Becky sitting in her car with the motor idling. The sky was somber and low, and the prior night's mist had glazed the pavement with a film of black ice—a bad day to be a wounded warrior. Once in the car, my mood improved with the scent of the daisies she'd brought to decorate the graves. That and the touch of her hand on my arm.

We eased out of the hospital parking lot and headed onto the VFW Parkway. Two traffic lights later, we turned at Baker Street, a road my father used to call cemetery row. There we passed a mile of graves, cemetery after cemetery, each of a different denomination—all God's children laid peacefully to rest, as long as they stayed in their realm.

Becky tapped on her brakes, eyeing the slick surface and all the pillared entrances. "So many cemeteries. How can you remember where your family's buried?"

"Easy," I said. "I've come here often enough."

Five times, though it seems like more.

I attended three funerals, came once before I left for active duty, and again on a three-day pass before shipping out to Iraq. I came not because the visits meant much, but because all of my buddies spent their last leave with loved ones. These grim gray stones were all I had left.

I found the entrance with no problem, and directed Becky down the narrow access road. Before we could reach the Williams' plot, however, we had to roll to a stop. Ahead, a row of parked cars lined one side, leaving barely enough space to pass. At their front sat a hearse. Beyond a waist-high stone wall, a funeral was in progress—a cluster of mourners, a casket draped with an American flag, seven Marines in dress blues standing at attention, feet at 45-degree angles, arms straight, and thumbs aligned with the seams of their pants.

Becky stepped out of the car, and I followed, huddling close more for warmth than support. We waited respectfully as the minister finished the eulogy.

While we listened, my attention drifted to the back of the cemetery, where a row of stately willows bordered the fence. They stood with browned branches bent low to the ground, like mourners with heads bowed, perpetual witnesses to an endless succession of funerals. The willow in front of us caught my eye. Darker than the others, it let no light pass through, and its branches quivered.

When the eulogy ended and the mournful sound of taps had faded to silence, an order was given, and the honor guard raised their carbines and aimed at the sky.

Out of habit, I snapped my right hand into a salute.

Seven cracks shattered the cold, and I jumped despite myself. Then again and again, and smoke from the three volleys rose and drifted away with the December breeze, as if carrying off the soul of the departed. Then I saw what had made the willow so dark. Out of the tree, a flock of starlings took flight as one, circled in a living cloud, and migrated to the next tree in the row. Their new resting place darkened, trembled, and settled to stillness, like the smoke from the honor guard's volley. It was a brief and moving moment, over too soon, like the life of the soldier.

Next, they removed the flag from the casket, folded and refolded it until only a thick triangle of stars remained, and one of the Marines presented it to the widow, holding it out stiffly in his white gloves.

I thought of Maria Sanchez at the archangel's funeral. He and the others were gone, while I stood here with a bum leg but alive. I longed to join them, to be embraced by the earth as well — to breathe no more, love no more, hurt no more.

Becky turned to me and took my hand in hers. It felt warm in the cold.

"Are you all right, Freddie? Talk to me. What are you thinking?"

"Do you really want to know?"

"Yes."

"I wish it were me in that coffin."

She squeezed my hand harder and lifted it to her cheek. "Well, I'm glad it's not."

When the ceremony finished and the mourners shifted from their folded chairs to a mingling crowd, we went back into the car and lumbered along the rutted road to the far end of the cemetery. I found the wrought iron gate that led to our family plot, which I'd purchased as a fifteen-year-old after my father died, and while my mother sat in our living room paralyzed with grief.

I recalled the first time I saw it, how I'd memorized the markings on the archway so I'd be able to find my way back. At the time, I thought they were magic runes, something from a fantasy game. Now, they looked more like souls writhing in hell.

I paused before passing through. In the distance, I could see the graves of my family, three vaults containing their remains.

With my mother's fear of being buried alive, she'd insisted Dad be placed in an above-ground vault. Even at fifteen, I'd argued with her—it was more than we could afford—but she used almost half of my father's life insurance for the funeral. When Joey died, we couldn't very well give him less. After Mom passed, I figured what the hell, and took out a loan on the house to give her the funeral she wanted. I could always pay for college by joining ROTC.

I tried to count vaults. From this angle, one blocked the other, but I was pretty sure there were no more than three. I was naïve to expect a fourth. Even if Richie's remains had found their way to the family plot, no stranger would have borne the cost of a vault.

Becky dragged me back from my memories. "Shall we go look?"

I nodded, unable to answer.

She locked arms with me and led the way.

The wind had died down, and the cold no longer stung. After a couple of dozen cautious steps on the frozen grass, clutching the eagle cane and hanging on to Becky, we reached the plot. Above the three unadorned vaults, a granite marker bore the family name: *Williams*. I couldn't take my eyes off it, afraid to look down.

Becky looked for me. "There's nothing, Freddie—no grave, no headstone, no mound that's been recently turned. He's not here."

I held onto her, wobbling a bit but unwilling to leave. My knee had begun to throb as if she had just stretched it, and I felt unsteady. I felt empty too, and strangely heavy, as if the planet had amplified its gravity and was pulling me toward the earth.

A little ways off, I spotted a marble bench, part of a nearby plot. I motioned to it, and Becky brought me there.

I patted the space next to me, hoping she'd sit, but instead she turned and raced off across the frosted grass.

"The daisies," she said. "Be back in a minute."

She ran through the wrought iron gate with a lightness that made me and my injured leg jealous, then retrieved the bouquet at a more respectful pace. Her little dash had infused color into her cheeks, and puffs of steam emerged from her lips. She lowered the bouquet to her waist and proceeded more slowly toward the graves of my family, taking small shuffling steps as she came closer. Except for the gloves and the parka, she might have been a bride approaching the altar at a wedding.

At the plot, she separated the flowers into clusters, one for each of the three vaults.

Only three vaults.

I sat steps away from where my parents and Joey were buried, thinking not of them, but of Richie. Before the Cape, we lived in a small apartment not far from the VA hospital, on the fourth floor, with a claw-foot tub and a trundle bed that Richie and I shared. He was two years older but followed me everywhere, a big brother until the differences began to show, and then a little kid who looked up to me and trusted me as we grew—as Mrs. Miller had said, two peas in a pod. Whatever happened, he thought I'd make everything turn out right.

Like the men in my squad.

Then it struck me. I used to be like Becky, always telling others that everything would turn out fine.

She arranged the daisies, smelling each before placing it on the vault. When she finished, she came back and settled beside me on the bench, but stayed quiet, as if observing a moment of silence.

When she finally spoke, she did so with a muted voice, the way people talk in cemeteries. "What was she like, your mother?"

My mother.

I tried to conjure her up, but had a hard time. My memory of her had begun to dim even before the war. Now, after all that had happened, she had become just another in a line of ghosts, a wraith of a woman who died when I was so much younger and full of hope. I mostly remembered her from the faded black-and-white picture from my dad's wallet, a young woman holding me in her arms. Her face was blurred, like a cathedral painting of a saint in the light of a candle.

An image that quickly fades.

"She was a slight woman," I said. "Probably why I was too short to dunk. Before her world collapsed, she laughed easily and was a pleasure to be around. Not the woman who wasted away, listening over and over to that damned Christmas carol. She cared most about three things: her family, the ocean, and God, in that order. Gradually, the things she loved were taken from her, until nothing was left but me and the round window in the garret, where she could see the ocean."

Becky released the long sigh of a patient teacher whose favorite student still didn't get it. "You're not like that. That isn't you. You can replace the things that were taken away with something new. I believe that. Do you?"

When I hesitated, she placed a hand on my cheek and forced me to face her. "Say it, Freddie. I need to hear it from you."

I wanted to be positive, like her, and to please her, but the ghosts in the cemetery weighed me down. "How would you know, Miss Sunshine and Light? What's ever been taken from you?"

She withdrew her hand and turned away, looking back to the funeral that had just concluded, to the mourners returning to their cars, eager to get out of the cold.

I thought for a second she might go back to her car too, and leave me on that bench surrounded by graves and frosted grass. I probably deserved it.

Instead, she turned back, the sunshine gone. Her voice took on an edge. "What is it, Freddie? You need to break scar tissue too? Well, I have some of my own, but I'm not going to share it with you. You have enough problems. My job is to pump you up, not bring you down."

"Fuck your job."

"What?" Her expression wavered between anger and laughter. "My job's the reason you can walk again. You don't care about my job?"

"I do, but I care more about you."

In the distance, the engine of the hearse started up, the last of the funeral procession to leave. We both turned to watch as it sped away, the need to drive with dignity gone. As it faded down the road, the starlings took flight again, a wave billowing toward us, flowing from tree to tree until they settled on the last of the willows, the one nearest us.

When the flock came to rest, I looked at Becky, and she looked back at me. She nodded just once—no words needed. Then she made the slightest motion in my direction, or perhaps it was just my imagination, but I moved too, and in an instant we were locked in an embrace. I held on as if by coming together, we might thwart our demons, mine and hers, whatever they may be.

When we separated, our eyes stayed fixed on each other, and our fingers intertwined.

"How is it," I finally managed to say, "that I'm not allowed to keep secrets from you, but you can keep them from me?"

Her smile was back, but weaker now. "It's because you're not ready to hear them."

"Tell me," I said as sternly as I could.

"And have you say I sound like a fortune cookie?"

"I promise I won't make fun of you."

She shook her head. "Not here. Not now. But you can promise me something else." Her gray-green eyes grabbed me and held.

I took a complete breath, in and out, and let the steam bursting from my lips fill the space between us. "What's that?"

"Never again wish it was you in the coffin."

Just then, the starlings rose into the air again, a majestic black cloud that spiraled and swirled, forsaking the cemetery and flying away to their roost, leaving Becky and me alone in the silence.

Dragons
and
Unicorns

32

THE FOLLOWING MONDAY, I MADE UP my mind—
no more cemeteries, no more ghosts. I marched into my
caseworker's office and filled out the necessary paperwork. All
that was left was to tell Becky, so I went from the caseworker's
office directly to the fourth floor, to the physical therapy room,
even though it wasn't my scheduled time.

Becky worked with another patient, an amputee who'd just
been fitted with an artificial limb. She was her usual self, cajoling
and comforting, giving hope.

I leaned against the wall in the hallway, out of sight but close
enough to listen, trying to hear what she was saying—physical
therapist talk, nothing more.

As they were about to finish, Ralph arrived to bring the
patient back to his room. He eyed me curiously. "Now, I know
you're not supposed to be here yet," he said in his rumbling
voice, "because I'm bringing Becky's next victim down in five
minutes."

I waved my free hand to hush him.

He managed to lower his voice. "Everything okay, Freddie?"

I nodded and whispered. "I came to see Becky."

"Uh-huh." He winked at me. "I knew it was only a matter of time."

I glared at him, as angry as I could be at a gentle soul who stood a foot taller than me. I was tempted to ask if he'd ever dunked, but then Becky came bustling through the door, pushing the young amputee in a wheelchair.

When Ralph saw her, he laughed and whisked the young man away.

"What was that all about?" Becky said.

"Just Ralph being Ralph."

She looked at her watch. "You're not due till this afternoon."

"I know."

"Then what are you doing here?"

"I needed to talk to you."

"Oh, Freddie, I can't. My next appointment's in five minutes and I need to prep."

She turned to go, but I reached out and grabbed her wrist.

She seemed surprised I could move that fast.

"I wanted to tell you myself, before the paperwork came down and you heard it through channels."

"Heard what?"

I took a breath so deep, and my shoulders heaved and sagged. "I've requested a change, a different therapist."

She flicked away a strand of hair in that way she had, and blew out a stream of air. "Did I do something wrong?"

"Nothing wrong. It's that regulation, the one that says no fraternizing. I don't want you to be just my therapist. I want something more."

I watched her closely, studying the way her hands moved with a nervous energy, searching for a hint of what she was thinking, but before she could respond, a bell sounded and the elevator door slid open.

Ralph emerged with a new patient, a kid who looked hardly

eighteen. The pall of war still shrouded his face, and he was missing a leg.

Becky shifted at once into therapist mode, went over, and touched the young soldier on the arm. He glanced up at her, and she showed him the kind of look that melts bad moods away, even for those who have all the right in the world to indulge them. She assured him things would get better, more a healing angel than the angels my mother had heard on high.

I backed away, swallowed hard, and left her to her work.

I was finished anyway. I'd said as much as I could but less than I'd intended. What I wanted to tell her was this: "I no longer need your magic touch. I need you."

Later that afternoon, I finished my first workout with Chuck, a muscular ex-Marine turned therapist. He'd given me a tough but first-rate program—weights, treadmill, balancing beam. I was toweling off when Becky appeared at the door.

She nodded to her fellow therapist, who took the hint and went off to reorganize the supply closet. Becky waited until the door closed behind him. "The Boston Common," she said.

"What?"

"When I was little, we'd go there every year to see the Christmas lights and the ice sculptures. It's like your gingerbread house, a special place for me. Come with me, Freddie. Friday night. I'll pick you up at six. The usual place."

She raced off to her next appointment without waiting for a response.

Becky's car pulled up to the advanced rehabilitation facility well past sunset.

I was too eager to see her and made a rookie mistake, staring directly into the headlights. The penalty? My night vision was shot. We'd done plenty of night patrols in Iraq, but this was my first time out after dark since the attack, and now I was half-blind. I gawked at the shadows wriggling behind the car and around the corners of the building, wishing I had night-vision goggles.

Becky leaned over and swung the passenger door open. "What are you waiting for? Get in."

I stuck my head through the door and peeked past the headrest. Resting in the middle of the backseat was a package wrapped in holiday paper, with a red ribbon and silver bow.

"What's that?"

"A Christmas present for you. I was going to surprise you later, but since you've already seen it, I might as well give it to you now."

She reached back and retrieved the package while I slid onto the seat, carefully lifting my damaged leg over the lip of the doorframe with both hands. Once I'd settled, she set the package on my lap. I let my fingertips glide over the paper and across the ribbon and bow. It'd been a long time since anyone had given me a present.

"Well, go ahead and open it." When I hesitated, she laughed. "It's been cleared by ordnance, I promise."

I waited another second, trying to think what to say, then ripped off the paper. Inside was one of those picture books people leave on the coffee table in their living room. Its title was *Cape Cod Gingerbread Gems*, a photo album of the kind of houses I once dreamed of designing.

She started the engine and we rolled across the parking lot.

As we left the VA hospital behind, I glanced back at the building—the first time I'd seen it at night. The turret stood out against the black of the sky, illuminated by spotlights. Yellow beams shone from the arched windows, as if someone in there stood watch.

After we merged onto the VFW Parkway, she broke the silence. "Do you like it?"

I nodded, but realizing she couldn't see me with her eyes on the road, I said, "It's good."

"Then why do you sound so tongue-tied?"

"It's just that no one else knows me that well. No one else would have...." I found myself having to swallow before more words could come out. Finally, I said, "Thank you."

"You're welcome."

"But how can I reciprocate? I wouldn't know what to get you."

"Someday," she said, "when you're on your own, find me a book on ice sculptures, like the ones we're going to see tonight."

Once downtown, we parked in the Common underground garage, a dimly lit place of concrete and columns with lots of places to hide. I stepped out of the car into a forest of steel coated with blast mitigation foam, the kind we used to spray on our Humvees. As we wandered around searching for an elevator, the click of our heels and the tap of my cane merged with the drone of the ventilation system. I began to hear whispers in the shadows, voices murmuring in the gloom. I breathed a lot easier when we were back above ground.

"That was as close as we could park," she said. "You okay crossing the Common?"

I puffed out my chest and held up my cane. "After a week with Chuck, anything will seem easy."

We had a long trek across the Common, up and down hills. Piles of slush lined the edges of the pathways, but the pavement was clear. In the distance, I could see the glow from the Christmas display, but mostly I concentrated on my footsteps. The nearer we came to the display, the denser the crowds. My pace slowed, not because of my injured leg, but because of all the strangers around me caused my skin to prickle.

Then shouts rose behind me, accompanied by the rattle of metal approaching. I spun around, braced for the attack, and....

Shit.

Just a young mother, pulling a wagon with two little boys huddled inside.

My mind flashed to another winter day, a long time ago, a memory I'd forgotten from before we moved to the Cape. Newly fallen snow blanketed the ground, and my mother pulled Richie and me on a sled across a park, breaking fresh tracks, singing in her little girl voice. *"Dashing through the snow, in a one-horse open sleigh."* Richie giggled and tried to sing along, and little brother Freddie sat so still, afraid to move for fear of startling the happiness away.

I stayed still now and held my breath, taking in this new winter scene, afraid to startle it away.

Becky noticed. "Are you all right?"

I nodded and reached out my hand, and she took it.

We continued on, past the obelisk at the high point of the Common, and down to a recess, where we stopped to watch the skaters on the frog pond. Colored lanterns lined the rink, casting a rosy blush onto the faces of the crowd. The skaters ranged from toddlers, giggling as they bounced off the boards in their padded snowsuits, to an older couple skating arm in arm, as if dancing to a Strauss waltz in their heads.

Many had come in costume—angels and ballerinas, Santas and elves—and surrounding them all, the glow of the lights in the trees.

From the frog pond, we climbed the last hill to where the ice sculptures were laid out in a row. The first one we encountered was a dragon looming almost ten feet tall. The artist had placed a green spotlight with a revolving filter at the base, so the light flickered through the ice, making the dragon seem alive.

At the foot of the dragon pranced a smaller sculpture, a life-size unicorn rearing up on its hind legs. Beyond them stood two swans facing each other, a hawk in flight, a winged griffin and a centaur, a mermaid and a reindeer, a miniature Cinderella castle and two lovers embracing.

And all I could do was stare up at the trees.

The Christmas decorations were destroying my night vision. I narrowed my eyes, trying to block out the glare. I squinted so hard that the lights blurred, conspiring with the branches to spawn an enemy hidden among them.

Becky caught me staring and breathed in the cold air. "The lights are beautiful, aren't they?"

I nodded. How could I tell her I wasn't admiring the lights but searching for snipers in the trees?

"It's like a dream from a fantasy world," she said.

"No, Becky, fantasy worlds aren't this nice."

Then, from a couple of blocks away, the voices of carolers wafted on the breeze, and Becky pulled me toward them.

As we approached the sidewalk that lined Tremont Street, the crowds grew. Most seemed to be shoppers, bearing bags of brightly painted packages and moving with a purpose, focused on their own lives—oblivious that we were still at war. The holiday colors they wore contrasted with the paler colors of our desert camouflage and the gun-metal gray of our rifles, or the dishdashas of the Iraqi men made drab by the sand and the heat—men I'd learned to suspect.

My heart began to pound, my hands to sweat. I stopped and pulled away.

"Is something wrong, Freddie?"

I searched around for an excuse, afraid to tell her what was happening to me, hardly able to understand it myself, and noticed the uneven sidewalk at my feet. "Cobblestones," I lied. "Just what I need with a cane."

"No problem. Hold on to me."

She looped her arm around mine and we crossed. My panic kept increasing, but I liked being held so close.

On the far side of Tremont Street, on the way to the carolers, we passed an alley, and my combat antennae began to twitch. When I searched in the shadows, the alarm I'd so carefully nurtured in Iraq went off. Among the trash and old newspapers, a clump of rags beneath a loading dock shuddered and moved — not an imagined being, but a real person. Danger? Or some wino bedded down under the rags, trying to stay warm for the night?

Then I thought of Richie. What if that was him, or what was left of him?

Becky tried to pull me back. "It's just an alley, Freddie. The carolers are over here."

I turned to go with her, but the crash of broken glass behind me pulled me back. The pile of rags had rolled over, flinging an empty bottle to the pavement.

"Fuck," I said loudly enough to attract a scowl from a passing woman, who sidestepped me as I stopped short on the crowded sidewalk. I yanked free of Becky and headed into the alley.

What if that's him?

I scanned the cavern of buildings and searched the rooftops, my eyes darting from window to window, watching for a muzzle flash. I jumped at a curtain pulled back, some guy glancing out to check the weather or the traffic before heading home. I studied doorways and dumpsters, and especially a garbage bin stuffed with bottles and cans, expecting....

Becky's physical therapist grip on my shoulder dragged me back to reality. "It's all right, Freddie."

"What's all right?"

"You were hyperventilating."

I spun around, ready to be angry. I didn't want to be pitied, but what I saw wasn't pity; it was more complex than that. Her look said, *"Give me your sadness. I'll take as much as you need. I'm here."*

I backed off from high alert, not to the way I was before the war, but enough to go on.

From there, we walked arm in arm, like the couple skating on the frog pond. We followed the sound of carolers, past Christmas displays in storefront windows and a street vendor roasting cinnamon sugar pecans. At the top of the marble steps of the Tremont Street Masonic Temple, between two statues of lions, a chorus presided over a crowd. They stood in formation, wearing old-fashioned top hats and mufflers, each holding a hymnal in their gloved hands. Their voices rose and spread into the night, a magnificent, ringing harmony of baritones and tenors, sopranos and basses — sounds of my childhood.

Above the carolers, pigeons nestled in the corners around columns, cooing along as if trying to harmonize with the music. On the sidewalk below, all around us, shoppers with bags of newly bought gifts closed in. I checked out the faces, gauging the risk.

Cheeks flush from the cold. Christmas cheer.

On the sides of the stairs, a few bums lay covered in cardboard to stay warm, enjoying the free show. In front of us, a bag lady with a shopping cart filled with rags bobbed her head to the tune.

The holiday season took over. I forgot about my family and the war and being trapped in a crowd of strangers. I looked down from the carolers and the stone lions to Becky, who was snuggling close and beaming up at the singers.

And then the music changed.

"Angels we have heard on high — "

An echo of my mother's sweet voice made me blink twice and shake my head, as I did when the ringing started in my ears, but the song persisted.

"Sweetly singing o'er the plains — "

In front of me, a boy about Richie's age sang along with the carolers.

I stretched out a finger and tapped his arm, and he turned. Not Richie. Richie was gone, along with Joey and the archangel and the others.

"And the mountains in reply – "

Slowly, the sound crept in—another day, the family together, faded music, flowered paper trying to brighten the room but failing, worn furniture, tired smiles. Where had they all gone? Then another scene appeared—a girl in a garden, a tower, a cluster of storm clouds forming over the distant mountains, an empty casket. I bit my lip.

"Echoing their joyous strain – "

This was real, not a memory of my mother's voice. This was here and now. My chest tightened and I had trouble breathing.

Suddenly, I saw dragons and unicorns.

My three days on the subway hadn't ended in failure, as the boy in the morgue wasn't Ritchie, and we found no grave in the cemetery.

What if that clump of rags in the alley is him?

I had to know.

I pulled away from Becky and elbowed my way through the crowd. Once free, I stepped off down the cobblestone sidewalk, moving faster than I had since the IED attack, ignoring the smell of roasting pecans, swinging my cane like a weapon. I must have had a wild look on my face, because the passersby spread before me like a wave.

Behind me, the carolers were stretching out the word: *"Gloooria."*

I muttered as I walked. "You want glory in your highest? Then let this be Richie."

A shout came from behind, barely audible above the carolers. "Freddie, come back!"

I reached the alleyway and skidded to a stop, too well trained to race in without body armor and a rifle at the ready, or a Kevlar helmet with night-vision goggles on top. I searched the rooftops again, and the windows. From one of them, an office worker with a coffee cup glared down at the alley, probably trying to decide whether to ignore me or call the police.

I took three quick breaths, oxygenating my blood, increasing my adrenaline, and rushed in.

The pile of rags still lay under the loading dock, not moving. I poked at it with my cane, and a hand flailed out, a gesture saying, "Leave me alone." The hand was too old to be Richie's.

The hell with reality. I have to be sure.

I reached out and grabbed a fistful of rags. My leg was gimpy but the months of rehab had built up my arms. I lifted and tugged until the man rolled over, confronting me with bloodshot eyes sunk deep into a haggard face. Liver spots mottled the skin, and matted clumps of gray stuck to the cheeks. Gnarled fingers flew up to protect the face.

"Richie?" I said, and shook my head, knowing it wasn't him, but finding it so hard to accept. "Richie?" I repeated more softly.

A hand touched my shoulder from behind. I whirled around and grasped at my waist for my rifle on its assault sling. When I found it missing, I groped at my hip for the hilt of a sword.

Even Becky was afraid of me now. "You're scaring that old man, Freddie. And frankly, you're frightening me."

I must have stared at her for a long time before my breathing slowed.

"It's me," she said.

"I know."

She swayed an inch in my direction, and I collapsed into her arms. Then I let her lead me out of the alley.

We found a doorway to duck into, and I steadied myself against the wall.

She took off a glove and touched my forehead with her fingertips. "You're sweating, Freddie, which is hard to do in this cold."

I just stared.

"It wasn't Richie."

"I know."

"Then why did you—"

"I know *now*." I didn't mean for my voice to be so loud. Shoppers passing by stopped to gawk, and I went quiet until they moved on. "But sometimes, Becky... sometimes, I don't know what's real."

"We all feel that way, Freddie. You think I don't feel it when I sit in the therapy room and watch kids brought in, one after the other, with limbs missing and a thousand-yard stare?"

"You don't understand. I don't know if *anything's* real—Richie, the war, all of this." I waved my hand to encompass Tremont Street, the stone lions and the carolers, the frog pond with the costumed skaters, the ice sculptures. I stuck my head out the doorway and gestured toward the alley some poor guy was sleeping in to get out of the cold, but I didn't look back at Becky, afraid to see what I'd find.

"Maybe we shouldn't do this again," I finally said.

"Do what?" She forced me to look at her. "Do what, Freddie? Come into the city? Go to see my favorite ice sculptures? Mingle with crowds? Listen to carolers who might sing your mother's favorite song? What is it we shouldn't do again? Or is it going out together, you and I? Because if that's it, I think I should have a say as well."

Her brows lifted, and she stood balanced in the moment, waiting for my answer.

My mind spun through images—the gingerbread house, my family, the war, a castle and crypt. I pulled away, putting just an arm's length between us, though it might as well have been a chasm. "I was wrong to ask you out. Take me back to the hospital... please."

For a long moment, she didn't respond. Then she put her glove back on, took my hand, and led me across the traffic on Tremont Street, past the ice sculptures and down by the frog pond, over the hill with the obelisk and into the dungeon of a garage. When we were both buckled safely in the car, she eased out of the parking space and, with a stab of her foot on the accelerator, lurched up the exit ramp.

She said not a word, not there and not on the ride back to the hospital.

As I listened to the rumble of the snow tires, I watched her hands clutching the steering wheel at ten and two o'clock. I stared at her set jaw, at her lips compressed into a thin line as she focused on the road ahead, and for the first time in years, I prayed to the Goddess, or to whoever would listen.

Don't let my demons drag her down.

The Dagger
of
Sorrow

33

DAY TWENTY-NINE. ONE MORE DAY before the end of all things. As I trudged down the path to the royal gardens, time itself seemed to be winding down, like the hands of an aging clock. No birds sang, the wailing of the wind had softened to a moan, and what passed for daylight these days had faded.

I'd reconsidered my plan, as the thought of bringing Rebecca to the crypt made my fists clench so tightly, the nails left marks in my palms. How could I have presumed to drag her down into my world of demons and assassins? Whatever course the final trial might take, it was something I had to do alone.

In the end, there was only me.

When I arrived at the gardens, I found her bustling about, organizing things that needed no organizing. She muttered to herself, checking off her list as she scurried about. "Prune the hydrangeas. Water the flowerbeds. Lock the tools in their shed so children playing in the garden won't harm themselves." It was as if she were leaving for the last time.

I stood by, silently admiring her energy.

When she noticed me, she turned and smoothed her dress and expression in a single motion. "Oh, good morning, Milord. Or is it noon already?"

I made a bow as if *she* were the royalty. "It's noon, but I've had a change of heart. Now that the time is upon us, I'm loath to bring you with me. I'm sorry, Rebecca, but I should never have agreed to let you come. Whatever is to be done, I'll have to do it alone."

Her eyes flared and she planted both hands on her hips. "Now what kind of gardener would I be to go back on my vow to the Goddess? And you so forlorn on the watchtower steps, thrashing at the air with your staff and dropping your sword to the ground. I've seen the burden you bear, and won't let you bear it alone."

I watched as she confronted me, shoulders squared and feet rooted to the earth like a swordsman braced for battle. Her look challenged me, insisting this world was full of goodness, and let all the demons be damned. Then, inspired by that look, a melody began to play in my head, the tune from the globe with the angels. It started as an undertone but grew in strength, until I could no longer ignore it. At once, from deep within my memory, the words came back to me like a song from the cradle, words of glory and Goddesses on high.

Rebecca's magic at work? Or mine? Or better yet, magic from the both of us.

I began to nod, slowly at first, and then faster. "Very well. If you still insist."

I held out a hand but came no closer, still hoping she'd back away and return to the illusory safety of her village, but she filled the gap without hesitation, foregoing my hand and looping her arm around mine. We thus proceeded to our fate, not like two people at the edge of despair, but like a couple walking down the aisle at a coronation.

That changed once we crossed the threshold to the crypt.

Rebecca's pace slowed until she was barely inching along. Her gaze flitted everywhere, up to the vaulted arches and across to the tombs of the kings.

I tried to hurry her along, knowing the less time we spent in the crypt, the better, but as we walked through the wrought iron gate and down the tunnel to the first chamber, her breathing became shallow and labored.

I paused at the end to let her rest. "Not exactly a garden. You can still turn back."

She gave a violent shake of her head, gripped my arm tighter, and drew me on. When we came to the caskets of my parents, she stopped. "It's the king. Your father."

"And beside him, my mother, the queen."

She dipped a knee, a curtsy of respect, and then her eyes widened as she took in the blush of youth on my mother's cheek. "But, Milord, your mother—" She struggled to breathe.

I finished what she was unable to say. "Has been dead for many a year."

"Then how is it she looks so alive?"

I drew in a gulp of air, trying to breathe for the two of us. "I warned you, Rebecca. The demons are devious. They show her like this to remind me how much I've lost."

I urged her to keep going. My family was only the first of the trials, and we had more to see. At the locked door, I slid my fingertips along the brass plate in the shape of a hawk, feeling for the keyhole, slipped the roots of the World Tree inside, and twisted. The lock released with a snap, and the door swung open.

"The second trial," I said, as we stepped inside. "The Hall of Heroes."

We passed the archangel and the four spears with the helmets on top. At the row of coffins, I bent my head, and Rebecca followed with a deeper bow.

Though I tried to encourage her along, she lagged behind, dragging her feet on the ground and gaping at each of the corpses. She gasped at the last one when she saw the void where a face should be.

"To overcome this trial," I said, "I had to embrace the shadows. These are the heroes who were lost, all known to me now and revered."

I led her on until the stone wall blocked our way.

"What now, Milord?"

As if in answer, the blue soldier appeared, his arm outstretched and beckoning.

I raised my staff and tapped the wall, grasping the gardener's hand and praying the eagle's magic would extend to us both.

It did. The two of us drifted through the wall like wraiths doomed to wander between life and perpetual sleep. On the far side, we rested beside the casket with the stranger inside.

As icy fingers of mist swirled about our ankles, Rebecca shivered and huddled close. When she spoke, her voice sounded as if muffled by the fog. "Is this the final trial?"

"Not yet. There's one more." I turned and pointed to the far side, at what I still believed to be an empty coffin. "There, the place I spoke of, so near but beyond my reach. Now we'll see how strong the power of our alliance may be."

I pulled out Kingsbane, feeling its sorrow add to the gloom of the crypt. I shook it off, raised my hand above my shoulder, and flung the dagger across the chamber, expecting it to bounce off the barrier as it had done before.

This time, it sailed through and landed on the ground by the coffin.

As I marveled at what we'd accomplished together, a bloodless hand reached down and picked up the dagger.

The assassin.

He greeted me like a friend he'd chanced upon in the courtyard on a summer day. His lips curled upward, but the empty sockets showed no sign of joy.

Then he turned to the gardener. "And so, my dear, we meet again, this time in the darkness of my world. Such darkness is not right for one such as you, who awakens each morning expecting the sun to shine. Perhaps, we need something brighter."

He twirled a hand, and an indigo glow appeared, replacing the gloom and letting me see more clearly. To my horror, the final coffin was no longer empty. The simpleton lay inside, his hands bound and his blue eyes open wide. The innocent smile still graced his lips, and at his feet rested the purple monkshood.

The assassin took the dagger and strode to the flower. "Time grows short, and this is the final trial. Now you will have to choose."

With a flick of his wrist, he stuck the dagger's point into the stem of the flower and dragged it downward, making a gash that oozed with sap. When he raised the dagger, its tip glowed moist in the blue light.

I stepped in front of Rebecca and drew my sword, but the assassin only laughed, a hollow sound that rose to the arches and scattered among their shadows until it faded away like a hiss.

"It's your dagger, Milord," he said, mocking the gardener. "Do with it as you wish." He spun the dagger around so the handle faced me, and offered it back.

I glowered at him. "If you return this to me, have no doubt what I'll do with it."

"If you mean to use it on your humble servant, you're more fool than I thought. Haven't you learned from our prior encounters? I'm nothing but air, an invention of your imagination, a non-player character in a game. Even if you kill me, I'd be back again the next time you entered this chamber. But this boy...."

He turned and gestured to the casket, stretching out a hand like the blue soldier beckoning.

"You expect me to slay the boy?"

"You've done it before."

I felt the blood rush to my cheeks. "Never. That's a lie."

"In your mind. To sacrifice the boy so you might become king. Such a small price. But it's not for me to decide. The choice is yours."

The moment had arrived, the end of the trials, my chance to save the world from the Horde. The small hairs on the nape of my neck stood up, and I was struck by a solitude so profound that my knees buckled. I recalled my father's words from long ago, as recorded by his advisor. There was only me and, like my father before me, I had to choose.

"The sap has great power," the assassin said. "All it will take is a scratch."

I reached out, accepted the dagger, and stepped toward the boy. I raised my arm, but before I could strike, a gasp from behind drew my attention.

"No, Milord."

I spun around, expecting a look of condemnation, but instead, Rebecca beamed with hope. My mouth opened, but no words emerged.

She spoke for me. "It's wrong to destroy a flower while still in bloom. That's not the gardener's way."

I turned back to the assassin, who must have read the uncertainty in my face.

"Would you fail the final trial?" he said. "Save the boy and cast your world into darkness?"

I wavered, looking first at the gardener and then down at the casket.

The boy stared back at me with an unwarranted certainty that I'd save him.

"I have until sunset tomorrow to choose," I said. "One more day to find a better way."

"Ah, a better way." The assassin's smirk widened, causing dark creases around the empty sockets. "But what makes you believe tomorrow will be better? Tomorrow might bring a more difficult choice."

"How could any choice be more difficult than this?"

"Foolish dauphin. The dreadlord is bound by the treaty, but he's a gambler. He loves to raise the stakes. Something with a bigger reward, but at a greater cost."

"And that is?"

He pointed a withered finger. "The gardener."

I froze. A sound escaped behind me, a combination of gasp and groan. My mouth became dry as wool, and my stomach filled with wasps. The dagger in my hand turned to ice, its sorrow flowing up my arm and into the very chambers of my heart. I tried to let go, but my fingers seemed welded to its handle.

I turned slowly, terrified of what I might find, but she was gone. "What?"

The assassin waved a hand over the casket. The boy had vanished, replaced by the gardener.

"What evil is this?" I said. "And how could this be a bigger reward?"

The blue glow now shone through the assassin's eye sockets, a sign of pleasure. "One simple scratch, Milord, and the war between the Alliance and the Horde will be over, not only for a generation, but for all time. You have the dreadlord's word."

I bent low over the casket.

Rebecca wasn't frightened at all. Instead, her look said, "Give me your sadness. I'll take as much as you need."

All the sorrow that Kingsbane had absorbed became like a leaden weight, and the dagger slipped from my fingers. It clattered to the floor with an unnatural sound, an echo that did not abate.

I lifted the gardener from the casket and, with the eagle staff held high, swept her out of the crypt.

Dreams
of the
Cape

34

AFTER THE OUTING TO THE COMMON, I threw myself into my goals. I worked out daily, more than my new trainer Chuck had prescribed, pounding out repetitions as if punishing the weights. I ordered thick texts on architecture and stayed awake late into the night, prepping for grad school entrance exams. I even consulted the chaplain about my discharge.

But I stayed away from Becky.

At first, Ralph or Dinah would come by on their lunch break to see how I was doing, after which they'd drop off sealed envelopes from Becky, cards wishing me holiday joy.

The holidays came and went, and I couldn't bring myself to respond. For a time, the cards turned to messages on brightly colored notepaper.

> *Hope you're doing well, Freddie.*
> *Keep up your rehab.*
> *Believe in the future.*
> *Spring will come.*

Then even those stopped.

But not the flowers. Every Monday and Thursday, when I'd come back to my room after details, a fresh daisy would adorn a jelly-jar glass at my bedside, as if some elf had snuck in and placed it there. Accompanying it, leaning against the glass, would always be an unaddressed envelope. Each time, I'd squint at the daisy's petals, trying to make them glow in the fluorescent lighting while I decided what to do. Each time, after a minute, I'd give in and open the envelope. Each time, I'd find inside a hand-written note with two simple words.

I'm here.

The first week in January, a storm blew through, leaving a fresh coat of snow in its wake. The next morning, icicles hung from the eaves of the advanced rehabilitation facility, and ice glazed the branches of the trees, transforming the hospital grounds into a wonderland. All that was missing were the ice sculptures.

Despite the bitter cold, I put on my army jacket and went outside to look.

The sky was that certain shade of blue, the kind that appears only when there's hardly a drop of moisture in the air, and puffy clouds floated across it, so crisp they looked like cutouts from a storybook. As I glanced up toward the main hospital building, a glint of sunlight reflected off a window on the fourth floor—the physical therapy room.

It was almost 11 a.m., meaning Becky's third patient of the day would be arriving—some kid with a limb blown off and convinced his life was over, or a tough veteran cursing the brass and questioning if it had been worth it. Becky would greet them with her gentle touch and her faith in the future.

Should I go?

My eye followed the ribbon of black pavement that led to the door nearest PT, no more than a couple of hundred yards, but then I looked higher, to the topmost turret of the hospital, to the forbidding windows keeping watch over the land, and a raw wind gusted and tore through me. I kicked away a chunk of icicle that had fallen in my path, and turned back.

Like all things, the cold snap passed, followed by a drizzly thaw That reduced the wonderland to a grayish slush, which soon turned black from the exhaust of cars. I stopped going outside, or seeing anyone other than the guys on my detail.

Until one day, Ralph came by. He rapped on the doorjamb to give me a heads up. "I brought you a visitor, Freddie. Is that okay?"

I tensed, afraid of what I should wish for, but it wasn't Becky.

He brought in a stranger, a small balding man with a thin mustache. In his hand, he held a tweed cap, which he kept twisting as if wringing out a wet towel.

I'd hoped to be done with surprises, but couldn't be sure. I nodded politely and offered a pleasant smile—the kind that said, *"I don't think I know you, but just to be safe, I'm not going to let on one way or the other."*

Ralph introduced us. "This is Mr. Shapiro, Freddie. He came to the hospital because of this." He showed me a crinkled and slightly grimy newspaper that looked like he'd salvaged it from the trash. *The Cape Cod Times.* Below the fold was the picture of me receiving the Silver Star.

I looked back at Mr. Shapiro with my mouth open.

The man made a little bow but hesitated to shake hands, still too preoccupied with his cap. "An honor to meet you, Lieutenant. Wow. A real American hero. An honor indeed."

A fan? Just what I need.

I was about to thank him and explain how busy I was, but Ralph warned me off.

"He might have some news for you, Freddie."

News? I hadn't received much news in the past few years, and what little came my way had been bad. I ground my teeth and waited.

"May I have a seat?" Mr. Shapiro said. "This weather's bad for my arthritis."

I nodded and motioned to the one option in the room, a gray folding chair along the wall. He settled in, lowering himself slowly, and then looked around for a place to hang his cap. I was about to grab it from him when he settled it on his lap. Only when the cap was safe did he begin.

"I run a small business, Lieutenant—souvenirs, tchotchkes. Some people would call it junk, but tourists like it. I don't feel bad, you understand, because a lot of people get pleasure from my stuff, a cheap memory of a few good days on the Cape. Well, several years ago, my son got the idea to sell merchandise online. DreamsoftheCape.com. Do you believe it? Me, with a website. And you know what?"

He paused, hoping to build suspense.

"What?" I finally said, determined not to scream.

"It took off, became 87 percent of my business. So now I run a little year-round shipping operation in the back of my store. People love to get beach stuff for Christmas. Reminds them of summer."

"Excuse me, Mr. Shapiro, but what does this have to do with me?"

"Well, the agency sends me kids—I give them jobs other people don't want to do. I get stacks of old newspapers from the dump and have the kids wrap the tchotchkes for shipment, the ones that are breakable. The souvenirs, I mean, not the kids. I got this one boy, great kid, been with me two years. Does a nice job, never complains, always grinning.

"One day, he drops a tchotchke, a porcelain mermaid that shatters on the floor. Never happened before, so I don't get mad or nothing. I just tell him to sweep it up, but he's so upset. It was a picture in the newspaper, he said, an old copy of the *Cape Cod Times*. He claimed it was his brother and pointed to a wounded soldier receiving the Silver Star."

He asked Ralph for the newspaper, then smoothed out the wrinkles and looked from the picture to me, and back. "That's you, all right. I wanted to meet you first, didn't say anything to the kid yet. I didn't want to disappoint him."

"What...?" Something caught in my throat. I reached for a bottle of water I'd been sipping and took a long gulp. "What's his name?"

"They call him Andy." I must have flinched because he quickly explained. "A nickname. I guess they thought he had a grin like Andy Griffith. You know, the guy on that TV show, the sheriff of Mayberry." When I gaped at him, he dismissed me with a wave. "Ah, you're too young. You wouldn't remember." I must have looked disappointed, because he added, "I'm sorry. I don't know his real name. I'm not sure anyone does. I pay the agency, and they pay him. A lot of these kids come from tough backgrounds, so I try not to be too nosy."

"And what... does he look like?"

He fidgeted in the chair and reached into his pants' pocket to pull out a photo in a plastic sheath. He reached out his knobby fingers and offered it to me.

I craned my neck for a peek, then stood and took it from him. My heart was pounding harder than when I went on patrol.

There, in the palm of my hand, was a picture of a boy. The hair was the right color, but had grown too long, and merged with a beard to conceal most of the face. I tried staring into the eyes, hoping to see through them to my brother, but it had been over six years since Richie ran off. We both would have changed, and I was afraid to get my hopes up.

I looked for a long time, until Mr. Shapiro interrupted. "You can keep that." He pulled a card out from his wallet. "Here's my number. If you think it might be him, give me a call and I'll tell you how to set up a meeting."

I accepted the card and shook his hand, trying not to squeeze too hard. Maybe my luck was changing, or maybe I was becoming a fool.

After Ralph escorted him out, I looked at the card. It was made of heavy stock and had raised letters with the words: Dreams of the Cape, Sam Shapiro, Proprietor. An etching of sand dunes adorned the background. It appeared more the card of a magician than that of a peddler of souvenirs.

Next, I rummaged through my night-table drawer and pulled out my own set of pictures, salvaged from the corpse of my father. I sat on the bed and compared the old, wallet-sized photos of my brother with this new picture, trying to see a resemblance.

I was still sitting there, staring at the pictures, when Ralph returned. "Is it him, Freddie?"

"Might be. I can't be sure."

"I hope so, for your sake. You're due for a miracle."

"I don't believe in miracles." I looked up at him. "Do you?"

"Aw, I don't know, but good things happen to people if they're open to them. You're gonna check him out, aren't you?"

"I don't have a car."

"Bullshit excuse. Any one of us would drive you in a New York minute. You know that."

I finally glanced up from the picture to the man looming over me, waiting for a response. As I marveled at his great height, a longstanding question resurfaced in my mind and became words.

"I always meant to ask you something. Did you ever play basketball?"

He laughed with that booming bass voice. "Haven't heard that one in a long time. I used to hear it all the time growing up. I was almost this size when I was thirteen. So everyone assumed—"

"But did you?"

He came in and sat opposite me, turning the gray folding chair around, straddling it so his long legs almost reached me. "A little. My high school coach recruited me for the team, even though I wasn't that interested. I couldn't stretch my arms very high over my head. Underdeveloped lats, he said. So he put me on an exercise program. I developed a half-decent shot, but I was slow as molasses. I lasted one season and never got into a game."

"Did you ever dunk?"

"Naw, I wasn't an athlete like you. I had bad knees, fallen arches, and could barely get off the ground."

"That's too bad."

"Too bad?" His voice rose half an octave, which still left him well within the baritone range. "Too bad to miss out on a game I didn't really like? It's not like I was going to the NBA. No, Freddie, too bad would be if I never got to help guys like you. Too bad would be you not going to meet this kid, who just might be your long-lost brother."

I glanced at the picture one last time, set it down on the bed, and studied my hands. "You're right, Ralph, but things haven't exactly gone my way the past few years. You get to expect disappointment after a while."

"You know what they say. Nothing ventured...."

I looked back up at him. "Would you take me?"

He thought for a moment, struggling with something, then got up and laid a great paw on my shoulder. "I know this is a big deal for you, and I'll be glad to take you, if that's what you want, but you and Becky seemed to have a good thing going. Shouldn't you ask her instead?"

He looked down at me with an impish grin. The brows that reached to the edge of his face fit the image, but he was way too tall to be an imp.

"You're pretty big to be playing cupid, aren't you?"

He almost blushed. "Can't blame a guy for trying to bring together two people he likes."

"Well, it's none of your business." The words came out more sharply than I'd intended; he'd only been trying to help.

For an instant, he stood there, face flushed, a pulse throbbing at his temple, looking as hurt as a guy almost seven feet tall could look. Then, without a word, he turned to go.

"I can't do it," I called after him. "I don't want to bring her into my messed-up world."

He stopped, his big shoulders filling the doorway, and rose up on the balls of his feet such that his head nearly hit the top of the frame. His eyes were wide and unblinking, aimed at mine as if linked by guide wires.

"Dr. B. was wrong about you, Freddie. He said you had a mild non-penetrating brain injury. That's what he wrote on your chart, but it's much worse than that."

I swallowed hard.

"You're just plain stupid." Then he pivoted around, nimble for a big man, and left the room.

Frederick
the
Fool

WHEN WE EMERGED FROM THE CRYPT into daylight, I set Rebecca down and held her close. I felt no tremor beneath the fabric of her dress, and sensed no fear.

Her soft, bottomless eyes locked on mine. "Some magic," she said with a weak smile. "Perhaps I should stick to gardening."

I reached out and brushed away a smudge of soot from her cheek. "I'm glad to see your spirit's intact and not tainted by the assassin's touch."

"The assassin." Her smile faded, and the color drained from her face. "But why, Milord, didn't you accept his offer? Peace for all time, and at such a small price."

"The demon can't be trusted," I said. "How could so much good come from such a wicked choice?"

"Then what will you do with time so short?"

"I don't know. That decision's for tomorrow, but your sacrifice won't be part of it." I looked down at my walking stick and into the eagle's wooden eyes. He seemed to approve.

Rebecca leaned in, rose on her tiptoes, and kissed me on

the lips. "Well, Milord, this gardener's not displeased to be alive, but should you change your mind, I'm here."

From there, I brought her to the royal chambers and placed her in the care of a maid-in-waiting—better than sending her back to her village. At least in Stormwind, she'd have protection from the castle walls, if only for one more day.

As I left, a panic arose within me—that if I took one more step or turned one more corner, the hope of seeing her again would fade. Nonetheless, I retreated to the privacy of my bedchamber, locked the door, and tried to think. I couldn't go back to the crypt with nothing but staff and sword. I needed something stronger, an enchantment or charm powerful enough to overcome the demon.

Where shall I find it?

For the rest of that afternoon, I stayed in bed, staring up at the mural on the domed ceiling. The painted dauphin stared back at me, the primal image of my youth. That dauphin had been helped by both Goddess and elf. I too had been advised by the elf, but where was my Goddess, and why had she forsaken me to go through the trials alone? For an instant, I wondered if the gardener might be the Goddess incarnate, descended from the heavens to guide me. Perhaps the staged sacrifice of an immortal was a ploy to test my resolve.

How could I take such a chance? Besides, if I were to survive the trials and go on with my life, I preferred she not be immortal, but real and flawed like me. I'd wish no other by my side.

What of Malfurion Stormrage? The great elf had appeared to me twice, on the stairway to the watchtower and before the locked door in the crypt. Though he'd counseled in riddles, he'd helped me overcome the first two trials. Now, in my hour of need, could he be the ally I sought? I made up my mind. Unless the Goddess sprang forth from the plaster in the mural and came to life, I had no choice but to seek out the elf.

I rolled onto my side and swung my legs to the floor with a grunt, then grabbed my staff and limped off to the watchtower.

As I headed across the parapet, the lengthening shadows made me pause. It was an hour before sunset, that time of day when the fading light made the world appear cloaked in scrim. When I was little, this had been my favorite part of the day, an in-between time when my schooling had ended and I had yet to be called to my royal duties. It always seemed to last longer than it should, a time of wonder, a bridge between worlds.

At the base of the watchtower, I violated the adviser's rule and chose the morning stairs, the most direct route to where I'd first met the elf. Twenty steps from the top, I stopped and searched the stone for the mark in the shape of an owl. When I found it, I pounded on the wall with my staff.

"Malfurion Stormrage," I cried. "Shan'do, honored teacher, appear and advise."

I shouted until the stairway echoed, and the words flying between the walls demolished each other into silence. When my energy waned, I slumped on a stair and rested my chin on the eagle's head, brooding until the light from the archway above took on an orange hue.

Sunset was at hand.

I trudged up the few remaining stairs and entered the chamber. Always before, I'd arrived just in time for my session, but now I had a few minutes to look around.

To the west, the sun shone red and fat on the horizon, streaming through a thumb-width crack in the clouds above the mountains. Its rays passed through the gems in the wheel and cast a rainbow on the opposite wall. I marveled at it. How could a lens to so much evil paint such a splendid glow?

To the east, the land spread darkly, and the sunrise oculus gaped black in the midst of the rainbow, an inviting maw drawing me toward it. I gripped the rim of the stone and leaned out over its edge. Below, in the shadow of the watchtower, the dying light did not reach. I could barely make out the drawbridge and the river raging below.

How simple it would have been to shift my weight and pitch out onto that river, with its jagged rocks, to be embraced by its flow and become another voice of the damned.

I wavered, balancing in the moment, but became distracted as the light around me came alive. The wheel had begun to spin, and a reflection of the dream started to play out on the eastern wall, replacing the rainbow. I watched the vision unfold, a dream I could remember.

I beheld the gardener in the casket, her eyes gazing up at me as I raised the poisoned blade. Before I could strike, the vision flickered and changed. Now I saw a different place—not a castle, but a lesser structure, a poor imitation of Stormwind. The vision breached the walls and glided down the corridor like a hawk riding the breeze. I saw people young and old, many with terrible wounds, but I also saw the care they were given, the good being done. I reached a room filled with flowers and, at its center, the gardener. She saw me and spoke two words. "I'm here."

Ignoring my obligations, I spun around and fled the watchtower.

As I hobbled down the sunrise stairs, preoccupied with what I'd seen, my thoughts were interrupted by a wind coming from the inner core, from a place where no wind should be. I stared spellbound as a candle wavered and smoked.

The gray wall swelled and Malfurion Stormrage reappeared. He loomed over me, his amber eyes boring into my mind. "Why," he said in his booming voice, "have you summoned me?"

I bowed and told him of the encounter in the crypt, and of the demon's unholy offer. "I beg your help, some magic to vanquish the assassin without costing the gardener her life."

He slowly shook his head. "You rely too much on magic. These are *your* trials, Dauphin, born out of *your* hopes and fears. Only *you* can make that choice."

My shoulders slumped, my final hope denied. "Sorrow's been my fate since I was a child, a fate I never chose. Can you, who have stared into the well of eternity, at least tell me why?"

"None of us choose our fate, yet sorrow is not preordained by the gods."

The blood rushed to my face, and I shook the eagle staff at the great elf, all my deference gone. "Enough with elfish wisdom! Not preordained? Then explain all that's happened—to my family, to the archangel, to the heroes and the boy with the innocent smile."

"What's happened is past. Not every future is dark."

"What could be darker than the death of the gardener by my own hand?"

"It's your trial, Dauphin. You, not fate, control its outcome. I can help no more." He turned so sharply, the breeze caused by the swish of his lavender cloak made the candle flame shiver.

I clutched at a corner of the fabric and held on until he'd dragged me off the stair. I fell to my knees at his feet and begged, "One enchantment. One spell to defeat the assassin."

He pulled away, unmoved by me, a mere mortal who'd soon be gone. "No need of spells to defeat the assassin," he said. "He's your own creation. All you need is to understand what he is."

"If it's that simple, then tell me. Tell me, and I'll do what I must."

His amber eyes softened as he pondered my request. Finally, he spoke. "The assassin is the ghost of your own past. You must learn to laugh in his teeth."

That evening, I prayed through the darkness to the Goddess on the dome, hoping she'd grant me wisdom. I faced a terrible choice, and was afraid of making it wrong.

The night passed slowly, a procession in shades of gray. When the black of midnight had lightened to charcoal, and then to slate, I arose. I'd get no sleep that night, nor would I be struck by a flash of divine insight. I knew two things for certain: I'd never harm the gardener; and I'd refuse to return to the watchtower.

What use are its dreams to me now?

I decided to trade the comfort of my bedchamber for a more restful place. With the eagle held high like a second set of eyes, I slipped out the doorway, down the hall, and across the courtyard to the crypt.

That chamber of death had always been gloomy, but now, in the wee hours of the morning, it seemed as if no light had ever graced its inner depths. I took a candle from a sconce by the entrance and went in. In its glow, the faces of the dead took on a reddish hue, and all seemed to be staring as I passed. When I arrived at the barrier to the final trial, the assassin's magic let me through, though the gardener no longer stood at my side. I knew it would, for I'd come to understand what the demon desired— neither the boy nor the gardener, but my despair.

At last, I arrived.

The final casket stood empty, as when I first beheld it, waiting for an occupant, but now it bore a newly engraved plaque:

Here lies Prince Frederick, the Fool.

Resting on the edge of the frame, Kingsbane, the dagger of sorrow, still gleamed with the sap of the monkshood on its tip.

I crept closer and grasped the dagger, feeling its heft in my hand, but nearly dropped it at the unmistakable scrape of footsteps on the hard ground.

A voice behind me spoke. "The eternal choice."

I turned, careful to keep the dagger's point at arm's length.

Before me stood the assassin. No expression graced his lifeless face, just as no inflection ennobled his words. "If you do this, the dreadlord will leave your world in peace."

"And the gardener as well? A long and happy life?"

He nodded, almost a bow. "Long, I can say. Happy will be up to her."

I raised Kingsbane into the glow of the candlelight. The dagger had already killed a king. How much easier to kill a prince? Then I thought of the gardener awaiting my return.

I set the dagger down on the rim of the casket and turned to the demon. "I have till sunset this day to make my farewells. I'll return before then."

The assassin bunched his cheeks and brow, narrowing the hollow sockets in what would have been a look of sadness if he had eyes. In a voice less than a whisper — no echo, no air — he said, "I'll be waiting."

The View
from the
Watchtower

THE NIGHT FOLLOWING MR. SHAPIRO'S VISIT, I tossed and turned, bothered by dreams. Done with sleep well before sunrise, I lay awake, staring at the ceiling and thinking about the war. When I'd been in Iraq, I lived minute to minute — no past, no future, only survival and now. Everything I saw or did, every person I fought with or against, displaced all the moments and all the people that came before, like living in an alternate reality.

Back in the States and recovering from my wounds, the war seemed like a fantasy. All I had left of it was a bum leg, the archangel's medallion, and two medals I didn't deserve. I wondered why I was still alive when so many were gone.

But what kind of life was it? I lingered, stuck in a twilight state in the shadow of the turret of the VA hospital, with no real connection to my past and no clear picture of my future. I led a foggy existence surrounded by dark mountains, with thunderclouds looming over their summits and demons waiting on the far side.

Through it all, on the horizon, like the sunset trying to break through, glimmers danced at the crest of the ridge — my leg getting stronger, my studies resuming, the possibility of finding Richie.

And Becky. She'd insisted the future was in my control, laid out like a blank canvas. I had only to choose between palettes — the one with bright colors and hope, or the other with grim memories and death.

I tried to focus on the colorful palette, recalling the style of the gingerbread houses around the green. I loved to sketch them, meticulously drawing the trim beneath each roofline, and the carvings that embellished them. I rattled off the names of the neighbors who lived in them, and when I'd recounted them all, it was still not daylight. I moved on to my basketball team, to those I played with my senior year, and the scores of the few games we won.

My thoughts kept returning to Richie, though, And to autumn days when my mother would take us apple picking. I recalled how we'd climb the hill in the orchard, to where the apples were ripest and dangling just above our heads, how I'd select the perfect apple for Richie and let him jump up and pick it. I thought of winters past, of Christmas mornings with the few presents my parents were able to make or buy, and of how Richie thought they were magic.

Is he the boy in the photograph?

I began to believe Mr. Shapiro was like a quest giver in *World of Warcraft*, with a gold exclamation point above his head, inviting me on a high-risk quest. If I chose to accept, and played well, my life would level up. If not, I would fall into endless despair.

When morning finally arrived, after the usual work details to clean out the common room and remove trash from the night before, I hung out with the guys, not wanting to be alone. Several of them were gamers, like me, and took the opportunity to jump online. They'd invited me a number of times to become a member of their guild, but I'd always turned them down and gone back to the cloister of my room. My reality was muddled enough without role-playing in a fantasy world.

This time, when I heard the familiar music start up, something drew me in. The kettledrums, the clash of cymbals, the trumpets, and the chorus, a tune I hadn't heard since Iraq—the call to a hero's quest.

I had no role in this new realm, so I went first to the character creation screen, a chance to shape a new identity. My old character had been a human warrior, bold and brawny with a prominent forehead and a shock of golden hair. This time, I chose something gentler. For my race, a Draenei, one of the exiled ones, blessed with an unshakeable faith in the Light. For my class, a priest and healer like the archangel—I'd had enough of damage dealing. For my name, I chose RichieW.

I took a minute to fine-tune my character, fiddling with the hair and skin color, trying out several funky beards and settling on none at all, switching briefly to female and back to male. When finished, I admired my new creation, slid the cursor over the "Enter World" button, and clicked.

At once, I found myself at the crash site of the satellite ship Exodar on Azuremyst Isle. I brought up my stats by habit, checking armor, strength, and stamina. Then, remembering I was no longer a warrior, I reviewed the more priestly virtues of spirit and intellect. I checked the contents of my spell book and bag—not much there. I hadn't been this weak in a long time—like in the real world. I shook my head, closed down everything, and set off to explore.

My choice of character had been a good one. The home of the Draenei was a calming place, a proper setting to roam around in during an unsettled period in my real world. The mist that gave the island its name rose up from the river and gave a blue tinge to the pines that lined my path. A purple haze veiled the mountains in the distance.

As I wandered through the landscape, searching for quests and hoping to find gold, weapons, spells, or anything else that would ramp up my experience, I ran into another player character, a female human mage.

This avatar had soft blue eyes, full red lips, and arched brows that disappeared under a mane of auburn hair—an image beautifully rendered. In one hand, she gripped a staff with a golden orb on top. Her other hand, open with delicate fingers, extended to me in greeting.

I laughed, knowing how role-playing could be. That lovely avatar could easily have been Chuck or Ralph. Nevertheless, I stopped to admire her. When I got no immediate reaction, I clicked to move on, but before I could step past, the chat window popped opened in the lower left corner of the screen.

"Where are you going in such a rush?" she whispered so only I could hear.

I positioned the cursor over the text box and typed, "I seek oblivion."

"Bad goal," she replied. "Believe in the future instead."

My mouth opened and I almost said, "Becky," even though I hadn't enabled my voice chat. I slid the cursor beneath her words, intending to respond, but my fingers froze over the keyboard. After a moment, I yanked the cursor away, clicked open the menu, and exited the game.

No more fantasy. Decision made.

I grabbed my jacket and rushed outside, pausing only long enough to check if the walkway to the main building was free of ice. Halfway across the common, a crow circled and landed at my feet. It had a sleek head feathered in black, and talons that clacked on the pavement as it hopped about, gaping at me with that strange round eye on the side of its head. I watched it with suspicion.

An omen?

I shook off the mood and shooed it away with a flick of my cane. It squawked once, spread its wings, and flew off to the horizon without looking back.

Once inside the lobby, I punched the call button six times, trying to make the elevator come faster. On the ride up, I held my breath as the cab bumped and rattled against the sides of the shaft. When the bell signaled my arrival on the fourth floor, the doors took forever to open. As I waited, I almost expected to see the candlelit wall of a castle.

I navigated the familiar green tile and fluorescent lighting of the hospital, advancing deliberately down the corridor, counting the doors to PT—the same as always.

The door was closed and locked. I tapped with the eagle's beak on the window, but to no avail.

It had been almost three weeks since I'd last seen Becky. Maybe she had finally given up on me.

I stared through the glass into the darkness, trying to see if the flowers were there, but I saw only my reflection. Then a thought occurred to me.

Ralph will know.

I rushed back to the elevator only to find it gone. I checked the lights above the door. Someone had summoned the elevator after me. The numbers from one to twenty remained dark, with only the topmost floor lit, the mysterious "RA." I wondered if it led to the tower with the arched windows. I punched the "up" button and waited, but no whirring, no motion. The light stayed stuck on "RA."

Out of a combination of impatience and stubbornness, I headed for the stairs. Eleven flights up to my old home on the fifteenth floor—nothing my cane and surgically repaired leg couldn't handle.

The stairway was gloomy, with concrete block walls and prison-style handrails, a place for emergencies and exercise. I leaned out over the handrail and glanced up the well, trying to see to the top, and began to climb, counting stairs as I went.

Nine stairs to a floor. Ninety-nine to my destination. Plus one to get into the landing and one to get out. A total of a hundred and one.

Despite all my rehab, I was winded by the fifteenth floor. Before exiting the stairwell, I stopped to catch my breath, not wanting to seem desperate when I found Ralph. At least that's what I told myself. More likely, I was procrastinating, hesitant to cross a portal into what might be a different world.

I opened the door.

On the far side, the usual scene appeared—nurses and health aids bustling about, patients with walkers and canes. I waited for a break in the flow before merging in. When I reached Ralph's office, I hovered at the threshold, trying to assimilate what I saw. A man sat at Ralph's desk, wearing hospital scrubs and tapping at his computer, but he was too slight to be Ralph, shorter by a foot or more.

"What are you doing here?" I blurted out, courtesy be damned.

"Just using the computer," he muttered without turning around. "Mine's on the fritz."

"Where's Ralph?"

"Don't know. Haven't seen him today." He swiveled around in his chair and took stock of me. "Can I help you?"

"No, thank you." I whirled around and left.

I was starting to get frantic—no Becky, no Ralph—and the exertion of the climb had made me lightheaded. I circled the corridor, the click of my cane on the floor getting faster and faster. I poked my head into patient rooms and peered into offices—no one I knew. I thought about taking the elevator to the "RA" floor.

What if Becky went up to the turret to keep watch through the arched windows, and to ward off evil from the world?

I raced around a corner and nearly wiped out Dinah.

She stretched out a hand for protection and steadied me. "My, aren't we getting mobile?" When I didn't answer, she straightened her glasses and looked at me through those Coke-bottle lenses. "Everything okay, Freddie?"

"I'm looking for Ralph."

"He's with a patient. Anything I can do?"

"Yes. No. I'm not sure."

"I'll tell you what... I was just heading for a break. Why don't I get us both a cup of coffee, and we can catch up in the solarium."

Moments later, the two of us sat blowing across the top of our steaming cups, staring out over the golf course and the cemeteries.

"So, why were you looking for Ralph?" she said.

"To find out what's happened to Becky. I went to look for her. Her room was dark and the door was locked."

"She's on vacation this week. We *do* get time off, you know. Most of us love our work, but it isn't easy."

"I know that."

"She'll be back on Monday." She studied me for a good five seconds, and tried out her next words as if easing onto thin ice, wondering how far she could go. "You two haven't seen each other in a while."

I nodded.

"Ralph told me about the kid who might be Richie. Is that why you're looking for Becky?"

"It's one reason."

"But you *are* going to check him out?"

"I... think so."

"Well, Dr. B. always says the first step in a diagnosis is to understand the problem. Is this about Richie? Or is it about you and Becky?"

A good question.

I'd made up my mind to try and find Richie, but what about Becky and me?

Dinah patiently watched me with the same kindness I saw when I first awoke from the coma.

"Maybe you *can* help," I said at last.

She took a sip, wincing when she found the coffee still too hot, and waited for me to continue.

"Becky once told me she had scars like me, but wouldn't tell me how she got them. She's always been so positive, like she's coasted through life. I know her parents are doing well and she had no siblings, but—"

"No siblings?" Dinah said. "That's not right. She had a sister."

"Had?"

"Yes. She died when Becky was a kid."

I blinked twice. There'd been storm clouds in Miss Sunshine's life. "Do you know what happened?"

"That's all she told me. I didn't think it was my place to pry."

A thought struck me, a way to find out more. "Do you remember how old Becky was when her sister died?"

"Fifteen, if I remember correctly. Yes, I'm sure she said she was only fifteen."

Fifteen. The same age I was when Dad died.

I pictured a teen-aged Becky dressed in black, standing in a receiving line in the basement of a church, surrounded by plates of chocolate chip cookies, and well-wishers assuring her everything would be fine.

I got up and looked out over the landscape, thinking of the first time Becky brought me here, the day she told me her simple goals—a home, a family, someone to love. I wondered where she was now, and what the view from the watchtower was like from behind those gray-green eyes.

Sand
in an
Hourglass

37

LATE THAT NIGHT, I SAT ALONE at a computer in the common room, playing a different kind of game: find out what happened to Becky's sister. I still had passwords to the sites I'd used to search for Richie, and I knew her sister's last name and the year she died. The rest was just work.

After two hours, the screen's glow had become oppressive, sucking in what little light remained in the room. My eyes watered, but no way would I give up.

Finally, I located an obituary giving me the first name, date, and place of death. Next, I went to the hospital records. Nothing.

I found what I was looking for among the police reports.

I stared at the words until the letters started wriggling across the screen. When I'd seen enough, I dragged the cursor over to logoff, but I was squeezing the mouse so hard, I overshot the button. It took three tries before I managed to steady my hand and click.

The screen went dark, and all the light in the room seemed to fade.

With Becky not due back until Monday, I decided to take matters into my own hands. I contacted Mr. Shapiro to get the phone number, and then called the halfway house. From the social worker in charge, I learned the boy they called Andy had been taken off the streets six years before—the right timing to be Richie. They'd found him wandering around with no identification, and he always refused to give anyone a name.

The only way to find out was to set up a meeting, so I located Ralph and asked if his offer of a ride still stood.

We left the hospital at ten on Saturday, a gloomy morning with a low gray sky and just enough snowflakes to force Ralph to fuss with the intermittent wiper control, trying to keep the blades from squeaking across the glass. As we approached the bridge over the canal, a heavy mist concealed its supporting arches.

Not exactly a day for miracles.

Ralph and I talked about a lot of things on the hour-long drive: of the war and the veterans he'd worked with; of his parents who were looking forward to retirement; of a new patient he'd taken on recently, a kid only eighteen years old whose mind and body had been shattered in an IED attack not so different from mine. When I began to question why I'd been so lucky, he switched the subject to the future—to my upcoming discharge and my application to grad school.

We didn't discuss Richie until we rounded the rotary with the welcoming topiary in the shape of the words: "Cape Cod."

"It's gonna happen, Freddie," he said. "I can feel it."

I clasped the cane between my legs and smiled at the eagle. "I hope so, Ralph. I'm due for a wish come true."

He chanced a glance away from the road to look at me. "If I had the power, I'd grant you this one."

For the next ten minutes, we stayed quiet. I tried to count the snowflakes that landed on the windshield and match them to my breathing. Only when we exited the highway and veered onto a winding back road did my unspoken fear rise up from my chest and become words.

"What if we're each born with a certain amount of happiness, like sand in an hourglass? And once that sand runs out, that's it? What if I drew the short straw, too few grains, and they all ran out when I was a kid? And that's all there is?"

"It's not a video game, Freddie. Bad things happen—worse for some people than others, and you've had more than your share—but your future's not cast in stone. This kid may not be Richie, and you may never find him, but whether there's more happiness in the cards? That's up to you."

A few more turns and we pulled into the small dirt driveway of the halfway house, a two-story wooden structure that looked like a World War II barracks. Someone had taken the trouble to add a splash of color to the paint, and flowered curtains to the windows.

When we stopped, I opened the door and planted my feet on the ground, wiggling my shoes on the loose gravel to get a stable platform. I stepped out, but only after asking Ralph to wait in the car. I had to do this alone.

Inside, the empty entry hall had no formal reception, nothing to greet a visitor but a folding bridge table with a circular stain in the center—residue of some long-gone plant over-watered. Along the wall, radiators with peeling paint popped and steamed like miniature dragons. A narrow hallway extended out the back, with doors on either side, and at its end, a staircase spiraled its way up to a second story.

"Hello?" When only an echo answered me, I took out the cell phone Ralph had loaned me and called my contact.

A few seconds later, a man climbed down the stairs and stepped smartly along the hallway toward me. He had long hair and a beard, at a distance looking like he could be the boy in Mr. Shapiro's picture.

I studied him like a ghost approaching, but saw no hint of Richie.

He was too tall and at least twenty years older than the boy who would be my brother. The lines of his face curled upward, making the crow's feet at the corners of his eyes crinkle—a face that bore witness to the work he did, a mix of caring and concern. Like Becky, Ralph, and Dinah, he was one of the good people in the world.

When he reached me, he extended a hand. "Lieutenant Williams, I presume. Pleased to meet you. I'm Bob LaGuerre, the guy in charge of our little world. Can I get you anything? Something to drink?"

I said an abrupt no, and then, more tactfully, explained that I was anxious to meet the boy who'd seen my picture in the newspaper.

My new friend Bob said he understood and headed off to fetch him, his footsteps clomping down the wooden hallway.

I waited, probably no more than a few minutes, but it felt like forever.

Finally, Bob LaGuerre returned, escorting the boy in the picture. He was dressed shabbier than my mother would have ever allowed, but was the appropriate age and height, and his gait looked about right, but....

It wasn't until he came closer that I knew.

He cocked his head to one side in that funny way he had, and looked me up and down. He stopped and stared when he noticed my cane with the handle in the shape of an eagle head.

I looked too, at its polished surface marked with the names of those who had died—the men of my squad, Mom, Dad, and Joey.

No need to add one more. Richie is alive.

"What's that?" he said.

"It's a cane I need to help me walk." When he kept staring at the eagle, I explained, "I hurt my leg in the war."

I braced for the question he'd asked every day when I'd come home from basketball practice.

This time, he worded it differently. "I guess you'll never dunk now, huh, Freddie?"

I nodded. I'd long since given up that dream, worried now not about myself, but about him. Just like when we were kids. I didn't want him to feel bad.

But he'd changed too. He broke into that special grin I knew so well, that magnificent innocence. "That's okay, Freddie. It's only a game."

The
Dreaded
Day

38

STILL WELL BEFORE DAWN, I RETURNED to my bedchamber to wait out the heat of the day. As I lay atop the quilt, swimming in my own sweat, I replayed my first meeting with the gardener: how the butterfly led me to her and landed so lightly on her wrist; how the mud formed a raven shape on her face; how she removed the torn apron to reveal a summery dress; how its fabric rustled against her skin. As exhaustion from the restless night overwhelmed me, I began to drift off, and while thinking of Rebecca surrounded by hydrangeas, I fell into a deep sleep.

I dreamed I was returning to the crypt for the final trial, but on my way, a tumult came from the main gate. I mounted the parapet, taking the stairs two at a time, and leaned over the wall to discover the cause of the noise.

Below, the people had begun to celebrate, assuming I would triumph and be anointed king. Many had raced out to line the road to the castle, where a squire led a white horse through the crowd toward the drawbridge across the moat. The horse bore no armor, but instead had a wreath of white roses about its neck, and on it, the gardener rode sidesaddle, a sprig of baby's breath in her hair. Overhead, the dark clouds had flown, replaced by the bluest of skies, and the sun shone as if there were no death.

Shunning the dawn, I slept till midmorning and awoke refreshed, but by midafternoon, I'd grown anxious, awaiting the end of the day. To help the time pass, I summoned a servant to draw me a bath, and within a few minutes, a stream of attendants appeared, each bearing a vessel of steaming water. After they'd filled the tub, I locked the door behind them and settled in to steep—a purification ritual, I told myself, for the final trial.

When I'd soaked enough, I dressed in my ceremonial robes, traditional attire reserved for state occasions. I put on a satin shirt, and the prince's tunic over it, taking small pride in how the gilded epaulets squared off my shoulders. I strapped on the belt with the burnished buckle and the six-rayed sapphire that glowed in its center. Last of all, I donned the dreamwalker wrist guards, said to increase intellect and spirit. While I preened in the mirror, I remained consumed by doubt.

Who is this person who stands before me? Hero or fool?

A pounding on the door stirred me from my reverie. I'd lost track of the time, but even with the clouds darkening Golgoreth, I could tell it was too early for sunset.

"Go away," I shouted.

Sir Gilly's gruff voice penetrated the thick wood. "Open the door, Frederick. For the sake of your father and mother, and all those who have gone before, let me in. The days of dread are coming to an end."

I moved from the mirror to the door, and grasped the latch, but stayed my hand, unsure whether to release it or not.

Suddenly, a flash and the great oaken door dissolved. When the smoke cleared, there stood Malfurion Stormrage, towering over the advisor. His staff with the bloodstone still smoldered from its latest spell, and his lavender robe flowed behind him with the force of his enchantment.

I gaped at the great elf.

"You begged for magic," he said, "and I have granted your wish."

I reached out, thinking he was about to offer me the staff.

At last, a weapon to defeat the assassin without sacrificing Rebecca or myself.

He pulled it back and turned aside.

Behind him, so much smaller, stood the gardener, dressed in a silken white gown and golden slippers. As in my dream, she wore a sprig of baby's breath in her hair.

She stepped forward wearing a mysterious smile, and when she spoke, she almost laughed. "You must come with me, Milord. Anointment's nearly done, and the coronation is at hand."

"The coronation?" I said. "But what of the final trial?"

"No need. I've seen a better way."

I couldn't take my eyes off her—so radiant, more princess than gardener—but I was loath to raise my hope. I longed to go with her... until I recalled the visions of the spinning wheel.

I stood my ground. "Return to your flowers, Rebecca, and leave me to my fate. The affairs of the watchtower are not for such as you."

"But they are, Milord."

"How so?"

"Because I too have been to the watchtower."

My mouth opened but no words flowed forth.

She reached out and brushed my cheek with the back of her hand. "This morn of the final day, I was too troubled to sleep, and so I went to seek you, knowing where you'd be at dawn. When you were nowhere to be found, I crept up the hundred and one stairs, thinking you might have gone early to the watchtower, but when I reached the top, the chamber was empty. Then, as I stood there pondering your fate, the wheel began to spin. Though I knew it was forbidden, I sat on the stool and watched as the visions unfolded. Now that I've seen the view from there, I believe our fate's intertwined. Or will be, if you'll take my hand."

She stretched out her hand to me, fingers curled, not a gesture of beckoning but of joining.

I stared at it as if it were the hand of an angel from on high, and knew what I had to do.

While the tune from the globe played in my head, my hand swung toward hers, our fingers met, and we joined.

The Natural Order

39

MONDAY MORNING, AS SOON AS I'D completed my details, I went to the window to check the weather. Drips from the melting icicles had coursed down the glass and refrozen overnight, leaving a wavy film on the pane. The light that filtered through the resulting glaze made the hospital appear blanketed in haze, and the turret at the top seemed to rise up from the mist like a castle in a fantasy world. Undeterred, I threw on my army jacket, pulled up the collar, and stepped outside.

The temperature was barely above freezing, but the sun shone strong. Its beams baked down on the piles of old snow, wringing water from them that trickled across my path. I glanced up to the clock at the top of the tower, which read noon.

Lunch time.

I walked in the side entrance of the main building, through the green-tiled corridor, and across to the courtyard.

As expected, she sat on her favorite bench, surrounded by snowdrifts and bundled in a parka and gloves, the only one brave enough to take lunch outside. An empty brown bag lay open beside her, and she held a cup of tea in both hands. She'd closed her eyes and was letting the steam rise up and warm her face. The aroma of apples and cinnamon filled the air.

It was hard to believe so many days had passed since I'd seen her.

She turned when she heard me approach, and eyed my gait, always the physical therapist. "Well, look who's walking with hardly a limp. How come you still have the cane?"

"I like this cane. It reminds me of you."

She cut off her laughter and ended it with an edge. "You *need* a reminder. It's been a long time."

"I'm sorry. I didn't mean to—"

"Apology accepted—for now. Don't just stand there making me squint into the sun. Have a seat."

I settled next to her, but couldn't find the words to express what I needed to say.

She broke the silence first. "Ralph told me about Richie. I'm happy for you."

"Thanks."

She swished her tea around and took a sip, then spoke into the cup. "If I'd been here, I would've been glad to take you."

"I know."

I searched the courtyard for something to focus on. Across the way, an oddly shaped snow bank caught my eye, so covered in soot that, to a veteran fantasy player, it took on the appearance of a snarling black bear.

Becky shook me out of my daze, trying to keep me in the real world. "Don't space out on me, Freddie. Not now. Talk to me."

I slid closer to her on the bench. "I wanted to see you every day."

"You had a funny way of showing it. You didn't even bother to answer my notes." She laid a gloved hand on my knee and her expression softened. "Why'd you stay away so long?"

I covered her hand with mine, but avoided facing her, instead keeping watch on the snow bear. "My world's pretty messed up right now. I worried that being around me was bad for you."

"Isn't that for me to decide?"

I didn't know how to respond.

She slipped her hand out from under mine, placed it on my cheek, and turned me toward her. "Don't I at least have a say?"

"What if you don't really know me?"

"Don't know you? I spent five months massaging your leg and stretching your knee. We had lunch together most days. I've read your military records from start to finish, been to the house you grew up in, and even visited the graves of your family. Jeez, Freddie, you're only twenty-five. How much more could there be?"

"Maybe more than I know myself."

"What's that supposed to mean?"

I looked at her, her eyes no more than six inches from mine. The longer I looked, the longer I wanted to go on looking, but she was waiting for an answer.

"Whenever something bad happens, people pat you on the arm and say time heals. I'm not so sure. Like with my knee. Most of the scar tissue's gone, thanks to you, but my leg will never be the same. What if that's true of my brain as well? My wounds may have been non-penetrating, but I have scar tissue there too."

"What are you trying to tell me?"

"That I'll never be the person I was."

"What's that have to do with you and me? I never knew the person you were, and I like who you are now."

She took a last sip of tea from the cup and tossed it into the nearby trash bucket. Then she crumpled the paper bag into a ball, preparing to take her customary shot, but she hesitated.

"I have a good idea what you've been through, Freddie. What do you think I do here every day? You're right. Sometimes life sucks, but at some point, you have to move on. It's the natural order of things."

The blood rushed to my cheeks, burning in the cold. "The natural order? What was natural about my parents dying before their time? Or some insurgent putting rocks and nails in a canister filled with explosives?"

She gaped at me, paper bag ball still clutched in her hands.

My heart was pounding, and I heard a whooshing sound in my ears, as if I was so close to something important and afraid to screw it up.

I took the chance. "Or your sister dying like Joey, OD'ing on drugs?"

Her eyes widened, and I peered into them, trying to see what she was thinking, but they were like the frosted windows in the gingerbread house door, revealing little of what was inside. For a moment, I wished I could take it back.

She grimaced and sucked air in through her teeth. "How'd you find out?"

"I researched it, like you researched my background. But I want to hear what happened from you."

"All right, Freddie. You need to break scar tissue too. Well, here it is. I had an older sister. She died of an overdose. Killed herself, and I'll never know why. So I have my sad story too."

The puffs of her breath came faster now, and I held up a hand to stop her, but I'd opened the floodgates, and she needed to go on.

"I was fifteen, like you when your dad died. I remember everyone pushing forward, straining for a look in the casket before they closed it. My mother said her expression was peaceful, that her ordeal on Earth was over, but I didn't believe a word of it. My last memory? I smelled the scent of lilies as they closed the lid."

I stared at her, no longer Miss Sunshine and Light.

She looked back, eyes glistening. "I'm sorry. I knew you'd come back eventually. The last thing I wanted to do when I saw you was to drag you down. I'm so sorry...."

I couldn't tell if she was apologizing to me or to the universe. "How have you managed to stay so positive?"

She stood and wandered over to the far side of the courtyard, looking for a second like she was about to wrestle the snow bear, before glancing up to the highest turret of the hospital, as if hoping someone inside might give her a sign. After a sharp intake of breath, her shoulders shuddered. Then, she came back and looked down at me with those gray-green eyes.

"After my sister's funeral, I stayed in my room with the door closed for almost a week. I didn't want to get up, get dressed, or go to school ever again. Finally, my father came in. I thought he'd be mad, but instead, he settled on the bed next to me so softly, I hardly felt the mattress sag. He told me no one asked us to come into this world, nor did they tell us why we're here, so it's up to each of us to find a purpose. He said the only tragedy greater than death is to never find that purpose.

"After he left, I stayed in bed, tracing the cracks in the ceiling with my eyes, like walking a labyrinth. I didn't budge until I'd grasped what he said. He was right. The saddest thing about someone who dies is the possibilities lost. At that moment, I swore, as a gift to my sister, that I'd make the most of my life. And that's all I'm asking of you, to try to do the same."

There it was, an insight so basic, I was ashamed I'd missed it all these years. Give up, or make the most of my life. I nodded.

"Life isn't always pretty, Freddie. We all have losses. Sometimes it takes a leap of faith to go on, and you've never had a reason to make that leap. I hope you have one now."

"What's that?"

"Me." She turned with a purpose and stepped off her five paces to the trash bucket.

While she peeled off her gloves and lined up the shot, the machine in my brain began to whir. Everything that happened since that day in the gym, when I first heard about my father's accident, played out in my mind. Was there more I didn't remember? Memories good or bad I was missing?

Then I realized it: none of that mattered. The most important thing still missing was standing in front of me, holding a silly paper bag like a basketball and waiting for me to invite her into my world.

I went to her and placed a hand on her face, tracing her cheekbone down to her chin with my thumb. "I'll tell you what. Take that shot. If it goes in, I'll make the leap and be with you."

Her eyes took on a sparkle from the sunlight. She grinned and took the shot, but her confidence faltered. At the last second, a gust of wind blew through the courtyard. The bag rattled around the rim and bounced out.

She turned to me with a look of horror. "A bad omen?"

"Fuck omens!"

I laid down my cane on the bench, picked up the bag, and went around to the far side of the black bear snow pile, a shot of more than twenty feet. I flexed at the knees the way my father taught me, and flicked my wrist. The brown paper ball spun off the tips of my fingers, arced through the air, and sailed into the basket without touching the sides.

"Swish," I said. "We have a deal."

A Leap
of
Faith

WE MARCHED OFF TO THE CORONATION, the prince and the gardener dressed in royal garb, with the advisor and the elf trailing behind.

At the entrance to the tabernacle where the ceremony was to take place, Malfurion and Sir Gilly begged off, citing preparations yet to be done. They made their goodbyes and wished us well.

By tradition, the coronation would not start until one hour past sunset, and so we had time to wait. I brushed clear a spot on the steps for Rebecca, not wanting to soil her dress, and we settled there, just the two of us, guarded on either flank by a pair of marble lions.

She shifted sideways and glanced over her shoulder to the inside of the tabernacle. She'd never been there before, and now stared wide-eyed across the nave and up to the sanctuary, where a stained glass window shed the Goddess's divine light on the altar.

"So beautiful, Milord."

I followed her gaze. "As a young prince, I used to come here and hide in the pews. I'd study that window as the low afternoon sun shone through, and try to imagine the Goddess coming to life."

As we watched, a column of robed singers entered from the back of the sanctuary and filed one by one into the stalls to the right of the altar, readying for their final practice. Once they settled, the royal chorus master swept in and took his seat at the great organ. He struck a chord to allow the singers to find their key. When all was ready, he began to play.

At once, the haunting sound of the wooden pipes filled the nave and rose up through the vaulted arches—a song, I'd been told, used only at coronations.

I recognized it at once—the tune from the simpleton's globe.

"Angels we have heard on high — "

It was as if the song had unlocked an empty chamber in my heart, one that cried to be filled before I could ascend to the throne. I knew at once what I needed to do, one final task before the ceremony.

Rebecca read the change in my face. "What is it, Milord?"

"I must leave you now, but only for a short while."

I rose to go, but she grasped my wrist in her firm gardener's hand. "Not to the crypt."

I reached across with my free hand, unclenched her fingers one at a time, and raised her hand to my lips to kiss it. "I have to go, Rebecca. The days of dread are coming to an end, but the crypt will always be with me. I need to see it one more time."

Her eyes narrowed. "Then at least let me accompany you."

I pictured the assassin still lurking within, and shook my head. "This is something I have to do alone."

She stood and blocked my way. "If you go without me, I'll shout for the great elf and Sir Gilly."

I knew how stubborn she could be, and tried to think of a way out. "Very well," I said at last. "You may come with me, but no farther than the entrance."

She nodded. "The entrance it is."

"No going beyond the archway."

She made her little curtsy. "No entrance, no archway, Milord. I swear by the Goddess."

I spoke not another word as we headed for the crypt, as every attempt caught in my throat. When we came to the archway that formed the entrance, I paused and emptied my lungs—the end of the trials, at last. I kissed Rebecca on the lips and entered.

As I shuffled down the dank passageway, I fingered the key in the shape of the World Tree and raised the eagle staff high, bracing for the unknown. Instead of dark magic, I found the crypt had returned to normal, nothing more or less than a resting place for the dead. Like the stairway from the watershed and the archangel's chamber, all remnants of the trials had vanished.

No, not vanished. Everything had merely resumed its proper form. In the first chamber, the caskets of my parents were covered and closed, the dust of age blanketing them with sleep. Nearby, my comrades in arms rested peacefully, surrounded by fading banners, a fitting memorial for heroes.

"*Embrace the shadows,*" the elf had said. Only now did I understand what he meant.

They were gone, and I could do nothing more than honor them for what they'd done and who they were. For better or worse, I remained alive and needed to move on, but I would never abandon the memory of the trials, etched onto my soul like the scars of old battle wounds on my skin. The past had come and gone, but I was forever changed.

I bowed my head in the gloom and, for a brief moment, the old feeling of despair threatened to return. Then I heard the whisper of slippers in the passageway, and turned to see Rebecca peek around the bend.

"You gave the Goddess your vow," I said.

"I lied," she answered with a smile. "And now it's time to go. The coronation is at hand."

As I stepped toward her, the gauzy light of dusk filtered through from the entrance to the crypt. The days of dread were coming to an end, but my fear had strangely subsided, replaced by an unfamiliar calm.

When we passed back through the archway, out into the open air and up the steps to the parapet that led to the tabernacle, it came as no surprise that the clouds had cleared, as in my dream. The setting sun blazed unencumbered over the mountains of Golgoreth, a huge orange ball that sent its rays dancing along the ridge.

I squinted through split fingers at a world I hardly recognized. It was the same Elwynn forest and the same Goldshire — everything the same as before — but for the first time since my father's death, all was bathed in yellow light beneath a sky of endless blue. No trace remained of the twisted fog that, for me, had come to define the days of dread. The air had cooled too, more like a late summer evening than the harshness of noon.

Then, for an instant, the sky darkened above us, a shadow crossing the ground where we stood. I startled to a whistle and a whoosh overhead, and looked up to see a flock of birds sweep by, a majestic black cloud that spiraled and swirled. Not all shadows were demons. The starlings had returned.

Rebecca and I paused to marvel at their display. After they'd finished their twilight dance and turned homeward to their roost, I caught the dying light flicker across her face, and all became clear as the sky. I tightened my grip on her hand as I had the day before, when we both walked through solid stone in the crypt.

This journey would be different.

She squeezed back. "Shall we go? The ceremony awaits."

I nodded, smiled. Then my smile settled into thought. I lifted my eyes to the pathway of light in the western sky. "They will always be with me."

"I know, Frederick," she said. "But so shall I."

Then, ignoring for now the watchtower and the crypt, we stepped off into the future.

EPILOGUE

I WAS BREATHING HARD AND HAD the night sweats again. I knew because I could feel the damp on my pillow.

Which pillow is it? That of a troubled prince, or a wounded warrior who lost his family and failed his men?

I squeezed my eyes shut, afraid to find out what was real. I sniffed the air, relieved at first by the smell of flowers nearby, but were they sweet autumn clematis from the royal garden, or daisies in a jelly jar beside my bed?

A cry in the night drew me, a wailing, but not like a father who'd given up his dreams or a mother overcome with despair. Not like the anguish of war, but a more hopeful sound. I eased the tension in my eyes, but not enough to open them. Through the lids, I could sense the darkness, but only the darkness of night, not the end of the world.

The pad of footsteps approached, and the crying grew louder, followed by a voice.

"Wake up, sleepy head, we have company."

I opened my eyes to take in Becky holding the baby.

She settled beside me and gently placed our daughter between us, then reached across and touched my clammy forehead. "Are you okay?"

I nodded, not needing to say any more—she knew the answer. I stretched across and gave her a long kiss, then reached out and let the baby's tiny hand grip my finger.

Our daughter turned her head to me, and then to Becky, secure in the safety of her parents' bed, her world, like mine, for now at peace.

Acknowledgements

From start to finish, a novel is an enormous effort and would not be possible without a great team. It starts with my beta readers, including the members of my writing group, The Steeple Scholars from the Cape Cod Writers Center, and continues with the editing of Dave King and Lane Diamond. It finishes with the formatting by Lane Diamond and the cover art of Dale Robert Pease. Through it all, the encouragement of others kept me going, my friends and family, including my dear wife, who has put up with my writing aspiration through the good and bad years.

I also want to thank my son, Kevin, who tolerated my inept play in World of Warcraft, as we went on quests together while I did research for this book.

Hopefully, I paid proper tribute to the men and women of our armed services, who sacrifice so much for others.

For those interested in learning more about the effects of PTSD and brain trauma, here are some of the books I read for research:

Achilles in Vietnam: Combat Trauma and the Undoing of Character by Jonathan Shay
Until Tuesday by Luis Carlos Montalvan
In an Instant by Lee and Bob Woodruff
The Blue Cascade by Mike Scotti

Finally, I want to acknowledge my readers, who are, after all, the reason I write.

About the Author

The urge to write first struck when working on a newsletter at a youth encampment in the woods of northern Maine. It may have been the night when lightning flashed at sunset followed by northern lights rippling after dark. Or maybe it was the newsletter's editor, a girl with eyes the color of the ocean. But I was inspired to write about the blurry line between reality and the fantastic.

Using two fingers and lots of white-out, I religiously typed five pages a day throughout college and well into my twenties. Then life intervened. I paused to raise two sons and pursue a career, in the process becoming a well-known entrepreneur in the software industry, founding several successful companies. When I found time again to daydream, the urge to write returned.

My wife and I split our time between Cape Cod, Florida and anywhere else that catches our fancy. I no longer limit myself to five pages a day and am thankful every keystroke for the invention of the word processor.

You can find me at my website (www.DavidLitwack.com), where I blog about writing and post updates on my current works. I'm also on Twitter (@DavidLitwack) and Facebook (https://www.facebook.com/david.litwack.author). If you'd like quarterly updates with news about my books, my works in progress, and my thoughts on the universe, please sign up for my newsletter at www.subscribepage.com/davidlitwacksignup.

More from David Litwack

THE DAUGHTER OF THE SEA AND THE SKY

A thought-provoking look at the line between faith and fantasy, fanatics and followers, and religion and reason.

WINNER: Pinnacle Book Achievement Award - Best Fantasy
WINNER: Awesome Indies Seal of Excellence
WINNER: FAPA Gold Medal – Adult Fiction: General

Children of the Republic, Helena and Jason were inseparable in their youth, until fate sent them down different paths. Grief and duty sidetracked Helena's plans, and Jason came to detest the hollowness of his ambitions.

These two damaged souls are reunited when a tiny boat from the Blessed Lands crashes onto the rocks near Helena's home after an impossible journey across the forbidden ocean. On board is a single passenger, a nine-year-old girl named Kailani, who calls herself The Daughter of the Sea and the Sky. A new and perilous purpose binds Jason and Helena together again, as they vow to protect the lost innocent from the wrath of the authorities, no matter the risk to their future and freedom.

But is the mysterious child simply a troubled little girl longing to return home? Or is she a powerful prophet sent to unravel the fabric of a godless Republic, as the outlaw leader of an illegal religious sect would have them believe? Whatever the answer, it will change them all forever... and perhaps their world as well.

"Author David Litwack gracefully weaves together his message with alternating threads of the fantastic and the realistic.... The reader will find wisdom and grace in this beautifully written story." ~ *San Francisco Book Review*

THE SEEKERS (3-Book Series)

"But what are we without dreams?"

WINNER: Pinnacle Book Achievement Award - Best Sci-Fi
WINNER: Awesome Indies Seal of Excellence
WINNER: Feathered Quill – Gold Medal – Sci-Fi/Fantasy
WINNER: Readers' Favorite Book Awards – Medalist - Dystopia

THE CHILDREN OF DARKNESS
(Book 1)

A thousand years ago the Darkness came – a terrible time of violence, fear, and social collapse when technology ran rampant.

The vicars of the Temple of Light brought peace, ushering in an era of blessed simplicity. For ten centuries they have kept the madness at bay with "temple magic," and by eliminating forever the rush of progress that nearly caused the destruction of everything.

Childhood friends, Orah, Nathaniel, and Thomas have always lived in the tiny village of Little Pond, longing for more from life but unwilling to challenge the rigid status quo. When they're cast into the prisons of Temple City, they discover a terrible secret that launches the three on a journey to find the forbidden keep, placing their lives in jeopardy, for a truth from the past awaits that threatens the foundation of the Temple. If they reveal that truth, they might once again release the potential of their people.

Yet they would also incur the Temple's wrath, as it is written: "If there comes among you a prophet saying, 'Let us return to the darkness,' you shall stone him, because he has sought to thrust you away from the Light."

"The plot unfolds easily, swiftly, and never lets the readers' attention wane... After reading this one, it will be a real hardship to have to wait to see what happens next." ~ *Feathered Quill Book Awards (Gold Medal in Science Fiction & Fantasy)*

"A tightly executed first fantasy installment that champions the exploratory spirit." ~ *Kirkus Reviews*

THE STUFF OF STARS
(Book 2)

If the Seekers fail this time, they risk not a stoning, but losing themselves in the twilight of a never-ending dream.

Against all odds, Orah and Nathaniel have found the keep and revealed the truth about the darkness, initiating what they hoped would be a new age of enlightenment. But the people were more set in their ways than anticipated, and a faction of vicars whispered in their ears, urging a return to traditional ways.

Desperate to keep their movement alive, Orah and Nathaniel cross the ocean to seek the living descendants of the keepmasters' kin. Those they find on the distant shore are both more and less advanced than expected.

The seekers become caught between the two sides, and face the challenge of bringing them together to make a better world. The prize: a chance to bring home miracles and a more promising future for their people. The cost of failure: unimaginable.

THE LIGHT OF REASON
(Book 3)

Orah and Nathaniel return home with miracles from across the sea, hoping to bring a better life for their people. Instead, they find the world they left in chaos.

A new grand vicar, known as the usurper, has taken over the keep and is using its knowledge to reinforce his hold on power.

Despite their good intentions, the seekers find themselves leading an army, and for the first time in a millennium, their world experiences the horror of war.

But the keepmasters' science is no match for the dreamers, leaving Orah and Nathaniel their cruelest choice—face bloody defeat and the death of their enlightenment, or use the genius of the dreamers to tread the slippery slope back to the darkness.

More from Evolved Publishing

We offer great books across multiple genres, featuring hiqh-quality editing (which we believe is second-to-none) and fantastic covers.

As a hybrid small press, your support as loyal readers is so important to us, and we have strived, with tireless dedication and sheer determination, to deliver on the promise of our motto: **QUALITY IS PRIORITY #1!**

Please check out all of our great books, which you can find at this link: **www.EvolvedPub.com/Catalog/**

Thank you!